P9-DBY-813

9 days &
9 Nights

9 days & 9 nights

KATIE COTUGNO

BALZER + BRAY
An Imprint of HarperCollins*Publishers*

alloyentertainment
Production by Alloy Entertainment
1325 Avenue of the Americas, New York, NY 10019
www.alloyentertainment.com

Library of Congress Control Number: 2017954055
ISBN 978-0-06-267409-8 (hardcover)
ISBN 978-0-06-284243-5 (international edition)

Endpaper photography used under license from iStock, Brzozowska
(Paris croissants), Arthur Zogheib Pinatto (Temple Bar—Dublin), Nikada
(stairway—Paris), Andreka (corner cafe), Missing35mm (medieval Irish bridge),
littleny (London phone booth), Nikada (Westminster Bridge), Engamon
(Irish sheep), andhal (bike), lechatnoir (colorful French pastry), Rixipix
(Citroën H type), IakovKalinin (Eiffel Tower).

18 19 20 21 22   PC/LSCH   10 9 8 7 6 5 4 3 2 1
❖
First Edition

For my mom, who taught me how to be a feminist

DAY 1

Ian tells me he loves me for the first time in front of an enormous display of medieval torture devices, halfway through a tour of the Tower of London on the second morning of our trip.

"Shit," he says as soon as the words are out of his mouth, reaching down for my suddenly sweaty hand and tugging me gently toward the back of the group. He's sheepish and wide-eyed, his thick straight eyebrows hooked together with alarm. "I'm sorry. This is, like, the world's most awkward venue to be saying this to you."

For a moment I just gape at him. "No, no," I lie—though not, I suspect, super convincingly. Over the nicker of my own skittish heart I'm vaguely aware of our guide rattling cheerfully on in a crisp British accent: "While these were once thought to be the axes which beheaded Anne Boleyn, in fact history shows she died by the sword. Now, if you'll look over to your left . . ."

Ian grimaces and rests his warm, heavy palms on my bare shoulders, shifting me out of the path of a family speaking enthusiastic German and using a selfie stick to take a picture of themselves in front of a collection of antique flails. "I mean, it definitely is," he admits. "But honestly, I've been thinking it since we took off from Boston. I mean, before that too, but especially since we got here. And every time I opened my mouth I was worried it was going to come out at a wicked inopportune time."

I laugh at that, I can't help it. "Like now?" I ask as he takes my arm and moves me again, both of us edging aside as another gleeful gaggle of tourists jostles its way through the crowd, camera flashes exploding.

"I mean, yeah," Ian says, his pale face going pink under his Red Sox cap. He digs the complimentary Tower map out of his pocket and refolds it a couple of times, nervous. We've been in London since yesterday morning. We've been dating for five full months. "Like now." He makes a face. "Is that weird?"

"Oh yeah," I assure him, unable to hide a smile. Out the narrow window behind him I can see a raven flying in lazy circles against the blue-gray August sky, swooping low and then righting itself gracefully. The guide said there are seven of them living in the Tower, a creepily macabre brood of avian house pets. "But not in a bad way."

Ian tilts his head to the side, hope splashed all across his handsome face. "No?"

"No." I reach up and fuss with the sleeve of his T-shirt, suddenly shy myself. The skin of his upper arm is warm and solid and smooth. The truth is, I'm not so much shocked by the setting he's chosen for this particular declaration as I am by the fact that he's saying it at all. *You don't even* know *me*, I think, then push the notion away, banishing it to the place where I store all the messiest parts of my past. "Not in a bad way at all."

"Okay," Ian says, letting a breath out, scrubbing a hand through the day's worth of vacation beard on his chin and smiling a little uncertainly. "Damn, Molly. I should have at least waited till we got to the room with the Crown Jewels or something." He glances around, shaking his head. "It's really morbid in here, now that I'm looking. This was not a slick move on my part."

"No, come on, this is great." I giggle, motioning around at the empty suits of armor standing at attention along one wall, the reproductions of executioner's masks hanging up alongside some horrifying metal contraption with a million sharp teeth, the intended purpose of which I'd rather not contemplate. "You're really getting your William the Conqueror on."

"Shut up," Ian says, but he's laughing too now, his studious face cracking open. "That's not even the right time period."

"Oh, well, God forbid I mess up my *time* periods," I tease. That was one of the things I liked first and best about Ian, how silly and self-aware he could be for someone so serious; getting to know him was like finding a secret late-night dance party in the green-lampshade reading room at the Boston Public Library. "I love you too."

"Really?" For one second Ian looks completely, purely delighted; then, just as quickly, he shakes his head. "You don't have to say it back," he reassures me, shoving the map back into the pocket of his dorky cargo shorts. "I mean, you know that, obviously. But you don't."

"Yes, thank you." I wrinkle my nose. "I know that. But I want to."

Ian squints at me like he's looking for the punch line. "*Really?*" he asks again. He sounds very young even though he's two years ahead of me at college in Boston; he'll be a senior when we go back to campus in two weeks. "You do?"

I laugh, not a little nervously. "*Yeah*, nerd," I say, trying not to feel like a jerk at how shocked he sounds by the admission. He said it to me without expecting it back, I realize abruptly. He said it to me like an offering. "I do."

Ian grins at me for real then, slow and steady. You could light the whole London Eye with that smile. "Okay," he says. "Well. Good, then."

"Good," I echo, more certain than I was even just a moment ago when I blurted it out. I *do* love him, after all: I love his brain and his heart and the person I am when

4

I'm with him. The person he makes me want to be. And isn't that what love is, really? Wanting to be the best version of yourself for someone else? If that's the rubric that we're using, then I've been in love with Ian since the very first day we met.

I was in the library at BU one rainy Saturday morning in late October of last year, rain streaking down the tall, wide windowpanes and a forbidden cup of coffee from the café downstairs rapidly cooling on the desk in front of me. It was barely a week after the clinic visit and I still had faint stomach cramps, a feeling like someone periodically reaching a cold hand inside my body and squeezing as hard as they could. Still, as I sat there in the carrel in my sweatpants and ponytail, a bulky plaid scarf wrapped around my neck, I was calmer than I'd been in two full weeks. I'd been gravitating toward the library more and more the last few days, in between classes and after dinner, drawn to the tall shelves and stain-resistant armchairs and most of all to the immaculate, antiseptic silence. Boston is a pretty quiet city, all Unitarian churches and hipster coffee shops and cobblestone streets made uneven by tree roots, but lately it was all too bright and loud and overwhelming, like I was walking around with my organs on the outside of my body. Everything felt screamingly, ferociously raw.

I was halfway through a calc problem set that wasn't due until Tuesday when someone stopped next to my hard wooden chair and cleared his throat. I startled, blinking up at the sandy-haired guy casting a broad shadow over my notebook. He looked like everything I'd always pictured when I thought of Boston: broken-in corduroys and L.L.Bean boots unlaced halfway down, a plaid flannel shirt rolled up to his elbows. He was pushing a metal cart full of library books.

"Um," he said, motioning at my coffee cup and smiling a shy, sheepish smile. "You're really not supposed to have that in here."

"Oh!" I felt myself blush deep and red, shame flooding all the way down to the soles of my feet inside my sneakers. "Shoot, I'm sorry." It was such a small, *stupid* thing, a contraband coffee, but getting called out for it by a total stranger flew directly in the face of everything I was trying to be here, with my neatly organized planner and my soothing playlist of classical music and my homework done three days ahead of time: somebody who didn't cause any problems. Somebody who didn't break any hearts. "Um. You can take it, or I can go throw it away, or—"

I broke off, swallowing hard. I knew this was hormones, theoretically—the doctor had told me that might happen, a flood of emotion like PMS dialed up to a thousand—but suddenly I wasn't at all certain I wasn't about to burst into tears.

It must have been achingly clear on my face, because Library Boy blanched. "You know what, it's okay, actually," he assured me. Then he grimaced. "I mean, it really isn't, probably my boss is going to be kind of a dick about it if he sees you. But I won't tell."

I took a deep breath, bit my tongue until I tasted iron. God, I was not about to have a meltdown in front of this random person just because he'd been unlucky enough to talk to me. I was not going to have any more meltdowns at *all*, not ever, but I was most definitely not going to have one now. "I'm sorry," I said again, more calmly this time. "I'll get rid of it. I don't want to be a rule-breaker."

That made him smile. "Fair enough," he said, letting go of the cart handle and scrubbing a hand over his scruffy chin. "I don't want to be an enforcer, in case that wasn't abundantly clear."

"Is that your job?" I asked, the small talk steadying me a little. There was something about him, that stormy morning, that felt oddly, instinctively safe. "The library enforcer?"

He nodded seriously. "Do I look intimidating?"

I gazed at him for another minute, taking in his tortoiseshell glasses and the Red Sox T-shirt peeking out from underneath the collar of his flannel, the beat-up leather band of his Swiss Army watch around one wrist. "Not really," I admitted.

He grinned then, holding his hand out. "I didn't think so," he said with a shrug. "I'm Ian."

"I'm Molly," I said, and we shook.

After that I fell into a routine of Saturday mornings at the library: textbooks stacked neatly on the table, water bottle tucked safely away inside my bag. The following week, Ian smiled and waved when he saw me. The week after that, he recommended a Barbara Kingsolver book he thought I might like. The week after *that*, it occurred to me that I was looking forward to seeing him, glancing up from my notes every couple of minutes and scanning the stacks for his kind, serious face.

Still, after everything that had happened back in Star Lake and after, I definitely wasn't looking for anything romantic, on top of which I couldn't imagine who in their right mind would possibly want to date me if they knew the kind of skeletons I had rattling around in my dorm room closet. Which is why I was so surprised, right before Thanksgiving, when Ian came over to the carrel I'd started to think of as mine and asked, so haltingly it sort of broke my heart, if I wanted to go see a Springsteen cover band at the Paradise that night.

"Um," I said, taken aback and caught off guard and so deeply pleased I physically couldn't keep from smiling, like the Boss himself had shown up in the reference section, climbed up onto one of the study tables, and launched into "Born to Run." It occurred to me, somewhere at the very back of my secret heart, that I hadn't felt anything like that since Gabe. "Hm." I put a hand against the side of my face, felt the blood rushing there. "So here's the thing. It sounds really fun and I promise I'm not just saying that. But I'm—" I broke off. "Just . . . not really in a place to be dating anybody right now."

Ian raised his eyebrows. "What makes you think I'm trying to date you?" he asked. When I blanched, he grinned.

"I mean, I'm definitely trying to date you," he admitted, jamming his hands into the pockets of his olive-green khakis and rocking backward on the heels of his boots. "But if it's not on the table, I can respect that. Honestly, no pressure. I'd also really like to just be your friend."

I squinted at him, looking for the catch but not finding one. "Really?" I asked.

Ian nodded and held his hands out like one of the street magicians posted up by the T station in Harvard Square, *nothing here*. "Really."

"Okay," I said, nodding slowly. "Then let's be friends."

And that's how it started, as a friendship: turkey-melt lunches in the dining hall where he asked about my business classes and told me about the books he was reading for his Irish-American Writers seminar; a trip to the Ben and Jerry's on Newbury Street because somebody had left a stack of two-for-one coupons on top of the trash can in the hallway of my dorm building. "What's the deal with you guys?" my roommate, Roisin, asked the week before Christmas break, pulling me aside at student-discount ice-skating night on the Common. Her hat had a giant pom-pom bobbing on top of it; her brown skin was faintly rosy with the cold. "I feel like he's been staring at you piningly all night."

I shook my head, reaching out for the paper cup of hot

chocolate she was offering. "We're just friends," I told her, and I meant it; still, when Ian mentioned going on a few dates with a girl in his teaching cohort in the middle of January it put me in such a bad mood that I blew off the superhero movie we were supposed to go see and jammed my sneakers on my feet instead. I ran all the way to Jamaica Pond in the screaming, skin-cracking cold.

Don't be spoiled, I scolded myself as I swallowed down deep gulps of the dry, stinging winter air. After all, it wasn't like there was anything I could do about it. I wasn't ready. I didn't know if or when I would be. Ian might have thought he wanted to date me for a minute there, sure. But only because he didn't actually know me at all.

Still, as the weeks went by I saw him more than I didn't: we ate mushroom and ricotta slices at the trendy pizza chain across from the BU arena. We sat in the oversized chairs on the second floor of the student center and studied for exams. In March we went to an extremely long, extremely awkward improv show in the black box theater on campus, after which we stood bewildered on the sidewalk and tried to figure out what we'd just watched.

"Okay," Ian said, rubbing a palm over his face. He shuddered visibly, like a dog shaking off water after a bath. "Wow. That was . . ."

"Special?" I supplied.

"That's one word for it, certainly." Ian grinned. "I think I need a beer. You wanna come over for a beer?"

I looked at him for a moment, his cheeks ruddy in the streetlight, his hair growing out past the collar of his warm-looking woolen coat. "Sure," I said. "That sounds great."

We followed the trolley tracks back down toward Kenmore Square, still totally unable to get over the weirdness of it: "I think my favorite part was when that one guy sang the *Barney* theme song and then meowed like a cat for six minutes," Ian said thoughtfully, and I laughed. It was only a couple of weeks until spring break, but Boston was still freezing and damp, the winter clinging endlessly on; my mittens had long since gone gray and dingy, a hole in the webbing between my fingers and my thumb. It had snowed *again* a few days before, everyone in the dining hall looking out the window and groaning in unison as the fat flakes began to come down, and now I picked through the slushy black remains of it, water seeping into my ankle boots. "Easy," Ian said, catching my hand when I almost slipped on a patch of ice slicked over the cobblestone sidewalk. "I gotcha."

"Thanks," I said as I righted myself again, my whole body going pleasantly alert inside my parka.

Ian smiled a little shyly. His hand was improbably warm. "No problem." He started to let go, but before I knew what I was doing I tightened my grip, like a reflex. Ian's eyebrows shot up in the darkness, but he didn't comment. "It's just down here" was all he said, nodding at a quiet side street.

Ian lived with two roommates in a scuzzy student apartment near the Fens, a listing walk-up where the narrow stairwells reeked of weed and Bagel Bites and his mail was perpetually getting stolen. The living room was drafty and cavernous, with tall coffered ceilings and molding that had been painted thickly over so many times it had lost all its detail; in the hallway, the colorless carpet was worn completely bald. The linoleum was peeling up in the kitchen. The windows rattled inside their frames.

It was Friday, and Ian's roommates—a kid named Harvey who was studying engineering and stayed at his boyfriend's most nights, plus a girl named Sahar who played in a punk band in Somerville on the weekends—were both out; the apartment was quiet, save a faint, irregular scratching in the walls. "It's a mouse," Ian confirmed, when he caught me tilting my head to the side to listen for it. "He's basically our fourth roommate, I'm not going to lie to you. He doesn't even have the decency to scurry. He just, like, strolls through the room while you're watching TV or making a sandwich or something. Harvey calls him Old Chum." He grimaced. "You're rethinking your decision to come over here now, aren't you."

I looked at him evenly for a moment, then shook my head. "No."

Ian's ears got faintly red. "Okay," he said, clearing his throat a bit. "Well, good."

He got me a beer from the ancient fridge and burned some popcorn in the microwave; we sat on the sagging IKEA futon in the living room and watched a *Friends* rerun on cable. It was late, nearly time for the T to stop running, and I knew I should head home, but the longer I sat there the clearer it became that I didn't actually want to go back to my tall, sterile dorm building. I wanted to stay here, in this warm, scruffy place.

"Your socks are wet," Ian observed suddenly, reaching out and flicking the bottom of my foot; on TV, Joey and Chandler had just left a baby on a bus.

"My feet are freezing," I confessed, tucking them up under me.

"They are?" Ian made a face. "Why didn't you say something? Hang on, wait a sec." He got up off the couch and disappeared down the long, narrow hallway, his shoulders so broad he seemed to fill the entire space. When he came back he was holding a thick pair of navy blue socks.

"They're clean," he said, handing them over. "I'm not a monster."

That made me smile, surprised and delighted; then I felt my face fall. He was being too nice to me, I thought, suddenly as close to tears as I'd been that very first morning in the library. I didn't deserve it, after everything that had happened. I didn't deserve *him*. This was a guy who'd read to little kids at a Head Start for his senior service project and confessed to being the Dungeon Master for all his friends' D&D games one of the very first times we hung out together. He'd been honest and good from the beginning. The last thing he needed was me stomping into his calm, steady life

13

with my talent for drama and flair for catastrophe, leaving my muddy tracks across his floor.

I thought about leaving. I thought about getting up and making my excuses, calling an Uber and waving good-bye and keeping a safe distance from Ian's sturdy, affable self until this longing—and that's what it was, I realized as I watched his fingers curl around the neck of his beer bottle, longing, a physical ache in my chest—had passed.

Instead I waited for him to sit down beside me, and I swung my feet into his lap.

Ian looked at me for a long moment. Then he set the beer bottle down. He reached forward and peeled my wet socks off, pressing one careful thumb against my chilly instep; I shivered. "Your feet feel like a cadaver's," he informed me, smirking a little.

"Rude," I said, but I was smiling. He squeezed my toes once before sliding the wool socks on with a surprising gentleness, pulling them all the way up over the bottoms of my jeans.

"Better?" he asked, and I swallowed.

"Much."

Ian nodded. Outside it was snowing again, tiny flakes visible in the yellow glow cast by the streetlights outside his building. It felt like we were bears hunkering down for the winter, as if the world couldn't get us up here.

Ian looked down at his grip on my ankles, then back up again; the moment that passed between us was so heavy I felt like I could reach out and hold it in my two shaking hands. He smelled like off-brand boy soap from the drugstore. I wanted to wrap him around me like a coat.

"Ooookay," I said, suddenly breathless, sitting back on the futon. "I—huh. Okay."

Ian let go of me abruptly, like he was worried he'd read me wrong. "I'm sorry," he said. "I didn't mean—"

"No no no." I paused for a moment, trying to steady myself. "I know I told you I wanted to be friends," I said. "And I really like that you were so cool about it."

"Well, I'm cool," Ian joked, gesturing down at his work shirt and flannel-lined khakis. "I mean, clearly."

"No, I mean it," I said. "You can always tell when a guy is trying to make something that isn't supposed to be a date into a date, or when they're secretly annoyed that it isn't a date, and you just—you've never been like that."

Ian tilted his head to the side, lips twisting. "I'm trying to figure out if that's emasculating or not."

"Can you just take the compliment?" I asked, more shrilly than I meant to.

"Sorry," he said sheepishly. "Yes."

"Look," I said, leaning my head back against the futon, curling my knees up in front of me. "Here's the deal. Without sounding super dramatic or like I'm in a Lifetime movie or like I'm being really vague on purpose, there's stuff about myself that I don't necessarily . . . like to talk about. Stuff you don't know about me."

Ian nodded. "Without being super vague on purpose," he echoed pointedly.

"I'm serious!" Deep down I knew this was silly, that by virtue of being so mysterious I was probably turning my past into a bigger deal than it needed to be. But what was I supposed to tell him? *I spent the bulk of my high school career playing the hypotenuse of a ridiculous love triangle that you can read all about in my author mom's international bestseller?* "I'm not trying to be an asshole, I just—"

"Do you have a boyfriend?" Ian interrupted.

I huffed a bit, surprised and—absurdly—a tiny bit offended. "No."

"Do you have a girlfriend?"

"No." I smiled.

"Are you a Republican?"

That one made me laugh. "No," I said, kicking lightly at his thigh with one socked foot. "I'm not a Republican."

Ian shrugged. "Then whatever it is, I don't care."

"Easy for you to say now, maybe." I shook my head.

"You're wrong." Ian leaned forward. "Here's what I do know about you," he said, ticking the list off on his fingers. "You make me laugh. You're smart and cool and kind and driven." He smiled. "And you are, like. The prettiest girl I've ever seen."

I rolled my eyes, quietly pleased. "Well," I said finally, mirroring him, leaning in a little closer. "I don't know about *that.*"

"I do," Ian said calmly, then cupped the back of my skull in one hand and kissed me. He tasted like beer and like popcorn and like hope. And maybe this was how it happened, I thought to myself, eyes closed and heart creaking open. Maybe this was how I started over for real.

The next morning I went and cut all my hair off, then called my mom and got permission to swipe her credit card for a dye job to match. She was worried about me, though both of us had tacitly agreed not to talk about why beyond her careful, general probes into my emotions and a book about grief that she'd sent to my dorm. "Sure," she said cautiously; she was in Chicago on a book tour, the hotel TV chattering away in the background. "Whatever makes you happy."

Once I was finished at the salon I met Ian at a coffee shop not far from campus; he stood up from the table when he saw me, an expression on his face like I was a rare, delicate thing. "I like it," he said, reaching up and tugging on the ends, then blushing a little. "You look like you."

"I feel like me," I told him, though I wasn't entirely sure if that was true or not, and tipped my face up for a kiss.

Now, five months later and halfway across the globe, I reach for his hands and lace our fingers together, noting with a surge of affection that his are sweaty, too, his palms hot and damp. "Well, you big weirdo," I say, standing on my tiptoes to kiss him, "now that we've got that all settled, you wanna go look at some more horrifying weapons?" We've lost our Tower tour group, the guide having led them off in a shuffling, murmuring cluster, no doubt to gamely exclaim over an antique stretching rack for the efficient tearing of one limb from another or a ruby-encrusted dagger that belonged to Thomas Cromwell. "We're probably missing out on a live disembowelment right now."

But Ian shakes his head. "I feel like I've kind of learned enough about medieval interrogation tactics for one day," he confesses. "You wanna get out of here and find some food?"

I nod, the relief sharp and unexpected. It's claustrophobic in here all of a sudden—those ancient stone walls getting closer, history pressing in from all sides. The soles of my feet itch with the instinct to run. For a moment I'm not sure which I'm more afraid of: Henry VIII's wide and varied collection of bone-breaking apparatuses, or holding Ian's heart in my two clumsy hands. Still, I remind myself it's normal: of course those complicated old feelings would come roiling up now, my past tapping me naggingly on the shoulder. The last person I loved, after all, was—

"Yeah," I say before I can think it, scanning the room for the nearest escape. "Let's go."

Outside we find a crowded pub to have lunch in, sitting side by side at the bar over heavy plates of fried fish and mushy green peas. Afternoon sunlight streams in through stained-glass windows, the slightly dank smell of beer and old wood dense in the air. The restaurant is teeming with smartly dressed office workers and clusters of chattering girlfriends on their lunch breaks, a pack of noisy English bros in quarter-zip sweaters laughing over something on one of their phones. "Is it rude to ask for ketchup?" I ask quietly, leaning toward Ian and nodding at my heaping pile of thickly cut fries. "Like, is ketchup even a thing in England?"

Ian frowns. "I think vinegar is the thing here, actually."

"I was worried you were going to say that." I twist the cap off the bottle of malt vinegar on the bar and sprinkle a few drops over my fries anyway, then hand it to Ian, who does the same before taking a big gulp of his Guinness. "When in London, right?" I tease, lifting a fry in salute.

Ian grins back, dimple popping in his right cheek. I like that he's the kind of person who knows stuff like this: local customs and the right way to act in unfamiliar places, who to tip and how to navigate the Underground and what to order in a fancy restaurant. His family traveled a lot for his mom's job when he was a kid, he told me once, so he comes by it honestly, but he also reads more than anyone I know. At any given moment he's got at least three books on the go: a giant hardcover next to his bed, plus a paperback tucked into his schoolbag and something on his phone for unexpected emergencies. "Did you bring that 'cause you're worried I'm gonna get boring?" I teased once, spying a dog-eared copy of *Wonder Boys* peeking out from the back pocket of his corduroys on the way to dinner not long after we started dating. "Is that why you've always got backup entertainment available?"

I was only joking around, but Ian shook his head seriously. "Not at all," he promised. "But at some point you're gonna get up and pee, right?"

Now he nods at the bartender for the bill and sits back on his stool. "So what's next on the agenda?" he asks, gesturing at my phone, which I've set beside my plate for safekeeping.

I eye him over my pint of cider. "What makes you so sure I've got the next thing decided?"

Ian laughs out loud. "I mean, I've met you before, to start with."

"Yeah, yeah." I wrinkle my nose. The truth is I've planned every day of this trip down to the minute, complete with color-coded lists and preloaded Oyster cards for the train and an app on my phone to remind me what we're supposed to be doing and when, plus the best way to get there and what to look at once we arrive. It's really just a more concentrated version of the schedule I started keeping at school last fall, a training regimen for a brand-new me, but I can understand how it might be slightly overwhelming to the uninitiated.

Still, if I've learned anything over the last year it's the importance of a concrete plan, a comprehensive guide for moving through the world with as few false starts as possible. A system, I have found, can stave off chaos. A system, I have found, prevents mistakes.

I pick up my phone and scroll through today's itinerary,

tapping the tiny checkboxes next to *Tower of London* and *pub lunch*. "Westminster Abbey," I report after a moment, flicking to the next screen to double-check our route on the Underground. "So nothing as traumatic as this morning, hopefully."

"What, the prison?" Ian asks, swiping a leftover fry off my plate. "Or me saying I love you?"

"What?" My head snaps up. "I wasn't traumatized!"

Ian looks at me like, *nice try, buddy*. "When I first said it?" he asks gently. "You were *something*."

I shake my head, trying to reel my guilty, embarrassed self back in. "I was surprised," I tell him finally. "That's all." Then, reaching out and taking his bearded face between my two hands: "Hey. I am really, really happy to be here with you, do you know that?"

Ian smiles back, his hazel eyes warm and friendly, and I know he's willing to let me off the hook. "I mean, you should be," he says, the grin turning just the slightest bit wicked and his faint Boston accent getting a touch more pronounced. He turns his face to plant a kiss against my palm. "I'm really fucking fun."

Ian pays the bill and we amble out into the late summer sunshine, weaving through the crowd on the bustling sidewalk and down into the Underground station. "This is so much nicer than Boston," I comment as we sit down to wait on a bench in front of an ad for a fancy British department store. The T back at home is notoriously unreliable, rattling along aboveground tracks that are perpetually freezing over in the winter. "Why do you think—"

I break off all at once at the sight of a familiar set of shoulders across the platform; my whole body goes wary and watchful and still. For one sharp second it's like all the air has gone out of this tube station, whooshing down into the dark mouth of the tunnel and leaving me gasping for oxygen like a hooked, terrified fish. Standing on the other side of the tracks, his beat-up backpack slung over one narrow shoulder, is—

Gabe.

I blink. I'm hallucinating, I must be, jet lag or exhaustion or some kind of weird transatlantic madness. To conjure my ex-boyfriend on the other side of the world—an hour after my *new* boyfriend tells me he loves me? The cold reality is I haven't seen Gabe since our breakup last summer at home in Star Lake. We haven't even *talked*, for God's sake. And he made it clear that was exactly how he wanted it.

I force a deep, steadying breath, straightening my spine before squinting across the tracks one more time. The stranger looks like Gabe, that much is undeniable. The shaggy hair is gone, trademark curls cut close to his head, but the khaki shorts and the scruffy sneakers are achingly familiar. This guy even kind of *stands* like Gabe.

He's also, I realize with no small amount of horror as he turns around and faces my direction, wearing a hoodie with the Donnelly's Pizza logo on the front.

His dark eyes widen as our gazes lock across the train tracks, my heart like a house on fire and a mechanical jolt rattling deep inside my bones. I want to scream his name across the station. I want to ask him why he ever let me think we were okay. Instead I stand frozen and helpless as a million different emotions flicker like old home movies across his face: Shock. Confusion.

Heartbreak.

The train thunders into the station with a roar and a rumble, the doors sliding open on the opposite side and the crush of people obscuring any view I might have of him through the thick, smudgy windows. When it screeches off a scant moment later, he's gone.

Again.

I don't know how long I stand there before I realize Ian is looking at me—before I realize Ian is even still *standing* here, brow furrowed. "You okay?" he asks.

I nod, coming back to myself like a swimmer resurfacing from deep underwater, breathless and improperly depressurized. "Um," I say, reaching for his hand and pulling him closer, stepping safely into the circle of his strong, sturdy arms. "Yeah, absolutely. Sorry. I'm great."

Ian keeps looking. "You sure? You're, like, ghost white."

"Thanks a lot," I say, managing a skim-milk smile, scooping my hair up off my sweaty neck. Suddenly the idea of spending the afternoon shuffling through a dimly lit church with a million other tourists makes me bone-crushingly weary. I want to sit down on the floor of the station and never get up.

"Um," I say finally, my throat thick with something that is certainly—*certainly*—not tears. "I think maybe I'm just more jet-lagged than I thought." It's not a lie, exactly: last night I lay awake until it was nearly light out, watching the sun creep up outside the window of our rental apartment. "Or maybe it was that cider? I don't know." I shake my head. "Anyway, do you want to maybe skip the abbey and crash for a couple hours instead?"

Ian raises his eyebrows in exaggerated surprise. "You want to *abandon the itinerary?*" he teases. Then, off something in my expression: "Sure," he says, more quietly this time. "Of course."

It starts to drizzle as we're heading back to the apartment, fat drops landing on the sidewalk and the metallic smell of rain on concrete saturating the air. I cross my arms, glancing up at the dark clouds creeping over the city and trying not to take them as an omen.

"It's a vacation, remember?" Ian reminds me gently, taking my hand and squeezing. "Not the invasion of Normandy."

"No, I know." I nod, unsure how to explain to him why the idea of winging it, even a little, unsettles me so disproportionately much. From the beginning, I've been purposely vague about everything—and *everyone*—I left back in Star Lake; after all, "everybody in my charming, picturesque hometown thinks I'm a dumb, messy slut" doesn't exactly make for sexy new-relationship banter—but it's not like uptightness for uptightness's sake is a particularly attractive quality, either. "Of course."

"Here," he continues, shrugging out of his hoodie as it starts to rain harder, his T-shirt riding up so I can see the pale, broad planes of his lower back. "Take this."

I smile. "I'm prepared," I say, pulling a travel umbrella out of my purse and waggling it in his direction, "but thank you. That's very courtly."

Ian shrugs. "It's England, right?"

I bump his shoulder with mine, pleased. He's taller than me, though not dramatically so: mostly he's just solid and durable-looking, the kind of person you could imagine chopping wood or paddling a canoe down a river, although every time I say anything remotely like that Ian reminds me he's from Worcester. "Oh, is that why?" I tease. "You're getting into the costume drama of it all?"

"Totally," he replies immediately. "I packed pantaloons. They're in my bag back at the rental."

"Dork," I accuse, but I'm laughing. As we turn the corner toward our rental apartment, the slow, chilly drizzle tapers off.

We're staying in an Airbnb in Shoreditch, a studio with a tiny kitchenette and a kind of purposeful hipster griminess that would horrify my mom. The floors are lacquered concrete layered with frayed kilim rugs, bright and thread-bare; there are vintage army blankets on the bed. On the walls are unframed concert posters for the Rolling Stones and David Bowie, weighted down at the bottoms with binder clips to keep them from curling in the humid air.

I toe off my sandals and collapse backward onto the bed, barely resisting the urge to curl myself into a tiny ball on the starchy white sheets while Ian fills two glasses of water at the sink. "You okay?" he asks, handing one over as he stretches out onto the mattress beside me.

Well, I think I saw my ex-boyfriend on the subway, I imagine telling him; *I cheated on him with his brother, who was* also *my ex, and I thought we'd kind of worked it out, but then when I got to Boston I realized I was—*

"Just tired," I promise brightly, sitting up and gulping the water, tucking my hair behind my ears. I lie back down and rest my cheek on his chest, listening for the reassuring thud of his heart beating underneath the cotton and trying to stop thinking about Gabe. Ian rubs my back for a long moment, making swirls and loops and intricate patterns, before ever so slowly rucking up the side of my tank top, running one gentle finger along the bare skin above the waistband of my jeans.

"That cool?" he asks quietly.

I swallow, my stomach swooping. "Yeah," I tell him, smiling as he pushes himself up on one elbow, ducking his head to press a kiss against my mouth. I reach a hand up to scratch my fingers through the hair at the back of his neck, shifting to make room as he gets closer, his body heavy and dense and warm. "That's cool."

Ian nudges the strap of my tank top out of the way and plants a trail of kisses along my collarbone, dark beard rasping against my skin. I reach for the hem of his T-shirt and he hums. The anticipation sparks between us like a live wire, and I know he's wondering if this is the moment, same as I am: even though we've definitely fooled around a bunch over the last five months, we still haven't actually had sex.

"I want to," I promised him the first time we really talked about it, sitting on the lumpy mattress in his apartment last April, my bra strap slipping down my arm. "I think I just need some time."

"Yeah, of course," Ian said seriously, rubbing at his own bare, freckled shoulder. "Take as long as you need." The fact that he was so sincerely nice about it made me like him even more than I already did, although now it's almost the end of August and I know he can't have been expecting it to take quite this long. I'm just waiting for the perfect opportunity—for the stars to align and the lighting to turn golden, for that moment when I'm one hundred percent sure. God knows I've made more than my fair share of mistakes about this kind of thing in the past, breaking hearts and ruining relationships and making choices I couldn't take back. This time, I want to be absolutely certain I get it right.

I close my eyes and slide my palms over the muscles in

Ian's stomach, reaching around to count the ridges of his backbone and telling myself I'm not still thinking about Gabe. Ian's a good kisser, friendly, and his fingertips are gentle along the underwire of my bra; he's fumbling with the clasp when the reminder on my phone chimes out on the nightstand, the volume jacked loud and startling.

"Shoot," I say, letting a breath out, squeezing Ian's upper arms to call him off. "We're supposed to go to that happy hour, remember? The place with the hundred beers."

Ian groans. "Let's skip it," he says, ducking his head to nip at my shoulder.

"Can't," I murmur, grinning as I wriggle out from underneath him and reach for my tank top, enjoying the tease. "Gotta stick to the schedule."

Ian grumbles a bit more, but after a moment he gets up too, heading into the bathroom to brush his teeth while I dig through my suitcase for a silky black T-shirt dress, pushing the thought of Gabe standing there on that train platform out of my mind once and for all. Everybody has their secrets, I tell myself, fluffing my hair out and slicking on a pale swipe of lip gloss. The trick is to leave the past where it belongs.

"You ready?" Ian asks now, coming out of the bathroom and holding his hand out, pink-cheeked and scruffily handsome.

"Sure am," I say, then twist my fingers through his and squeeze. "Let's go."

DAY 2

We spend the next day playing tourists, Tower Bridge and the Rosetta Stone at the British Museum, popping up out of underground stations like subterranean animals after a long, cold winter. For lunch we slip into a tiny corner shop and pick up cheddar cheese sandwiches with mustard and pickles on bread so crusty you could break a tooth trying to eat it. I like traveling with Ian, I think again as we post up on a bench in Covent Garden to eat them: in spite of all my careful planning he's open to a kind of wandering, with a willingness to sit in one place for an hour at a time and watch the world go by. "We're not *seeing* anything," I protest when he suggests running across the street for ice cream.

"Take a breath, General," Ian tells me, nodding at the crowded plaza. "We're seeing plenty."

"Jerk," I tease, although truthfully, my new vacation

sandals are rubbing a blister on my pinky toe and I'm happy to have a break. In any case, it's not like he's wrong. When I follow his gaze I spy a deliveryman unloading a shipment of flowers from a truck and loading it into the service entrance of a nearby restaurant; I watch a pack of skateboarders in brightly colored T-shirts zipping through the throng. Across the street is a newsstand packed with gossip magazines, their covers splashed with lurid photos of Sabrina Hudson's latest nightclub meltdown, and I frown for a second, squinting to read the headlines: Sabrina Hudson was a huge TV star back when I was in middle school, and there was even chatter about her possibly playing Emily Green in my mom's *Driftwood* movie, but for the last year or so she's been on what seems like one long bender, getting fired from film projects and arrested for a DUI and embroiled in public knock-down-and-drag-outs with one sketchy boyfriend after another.

"I used to have a huge crush on Sabrina Hudson," Ian tells me now, nodding at the magazine racks with a grimace. "I mean, before she turned into a giant train wreck, clearly."

"You and everybody else," I tease, though I'm still peering distractedly at the tabloids. God, it must be awful to crash and burn like that in front of the whole entire world. "Okay," I say finally, smiling at him and reaching for my phone to check the schedule. "Let's get going."

In the afternoon we wander through the cluster of bookstores on Charing Cross Road, all low ceilings and narrow aisles and the smell of old paper and must, rare first editions locked safely into glass-front cabinets and fusty shopkeepers like something out of Harry Potter keeping a watchful eye on their wares. A bookstore cat darts across the end of the aisle, a flash of white paws and Bengal stripes, there and gone again. It's the kind of place I probably would have found boring a year ago, but Ian is so clearly in heaven that I find myself getting excited about it too, the two of us digging through the messy, overcrowded stacks with the enthusiasm of contestants on some kind of ultra-dorky game show.

"You're not going to have room for all of those in your backpack," I warn him finally, eyeing the growing haul tucked under his arm. Ian collects Vintage Contemporaries paperbacks from the eighties, the kind with tacky paint-by-numbers art on their covers and bright bands of color along their spines. I've seen them lined up on the bookshelves in his apartment, forming a rainbow nearly narcotic in its orderliness.

He shakes his head, looking confident. "Oh, I'll make room," he promises.

"You will, huh?" I ask, charmed. He raises his eyebrows in reply, then sets the books on a nearby shelf and kisses me, broad chest and beer-tasting tongue and both hands on my face. I love Ian's hands; they're oddly aristocratic compared to the rest of him, long and lean, with bitten-down nails that are all college dude. Watching him hold a pencil always strikes me as stupidly dear.

"This," he mutters against my mouth, "is how I want to die."

I laugh, flattening my palms against his T-shirt; I can feel his heart tapping steadily away underneath the cotton. Bookstores are holy sites for Ian—he's a double major in English and secondary education, the only guy in his teaching cohort. Back when we first started dating he used to bring me books instead of flowers, leaving them on my desk and in stacks at my door like offerings—Stephen King, Jane Austen, Chimamanda Ngozi Adichie. I've never been a huge reader, truthfully—not to mention the fact that after the *Driftwood* debacle I wanted to stay as far away from my mom's career as humanly possible—but I didn't want him to think I was a moron, and in the end I was surprised by how much I enjoyed them, dipping into a dozen different worlds in the sterile quiet of my dorm room. I wanted to know all the authors he'd fallen in love with. I wanted to read everything he'd read.

"Come on," I say now, pulling gently away. "We get kicked out of this place for unliterary activities, you're never going to forgive me."

"You're probably right," Ian says seriously—then kisses me back into the shadows, grabbing one last book off the shelf above my head.

For dinner we've got a reservation at a place I scoped out on one of the travel blogs I haunted all summer, a ten-table bistro with crispy chicken cooked under a brick and the best mashed potatoes in London. It's close enough to walk from the apartment, and we leave a little early, taking our time as we stroll past souvenir shops and coffee bars all closing up for the night, street vendors locking up their carts. It's clear and cool outside, that first hint of fall coming. The sky is a soft, velvety blue. The streets are lined with pubs and restaurants, their patios packed with a rowdy Friday-night crowd; I press my cheek against Ian's sturdy shoulder as we pass a street-corner busker picking out "Eleanor Rigby" on the guitar. The more time goes by, the more convinced I am that seeing Gabe was some kind of weird neurochemical aberration, my brain bending double and snapping back.

We're nearly to the restaurant when I stop short at the sound of music coming from a massive brick building on the corner of a quiet street, a converted warehouse bearing the faded logo of a canned goods company on one side. I've noticed this about London, the way new places and things are layered on top of old ones, like the whole city is a talented seamstress fashioning one-of-a-kind couture out of ancient thrift store finds. An alley to one side is strung with a canopy of old-fashioned white lights and leads to a beer garden on a back patio; I can see a jazz trio set up back there, a girl in thick glasses and red high heels plucking away at the double bass. "Oh," I say, before I can stop myself. *"Look."*

"That's fucking awesome," Ian says, a slow smile spreading across his face and his accent just detectable like it always is when he's excited about something. Then, taking my hand: "Let's check it out."

I hesitate for a moment—thinking, stubbornly, of the app on my phone—but Ian bumps my shoulder. "Come on," he urges. "It's a *kuddelmuddel*."

My eyes widen. "I'm sorry," I say, a laugh pulling at the corners of my mouth, "a *what*?"

"A kuddelmuddel," Ian repeats, grinning back at me. "It's German. It actually means, like, messy chaos? But my mom always uses it to describe what happens when you're traveling and you find something sort of good and unexpected that isn't part of the plan."

"A kuddelmuddel," I repeat, falling a little bit more in love with him. "Okay."

The restaurant is massive inside, all dark wood and basket-weave tile and one whole wall of windows flung wide open to the courtyard, the faint whiff of cigarette smoke on the breeze. A dozen framed mirrors hung behind the bar catch the candlelight flickering on the tiny bistro tables; at the back is a row of booths with dividing walls that stretch to the ceiling, deep-red curtains hung across each one. It smells like fried fish and dark beer and underneath that a certain not-unpleasant sourness, generations of spills mopped up on the wide, scratched floorboards. Also, it's *packed*.

"It'll be at least forty-five minutes," the hostess says, once we make our way through the crowd; she's got impossibly long lashes and cat-eye liner, a smart black dress paired with combat boots. "You could get a pint while you wait?"

"You wanna bail?" Ian asks, checking his watch and

glancing back toward the exit. "We can still make your reservation, if you want."

"Actually, no," I hear myself say, surprised by the urge to stray from my carefully curated itinerary. But there's something about the energy of this place that I like, a sense of possibility. I watch a burly, bearded waiter hurry by with a tray of bright-pink cocktails in delicate champagne coupes. "Let's stay."

Ian orders us a couple of beers and we find a spot to post up near the bar as the crowd thickens all around us, cologne and bright lipstick and plaid button-down shirts. We keep getting muscled into each other, my chest pressed up against Ian's. Behind me a girl who's already half drunk is telling a very enthusiastic story to her friends, all hand gestures and colorful British expletives; I duck out of her way, scooting from side to side to avoid a pint glass to the back of the head. After a while I've got a rhythm down—my hips rocking ever so slightly into Ian's, then back again, holding my glass up so I don't spill on my dress. Beer drips down onto my wrist. I lift my arm to lick it away and when I look back up Ian is staring at me, the intent on his face so overt it makes me shiver. He raises his eyebrows, something that just misses being a smile tweaking the corners of his mouth. "What are we, dancing?" he asks, head tipped down close to mine.

It takes me a minute to realize what he's getting at, that low swoop in my belly. Then I grin. "Why?" I ask, flirtatious. "You wanna dance?"

35

Ian shakes his head, mischievous. "I mean, not particularly."

"Well then," I tease. "What do you want?"

He's about to answer when the girl behind me swings her glass with particular vivacity; I overcorrect as I'm ducking out of her way, stepping directly onto the foot of the dark-haired guy standing to my right. "Whoops," I start, blushing like a clumsy tourist; I turn around guiltily, free hand held up in apology. "I'm sorry."

"Nah, it's cool," says a deep American voice I know in the cells of my bone marrow, a voice I know in the ventricles of my heart. "You're good."

He glances at me quickly, then immediately does a double take; for a moment both of us just freeze. I can't stop staring, struck silent by the shock and the horror and the fact that apparently I wasn't hallucinating yesterday in the tube station: it's *Gabe*, who I've known almost as long as I can remember. Gabe, whose family I destroyed for the second time last year. He's here in this pub in London in dark jeans and a soft-looking henley, a bottle of Amstel clutched in one hand.

And he's with a girl.

She was with him yesterday in the Underground station too, I realize now, though I didn't notice her at the time—as if my brain was protecting me somehow, only seeing what it wanted to see. It feels like this whole trip is reshuffling in front of my eyes like a deck of enchanted cards from an animated movie, becoming something other than the thing it was five minutes ago. It feels like my whole life is.

"Um," I manage finally, just the one idiotic syllable. "Hi."

"Hi," Gabe echoes, sounding just about as useless. "What are you doing here?"

"What am I—I'm on *vacation*," I retort, more snottily than I necessarily mean to. "What are *you* doing here?"

"Yeah," Gabe says, gesturing to the beautiful blonde beside him. "Us too."

Us. Right. I suddenly remember Ian waiting patiently at my side, watching the proceedings with a curious, quizzical expression. I hesitate for a moment, realizing abruptly that I have no idea how to explain what's going on here. "This is Gabe," I blurt roughly. "Gabe, this is my boyfriend, Ian."

Just for a second, what looks like the ghost of a reaction—surprise? Jealousy?—flares across Gabe's achingly handsome face. Then he grins, and just like that he's the King of Funtown, same as he always was back at home. "Wow, good to meet you, dude," he says easily, reaching his hand out for Ian's. "This is my girlfriend, Sadie." He turns to the blonde, lays a confident palm against her back. "Molly's from Star Lake," he explains smoothly. "She dated Patrick forever, way back in the Stone Age."

I blink. He's not wrong, certainly—I *did* date Gabe's brother, Patrick, forever—but that's definitely not our only connection. By the end of last summer he was the only Donnelly I had any interest in giving my heart to at all.

"Oh wow, *hi*," Sadie says. She's tall and toned, with a long waterfall of hair braided into a fishtail over one golden shoulder. Her handshake is firm as a bear trap. "It's so cool to meet you. How wild is this, right?"

"Seriously wild." I smile what I hope is the smile of a normal person and not an escaped convict whose haunted past is flashing before her eyes three thousand miles from the scene of the crime. It occurs to me that if we hustle, maybe Ian and I can still make our reservation at the chicken-under-a-brick place. Hell, maybe we can hop a flight to Burundi. Anything to get out of here.

I'm about to make an excuse—a migraine, a phone call, explosive uncontrollable diarrhea—when the hostess interrupts. "Any parties of four waiting for a table over here?" she calls, popping up on her toes and shouting over the din in the bar. "I could take a quad right now."

The chatter in the crowd gets more purposeful then, everybody peering around to see who's going to claim it. But there don't actually seem to be any four-person parties waiting; it's all couples like Ian and me—or Gabe and Sadie, I think with shocking sourness—and big, raucous groups. The quizzical hesitation is palpable as we look at each other, the four of us coming to the same obvious, horrifying conclusion at once.

Sadie's the one who says it. "Do you two want to double up?" she asks cautiously. There's a low midwestern lilt to her voice, Kansas maybe; it makes me think of wide-open spaces, of long afternoons running around in the grass. "I mean, were you waiting for a table?"

"Totally," Ian says. "Let's do it." He glances at me for confirmation, apparently oblivious to the panic and dread I'm sure must be radiating off me in a thick, noxious cloud. "That's cool, right? Honestly, I just want to sit down someplace. I'm about to eat my shoe."

"Um." I purposely don't look in Gabe's direction, same as I can tell he's purposely not looking at me; it feels like one stray second of eye contact might give up the game here, lay our whole sloppy history out for everyone to see. The last thing I want is to have dinner with him. I don't see how I *can* have dinner with him without one or the other of us somehow plowing up the past I've spent the last year keeping buried for everyone's benefit. I don't trust myself not to lose my head and start screaming, to demand an explanation for why he ghosted like he did. *I needed you last fall,* I want to tell him. *I needed you, and you made sure I knew I didn't matter.*

It's that last thought that has my spine straightening: after all, if Gabe can act like there's never been anything worth remembering between us, then so can I. "Sure," I say brightly, tucking my hair behind my ears and smiling. "Absolutely."

Gabe looks shocked, then slightly irritated, like he was counting on me to come up with a plan for emergency evacuation and—just like always—I've let him down. Well, screw him, I think. At least one of us has to be a damn adult here. "Sounds like a plan" is all he says, raising his hand at the hostess and smiling his dazzling politician smile. "We're four."

The hostess nods briskly and leads us through the clusters of tables to one of the booths at the back; I slide in next to Ian and across from Gabe, still careful not to make eye contact.

"So when was the last time you guys saw each other?" Sadie asks as we get ourselves settled. She's got sharp blue eyes and a faint spray of freckles across her nose, with pale eyebrows and the kind of deep, even tan that tells the story of a summer spent outdoors. "Molly, is your family still in Star Lake?"

"Um, my mom is," I admit, glancing down at the menu, "but I don't get back there too often. We haven't seen each other since last year."

"Long time," Gabe agrees, scanning the beer list. Neither one of us volunteers any other details.

"Actually, dude," Ian says, nodding his chin at Gabe across the table, "you're exactly the right person to clear this up for me. Your town can't possibly be as bad as Molly makes it out to be, right? Whenever she talks about Star Lake, it's like it's situated directly on top of a hellmouth."

I wince. He's ribbing me, doing a little comedy routine for my benefit, but I definitely don't want Gabe, who's basically the mayor of Star Lake, to think I go around trash-talking it—especially considering the holy havoc I wreaked there last year. "I never said that," I protest.

"Oh, really?" Ian gives me a look like, *come on*; Gabe is eyeing me from across the table, all long eyelashes and inscrutable expression. "I think the exact words you used were—"

"Okay, okay, but Star Lake talk is boring," I interrupt, then turn to Sadie. "So are you also at Notre Dame?"

"Guilty as charged," she says, lifting her backpack off the booth to reveal a Fighting Irish water bottle hooked to one strap by a carabiner. She's premed just like Gabe, she tells us; they met in their organic chemistry class freshman year but didn't connect until last fall, when they were in the same Shakespeare gen-ed requirement they'd put off as long as humanly possible. "So there we were, these two science nerds trying to figure out what on earth was going on in *A Midsummer Night's Dream*," Sadie recalls. "It was comical, really."

"Hey, speak for yourself," Gabe says, smiling the first genuine smile I've seen out of him since our eyes locked in the bar; the sight of it sends a pang through my body. Of course he's smiling at her, I remind myself sharply. She's his *girlfriend*. I bury myself in my menu, mumbling something inane about shepherd's pie.

Sadie asks what we've seen in London so far and Ian gives her the rundown, thankfully only stopping to tease me a little about what a tight schedule I've got us on. "What about you guys?" he finishes, reaching for his pint glass. "When did you get into town?"

"Just a couple of days ago," Sadie says. They took the train out to Buckingham Palace yesterday, she continues, then snagged student rush tickets to a show in the West End. "We were in Scotland before that," she finishes. "We spent a few days hiking and camping near Edinburgh."

I look at Gabe in surprise: "Since when are you into *hiking*?" I blurt, before I can stop myself.

Gabe's eyes widen, just slightly. "Since always," he says, shrugging over his beer bottle and looking irritated. "I used to go all the time back home."

"In Star Lake?" That's a lie if ever I've heard one: Patrick is pretty outdoorsy, maybe, but Gabe has always been more of the "drinking beer at a party in the woods" type of nature appreciator. Still, it occurs to me all at once that this is dangerous ground to be crossing, and I turn to Sadie instead: "How was Scotland?" I ask her eagerly. "I mean, keep in mind, you could tell me literally anything and I'd believe you. Everything I know about it is from that sexy time-travel show."

Sadie shakes her sandy head, quizzical. "I don't know it."

"Oh man, my roommate and I were obsessed." I smile, launching into a detailed explanation of the broader plot points—labyrinthine palace intrigue, daring escapes from British prisons, rakishly handsome Highlanders in kilts. "You'd actually probably really like it," I tell her. "The main character is a woman doctor."

"Yeah," Sadie says, in a voice that's not unfriendly,

exactly, but also somehow manages to communicate the fact that I emphatically haven't sold her on the concept. "I guess I don't really watch a lot of stuff like that," she explains, holding one hand up like, *you know how it is.* "Girly stuff, I mean. I'm more into, like, grittier shows and documentaries, that kind of thing."

"Oh," I say, slightly taken aback. Something about the way she said it pings me, but debating Gabe's new girlfriend over the merits of a time-travel show seems like a stupid hill to die on. "Okay, yeah. I hear you."

"Molly loves documentaries," Ian puts in helpfully. Then, looking at me: "Didn't you say you once spent a year working your way through, like, every documentary on Netflix?"

"Um, yup," I admit, cringing. In fact, it was senior year of high school; I was away at boarding school in Arizona, hiding out after the *People* article about my mom's book—and, by extension, about me and Gabe and Patrick—hit newsstands. I did the same thing last summer back in Star Lake in an effort to avoid the wrath of Gabe's sister, Julia, chomping down on Red Vines and hibernating in my room. "That was me."

Thankfully, the curly-haired waitress shows up just then, notepad in hand, and once we've ordered I slide out of the booth and escape to the tiny, gilded ladies' room. I splash cold water on my face and stare hard into the fake-aged mirror above the sink: *Pull it together,* I order myself, and I almost think that I have until the moment I open the bathroom door and find Gabe waiting in the hallway on the other side of it.

"I had to pee," he says immediately, jaw jutted out and a voice like he thinks I'm about to accuse him of something. "I didn't just, like, follow you back here."

Oh, for Pete's sake. "Okay," I say, shrugging. "I didn't say you did."

Gabe's eyes narrow as if he's going to argue, but in the end he just kind of droops. "Sorry," he says, looking a little ashamed of himself. "This is really fucking weird."

That makes me laugh, a noisy half-hysterical cackle. "Yeah," I agree, "no kidding."

"I mean—" Gabe breaks off and for a moment we just stand there, looking at each other in the narrow, darkened hallway. His short hair makes his face seem sharper, more grown-up. "So, um," he says, after a beat too long for it not to be awkward. "You called me."

My face flushes; I'm surprised he brought it up. I remember the night I did it, perched at the top of the tiny fire stairwell in my dorm building last September, one arm wrapped around my stubbly knees: *I need to talk to you,* I said into his voicemail. *It's important.* The memory feels like a bone bruise, ugly and deep.

"Um," I say finally. For an instant I think about telling him everything: the way my sneakers squeaked against the shiny linoleum floor of the clinic in Boston, the feeling of the doctor's gentle, sandpapery hands. Watching the

44

bright-orange trees out the window once it was over, leaning back in the passenger seat of my mom's car. Then I shake my head. There's no way for me to tell him in this crowded bar halfway across the universe. It's possible there's no way to tell him at all. "Yeah."

"And I didn't call you back."

I nod. "That's true, too."

Gabe exhales. "I'm sorry," he says, jamming his hands into his pockets. "I just . . . was caught up with school stuff, I guess."

I swallow. "I get it," I lie hurriedly, waving my hand like it's no big deal and deciding not to mention that it's right up there with dogs and homework for the flimsiest excuse I've ever heard in my life. "I mean, I probably wouldn't have called me back either if I were you."

Even as I'm saying it, it occurs to me that it isn't true, not really. Gabe and I had the world's messiest breakup, that much is undeniable—I spent all of last summer somersaulting wildly between Patrick and him, oblivious to the fact that I was more or less the latest prize in some long-running brotherly pissing contest. But we talked it out before I headed up to Boston, the two of us sitting side by side on the sunbaked hood of his beat-up station wagon on the very last day of summer break, and I honestly thought we were, if not exactly okay, then definitely on the road to getting there. I even wondered if there was a chance we might be able to make things work between us someday. Of *course* I would have called him back, if the situation were reversed. Of course I would have come.

"Anyway," I say, tucking my hair behind my ears and smiling as bright as I can muster. "It's all over now, right?"

"Yeah," Gabe agrees, after another long moment. "I guess it is."

"Good." I let a breath out. "So we're cool?"

Gabe nods at that, but he's still looking at me with that unconvinced expression on his face, like I'm one of those human statues on a street corner and he's waiting for me to break and move. "What?" I demand finally. My face gets hot, though that could be the bar or the beer or any number of acceptable, non-Gabe-related things. "You wanna fist-bump on it or something?"

That makes him smile, wide and easy; just for a second, he's the Gabe I know again. "Sure, actually," he says. "Let's fist-bump on it."

We do, clumsy, both of us laughing. "You didn't explode it," I protest.

"I didn't," he agrees, making a face at me. "Come on, let's go before they start wondering where we are."

I follow him back to the booth, where Ian and Sadie are deeply engrossed in a conversation about a *New Yorker* article they both read about fracking, which I suppose is more serious than time-traveling lady doctors. One of Ian's great talents is his ability to hold forth with anyone on basically any topic, from Patriots football to the midterm elections to the complex machinery behind nineties boy bands. It should make him obnoxious—it would make most people obnoxious, I think—but it doesn't, for some reason. Instead it just makes him fun to talk to. "That same guy wrote a book about deforestation that'll make you crap your pants," Ian's telling her excitedly.

"Ian likes to read," I tell Sadie, reaching for the pitcher on the table and splashing some more beer into my glass. "Just in case that wasn't abundantly clear."

"You know, I've been getting that impression?" Sadie laughs. "Who's your favorite author?"

Ian smiles bashfully. "I mean, how long do you have?"

It should be awkward. It should be *awful*. An impromptu double date with my ex and his new girlfriend? It's like something out of a bad student play. But the longer we sit there—and the more pitchers of beer we order—the more surprised I am by how easy it starts to feel. Sadie is a big talker, full of stories about Notre Dame and the wilderness camp she worked at this summer and her four brothers back at home in Omaha, all of whom also have names that start with the letter *S*. Even Gabe warms up a bit, chiming in with a story about the two of them landing at Heathrow and riding six blocks in the backseat of a car before realizing it wasn't an Uber.

"Once the poor guy figured out he wasn't being carjacked I thought he was going to murder us," Gabe admits, grinning; Ian is laughing so hard he's about to snort his beer.

"We basically grabbed our stuff and jumped out into moving traffic."

It's normal, sort of; more than that, it's *nice*. Still, I know just sitting at this table is pushing my luck in a pretty spectacular fashion, and I mean to pull Ian away as soon as we've eaten—to head back to our rental or even another bar, a place that's just the two of us. But right as we're about to ask for the bill the jazz trio out in the courtyard is replaced by a rough-around-the-edges cover band, and before I know it the whole place is rocking with the sound of a slightly out-of-tune British Bon Jovi cover.

"Well, now we have to dance," Ian says, in a voice like he's delivering truth from a higher power, which as far as he's concerned he basically is: Ian loves to dance. Already he's moving around in his seat a bit, broad shoulders bopping up and down like a little kid in a bounce house. He looks across the table at Gabe and Sadie. "You guys? You in?"

Right away, Gabe shakes his head. "That . . . is a hard pass," he says, sitting back in the booth; he's smiling, ostensibly good-natured, but he's also got his arms folded with a mulishness I don't recognize. "Thanks, though."

I raise my eyebrows, frowning at him across the table before I can quell the impulse. I've always thought of Gabe as incredibly game, the first guy to order a five-alarm chili burger or jump in the lake in the middle of January or run across campus in a pair of tighty-whiteys on a dare; the kind of person who's always been confident enough never to worry about the possibility of looking dumb. I can't tell if it's the company—namely, me—turning him guarded and reluctant, or if there's something else going on. Either way, I remind myself, it isn't my problem anymore.

"Do you guys want to get the check, then?" I start to ask, but Sadie is already sliding out of the booth, all long limbs and maxi skirt, a worn-in pair of Birkenstocks on her feet.

"Oh, come on," she says, holding her hand out for Gabe's, "it's vacation." She gestures at me. "Molly thinks you should."

Gabe's eyebrows twitch, infinitesimal. "Is that what Molly thinks?" he asks quietly, then sighs and puts his palms on the table, making to get up. "All right," he says, "twist my arm."

We head out into the crowd on the patio, Ian's hands warm and clumsy as he twirls me around on the densely packed floor. "You are a really, really bad dancer," I tell him, laughing.

"Fuck you!" Ian says, pulling me closer and pressing a kiss against my mouth as the band segues into an old Coldplay song. He's a little drunk, expansive and good-natured, his fingertips settling low on my hips. "I'm blowing your mind."

"Oh, is that what you're doing?" I tease, thinking of the loaded moment that passed between us earlier. I scratch lightly at his shoulder through his warm, wrinkly button-down, purposely not tracking Gabe and Sadie on the other side of the room. "I wasn't sure."

Finally the band takes a break and the four of us collapse

back into the booth, the waitress dropping another pitcher of beer onto the table between us. "So what's your plan for the rest of the trip?" Sadie asks, rosy-cheeked and a little breathless. "Where to next?"

"Ireland and then Paris," I tell her. Then, to Gabe, "Imogen is in Ireland, did you know that? She got an art fellowship, she's living in a convent or something and studying feminist art from the twelfth century."

Gabe grins. "Sounds like Imogen," he says.

"We were dying to go to Ireland," Sadie puts in, tilting her blond head in Gabe's direction. "Gabe wanted to see the house where his grandpa used to live. But this trip was so expensive as it is, it felt like a bad idea to tack an extra country on."

"Where's your family from?" Ian asks Gabe, taking a sip of his beer. He's definitely a little drunk now, the tiniest bit of a slur to his vowels; his face is flushed pink and new-looking in the warm, humid bar.

"Well, my dad was born in New York," Gabe explains; if he's hit with the same twinge I always am at the mention of Chuck, who died when Gabe was a junior in high school, he doesn't let on. "But his family was from County Kerry."

"Wait, really?" Ian turns to look at me. "Did you know that?" I shake my head—I knew Gabe's grandparents came over from Ireland in the sixties, but not the specifics of where—but Ian's already turning back to Gabe: "That's where we're going."

Sadie's eyes go wide. "Seriously?"

Ian nods. "The convent is like an hour from Shannon," he tells her. Then his expression changes, going thoughtful and alert, and suddenly—horrifyingly—I know exactly what's coming. *Don't do it*, I plead silently. *Say anything, anything but—*

"You guys should come," Ian suggests.

I freeze, both shocked to the depths of my person and wholly, dully unsurprised: in fact, this is exactly like him. Ian loves both big groups and unexpected situations, is forever inviting some random kid from his James Joyce seminar out for a bowling night in Southie or organizing a party bus for a twenty-person trip to eat giant turkey legs at King Richard's Faire. I found it charming, back in Boston. Right now, not so much.

"*Really?*" Sadie asks, sounding delighted.

"Really?" Gabe says, looking significantly less so.

"Yeah!" Ian exclaims. I can see him getting more and more excited by the idea, the ingeniousness of it coalescing in his mind. "Why not? It's only a couple of days." He turns to me. "I mean, if you think that'd be okay with Imogen?"

"Yeah, no, totally, it's not that I don't think it'd be okay with Imogen, I just—" I stop short, frantic as an animal forced to chew its own leg off in a desperate attempt to free itself from a trap. I can feel the same cold panic radiating off Gabe from clear across the table. There's no way to explain why this is a horrible idea without outing ourselves, and it's too late for that now; my carefully assembled itinerary—my

51

neat, tidy plan—is dissolving in front of my face like so much cigarette smoke.

Still, through the soupy haze of hysteria in my brain I can't deny the delicious lick of something unexpected, the opening chords of a song I haven't heard in a very long time. It occurs to me that even after everything that happened, I've been waiting to see Gabe again since the day I said good-bye to him last summer.

"We definitely don't want to put anybody out," Sadie promises. She looks completely and obviously enamored by the idea of coming along, her pretty face lit up like her veins are full of neon. "But that sounds amazing, actually. Like, assuming you guys are for real and this isn't just a politeness offer, and we're not messing up your romantic vacation or anything like that." She looks at Gabe. "Isn't that the point of a backpacking trip?" she asks, sounding almost beseeching. "Like, going wherever the whim takes you?"

"Kuddelmuddel!" Ian bursts out like a contestant on a game show who knows he's got the winning answer. He looks to me for confirmation. "Right?"

Gabe's eyes narrow. "What?"

I shake my head. "Forget it."

For the first time all night, Gabe looks directly across the table at me. *What are you doing?* his expression seems to beg. After all, I could still save us; it wouldn't even take that much. I could weave a thousand excuses. I could tip my hand and tell the truth.

But I don't.

"It's a real invitation, dude," Ian declares, sitting back in the booth, his long limbs everywhere like he doesn't have a care in the breathing world. "We wouldn't ask if we didn't mean it."

"Ryanair flights are like thirty bucks right now," Sadie puts in. "Or thirty euro, but still. I was looking today," she explains, off Gabe's quizzical expression. "I thought we couldn't make it work 'cause we'd still have to pay for a hotel and car rental and all that stuff, but if we have a place to stay . . ." She mirrors his wide-eyed stare. "Oh, come on," she cajoles, hooking her arm around his and resting her sharp chin on his shoulder. "It'll be an adventure."

"An adventure, huh?" Gabe asks, lips twisting. But then, to my utter surprise, he nods. "Okay," he says slowly, like he knows he's outnumbered. "Fuck it. Why not, right? Let's go."

"Sweet!" Ian is grinning. "Glad to have you aboard, kids."

"To Ireland," Sadie says, raising her pint glass. "And new friends."

The rest of us raise our beers in a sloppy cheers, giddy; beer sloshes down my wrist as we clink. I look everywhere but at Gabe as the band starts up again, grateful that the music is too loud to think about what might happen next.

DAY 3

"Wake up, Drunky Brewster," Ian says the next morning, nudging me with one gentle knee and waving a paper cup of weak British coffee in front of my face. "We gotta go meet your friends at the airport."

I shake my head into the sheets. "What?" I mumble. My head is pounding, my stomach gurgling from all the beer we drank last night; for a second I'm completely disoriented. Then I remember:

Gabe. Sadie.

Ireland.

Oh my God, what have I done?

I scramble upright, head clearing as suddenly as if I'd fallen through thin ice into Star Lake in January. "Why did you do that?" I demand, trying not to sound too ear-splittingly shrill and knowing I'm missing by several octaves at least. "Just invite those guys to Imogen's last night without asking me first?"

"Wait, what?" Ian sets the coffee down on the nightstand, blinks at me. "Really? You're mad at me now? Last night you were totally into the idea."

"No, I wasn't," I tell him, though I know I can't actually blame him for assuming otherwise. I wanted so badly to convince him that everything was fine, and I overshot so hard that for a second I even managed to convince myself it was a good idea. "It's just, it's weird."

"Why is it weird?" Ian asks. "They're your friends. Or he is, at least. Isn't he?"

"No," I amend, "I mean, he *is*, but it just feels like an imposition on Imogen, and it wasn't part of our plan, and—" I break off, huffing a breath out. I can't believe I let him do that. I can't believe I let *myself.*

"Do you want to uninvite them?" Ian asks finally, sitting down on the edge of the mattress and looking faintly crestfallen. "You can just text them, right? Say you got some kind of rare European fever and the whole thing is canceled."

I smile in spite of myself, shake my head. "No," I say. "That just makes it weirder." I sigh, scrub my hands through my unwashed hair. "I'm sorry. I'm being a control freak."

"Something new for a change," Ian jokes, but there's a faint edge to his voice. I tuck my hair behind my ears, and just like that I'm my normal self again, bright and unruffled.

"You're right," I tell him. "I'm being ridiculous. It'll be

fun. The more the merrier, right?" I lean over and stamp a deranged kiss on his face before hopping out of bed and trotting toward the bathroom. "Good morning, PS. I'll call Imogen and let her know."

I shut the bathroom door and turn the water on, then scroll through the favorites on my phone until I find the number for Imogen's international cell. "It's you!" she says when she answers. "What's the matter?"

"What makes you think something is the matter?" I ask, sitting down on the cool tile floor and stretching my legs out in front of me.

Imogen laughs. "If nothing was the matter, you would have texted. You guys are still coming, right?"

"No no no, absolutely!" I promise. "Yes. There's just, like. A tiny wrinkle." I rest my head against the doorjamb, try to think how best to begin. "So, first of all, guess who's in London."

I explain the whole night as quickly and factually as possible, leaving out the part where seeing Gabe again set every cell in my skeleton humming like a juiced-up power grid and ending with Ian being Ian and inviting them to tag along. Once I'm finished, Imogen is silent for a moment. "So you're bringing Gabe and his new girlfriend to my nun house today?" she asks. "Is that what you're saying?"

"Um," I say sheepishly, squeezing my eyes shut. My head really hurts. "Yes? I'm sorry. I know it's a massive imposition, you can definitely tell me to go screw, I—"

"No, it's not that," Imogen interrupts. "Come on, I don't care about that. I just . . ." She trails off, the question hanging thick as London fog in the silence.

"I didn't tell him," I blurt. "I know that's what you're thinking, and you're not saying it out loud because you're polite, but—no. I didn't tell him."

"Are you going to?" Imogen asks. "I mean, for the record I don't actually think you're obligated, after the way he totally fell off the face of the planet back in the fall. But that's just me."

I huff a quiet laugh through my nose. "I don't *know*," I murmur, glancing over my shoulder at the closed bathroom door. "I wanted to back when it happened. You know I wanted to. But you're right. He made it pretty clear he didn't want anything to do with me after last summer. So I kind of don't see what it would accomplish at this point except dredging a bunch of ugly stuff up again."

"I mean, I *thought* he made it pretty clear," Imogen points out, "except for the part where apparently now he wants to embark on an international vacation with you and your new boyfriend like a giant weirdo." She sighs. "God, I don't even know where you all are going to *sleep*."

I smile at that, knowing this is about as much of a blessing as I'm likely to get. "Thank you, lady. I can't wait to see you. You're the best."

"I am, truly," Imogen agrees, and I can hear the wry smile in her voice. "But Molly?"

I close my eyes. "I know."

"I gotta say it anyway."

"I know."

"You're playing with fire."

I hesitate. I want to explain to her that I'm not that person anymore, that I've spent the year making and remaking myself until she'd hardly recognize the girl who blew through Star Lake like a category five hurricane last summer, knocking down houses and uprooting trees. What Gabe and I had was cozy and exhilarating and old-fashioned all at once somehow, a love like sitting next to a campfire wrapped in a blanket on a cool September night. But that's over now.

It has to be.

I tilt my head back against the doorjamb, humming my quiet assent into the phone. "I know," I promise again, a third time like a spell in a fairy tale. "But we're friends, Imogen. Or we're trying to be, maybe. That's all."

"If you say so," Imogen tells me, in a voice that lets me know she's not convinced, not really, but she's going to wait until she sees me in person to press me on it any more. "Either way, you better hurry up and get here before I change my mind."

I smile, climbing up off the tile and tucking my hair behind my ears. "I love you," I tell her. "I'll see you soon."

Ian and I pack our bags and use the app on my phone to find the train to the airport, my heart thrumming in a way

I'd rather not examine too closely; by the time we get to the terminal I can't keep myself from frantically scanning the crowd for familiar faces like a secret agent in a spy movie. There's a part of me that's hoping Gabe woke up full of the same existential dread that I did, that somehow he'll have managed to talk Sadie out of this whole doomed endeavor.

The other part of me can't wait to see him again.

In any event, the two of them are already sitting at the gate when we arrive, Sadie's sandaled feet resting on her bulging backpack; she's wearing denim shorts and an Outward Bound hoodie, her hair in a long French braid. "Hey," Ian calls, raising an easy hand in greeting. "You came."

"We came!" Sadie agrees cheerily. Gabe, for his part, looks less than convinced. Still, he seems game enough, chatting with Ian about the crummy fielding the Red Sox have been doing lately and asking if we want anything when he and Sadie get up to get coffee.

"Not so bad, right?" Ian asks me as they trot across the terminal, digging a Tana French mystery out of his bag and looking at me hopefully.

"No," I have to admit. "Not so bad."

I page through my own book while they're gone, losing myself a bit in the story of a fancy party full of diplomats held hostage by South American terrorists. By the time Gabe and Sadie turn up again it's nearly time to board. As Gabe's passing by he drops something in my lap; I startle, blinking down in surprise at a package of Red Vines. For a second I think, dumbly, that he brought them from Star Lake—that's how strongly I associate them with home—but when I look up at him in confusion he only shrugs.

"Saw them at the newsstand," he explains in a voice that pretty clearly communicates, *I am begging you not to make a big deal about this.* "Thought maybe you'd want 'em for the plane."

"Um." I clear my throat. "Thanks," I say, but he's already sitting down on the other side of Sadie, peering at something she's showing him on her phone. I might as well be vapor.

Ian glances over curiously. "I didn't know you liked those," he says.

"I used to, yeah." It's an understatement: I basically lived on Red Vines last summer, gnawing through them by the pallet load. I kept an emergency stash of them everywhere, my work locker and my nightstand and in the glove compartment of my car. I couldn't find them in Boston, though, not to mention the fact that I wasn't exactly hankering for culinary reminders of Star Lake after everything that happened. I haven't even thought about them in months.

But Gabe remembered.

"Attention, passengers," the gate attendant calls over the loudspeaker. I exhale, grateful for the distraction, and shove the Red Vines to the very bottom of my purse.

Imogen is staying in a caretaker's cottage on the grounds of a Sisters of the Resurrection convent on the west coast of Ireland, in County Kerry, where the hills are so green they're almost blue. From the airport we take a bus to another bus, then drag ourselves and our backpacks two long miles up a steep, narrow lane flanked on either side by fields dotted with tiny white stucco houses. A light, chilly rain is falling, the smell of it brackish and new.

"You guys regretting coming with us yet?" Ian calls over his shoulder, his grin wide and energized underneath his Sox cap. He loves an adventure more than anyone I've ever met—except maybe Sadie, whose body was apparently built for mountain climbing and high ropes courses and who looks like she could hike from here to Belfast without breaking a sweat.

"Not yet!" she calls cheerfully, her braid swinging back and forth like a horse's tail.

For his part, Gabe is quiet, one thumb hooked in the strap of the duffel slung over his shoulder; he hasn't had a ton to say since we got off the plane, and I can't exactly blame him.

"I do have to pee, though," Sadie continues, slowing down a bit to wait for me, then peering over my shoulder. "We getting close?"

"I think so?" I frown, puffing a bit from the long tromp up the hill. I'm following the map on my phone, but even with the international plan I sprung for my service is spotty here, fading in and out again. I'm starting to worry we've passed Imogen's turn altogether when a church finally rises up in the distance, tall and stone-clad and spired. Next door is a sprawling Tudor that must be the convent, flanked by a bright, teeming garden; beyond *that* is the tiny cottage that belongs to Imogen and the other fellows. In her emails she described it as her hobbit hole, and I see now she wasn't exaggerating: it looks half collapsed, crumbling mortar and mossy roof and a distinct list to one side, like it's one heavy rainstorm away from being absorbed back into the earth.

My heart stutters in pure anticipation: I haven't seen Imogen since she came to visit me in Boston last fall after everything happened, the two of us cuddled in my extra-long twin bed watching movies on my laptop and eating convenience-store Pop Tarts. My pace quickens as I hurry up the leaf-slicked walkway, my roller bag bouncing awkwardly along behind me. I'm just reaching out to knock on the peeling red door—there's no bell that I can see—when Imogen flings it open and squeals delightedly. "You made it!" she crows.

"There are *goats* on your lawn," I blurt out.

Imogen laughs. "There sure are," she agrees, apparently unfazed by their quiet bleating. "They belong to the ag kids, they're all named after Beatles." She steps back, smiling at the rest of my traveling party. "Come on in, guys."

Imogen has gained weight in a way that makes her look like a fifties pinup girl or a Botticelli angel, all milk-pale skin and jet-black bangs; she's barefoot in a long floral sundress, a million silver bracelets up one arm. She introduces herself to Ian and Sadie with a grown-up confidence, then holds her arms out to Gabe. "Gabriel," she says, mock formal. "Always a pleasure."

"Imogen," Gabe echoes, grinning wry and rueful. "Like-wise."

The inside of Imogen's cottage reminds me of the set of some whimsical, madcap romantic comedy, only ugly. It has low ceilings and exposed wooden beams and a rust-colored kitchen that hasn't seen any updates since the seventies at the latest; there's a teeny sitting room with an ash-filled fire-place, a faded rag rug covering the sagging hardwood floor. "I'm going to put you guys on the pullout, but I can't make any promises about how comfortable it is," she tells Gabe and Sadie, nodding at a flowered love seat that looks as though perhaps it was rescued from a nursing home sometime before any of us were born. "I hope that's okay."

"It's great," Sadie promises. "Thanks so much for having us, really."

Imogen laughs. "Let's see if you're still saying that once you've been here a couple of days," she warns. "The convent isn't exactly the kind of tourist attraction that draws people from miles around."

We shuffle down the dim, narrow hallway that leads to the pair of bedrooms at the back, Sadie peeling off into the tiny bathroom. "When you flush the toilet, there's always this moment you think you clogged it, but don't worry," Imogen instructs. "Just keep holding the handle down and eventually it'll work." She grimaces as the door shuts, lowers her voice. "I mean, like. Most of the time."

She leads us into a bedroom that smells strongly of cedar

and is outfitted with a pressboard bureau, an antique student's desk, and a gruesome painting of the Sacred Heart of Jesus. "My roommate just went home to Alberta," she explains, gesturing for Ian and me to drop our stuff on the narrow twin bed. "She was losing her shit about missing you, though, Mols—she's like your mom's biggest, creepiest fan. She brought all her books here in her suitcase to keep her from getting homesick."

"I didn't know your mom was an author," Sadie says, coming back out into the hallway. "That's so cool." Then, to Imogen: "You were right about the toilet, by the way." Back to me: "Has she written anything I'd know?"

"Um," I begin, purposely not looking over at Gabe. "Well—"

"Hey, did I tell you I bought wine and cheese like a damn adult?" Imogen interrupts loudly. "Come on, it's in the kitchen. We're going to have to drink the wine out of mugs with pictures of Saint Peter's Basilica on them, but that's okay." As soon as Sadie's back is turned she mouths *sorry*, and I shake my head; after all, it's not like I've never had to explain my way out of that particular situation before. It's an awkward occupational hazard of having your mom write a thinly disguised, hugely bestselling novel about your teenage love life.

I'd been dating Patrick for a little over a year when things started to go sour between us; we'd been best friends since we were little, but navigating an actual relationship was messier and more complicated than either one of us was necessarily prepared for. I never meant for anything to happen with Gabe. When it did, just once in the spring of my sophomore year, I blurted the whole thing out to my mom in a fit of guilt and panic; my mom, blocked and past deadline and four years out from the last successful book she'd published, closed the door of her office and committed it to paper.

It might not have needed to be such a disaster. After all, it's an author's job to make things up, to spin stories like spiderwebs right out of the air. But Diana Barlow's literary comeback arrived with a slew of publicity, including a spread in *People* magazine in which she confessed to filching from reality—namely, her daughter's relationship with two brothers from down the road.

That was when all hell broke loose.

Gabe was off at college in Indiana by then, so he ducked the worst of the blowback. Patrick dumped me so fast it all but bruised my tailbone, and their little sister, Julia, made it her mission to turn my life into a waking nightmare: enter boarding school in Arizona and the never-ending stream of Netflix documentaries. It wasn't until last summer that I braved the trip back home to Star Lake—and, true to form, wound up making all the same mistakes one more time.

But: *that was then*, I remind myself, following Ian down the hallway a full year later and clear on the other side of the world. I move through space more gently now. I'm careful about where I step.

Imogen opens the bottle of wine with impressive ease and digs a fat block of cheese out of the pint-size refrigerator, plunking it on a chipped flowered plate and handing me a knife. "So, what I didn't get is crackers," she says sheepishly. "Sorry, dudes."

Ian shakes his head. "I'm off carbs anyway," he says, and I grin. He's tickled by this place, I can tell, like it's straight out of one of the Roald Dahl books he devoured when he was in elementary school. I half expect there to be Twits living under the stairs.

"So explain this fellowship to me?" Gabe asks as we settle ourselves in the living room, Sadie and him on the love seat and Ian folded into a rocking chair that looks like it's constructed entirely of matchsticks. I lean against the sooty fireplace, ankles crossed in front of me. "I didn't think rural Ireland was, like, a hotbed of feminist art."

"Well, that just shows how little you know about the art world, my friend," Imogen says snootily, sitting down beside me and tucking her arm in mine. Then she laughs. "Nah. It was really just this one artist. She was a nun at the convent here who made all these Mary-centered paintings in the twelfth century. Really wild ones, too: Mary punching the devil in the face, Mary preaching in front of a big crowd of believers, Mary doing miracles. Women weren't supposed to be doing any kind of art back then—especially not nuns, and *especially* not, like, this supposedly heretical stuff, so she signed them with a man's name."

"What happened to her?" I ask.

Imogen shrugs. "Eventually she got found out and they burned her as a witch." She raises her wine mug, lips twisting ruefully. "Patriarchy!"

I snort. "I love you."

"And I you," Imogen says. "Anyway, the church sold the property to some hippie university in Vermont in the eighties to use as a study-abroad site—it's mostly botany and agriculture majors on account of the garden and the animals and whatnot, but they also have three women artists come here every summer to, like, do the old art thing." She shrugs. "It's the randomest, I know."

"Random, but amazing," I remind her, nudging her in the side with a gentle elbow. "Like a hundred other artists applied," I tell Gabe.

"Thanks, Mom," Imogen says in a dopey voice. Then she smiles. "I really do love it here," she confesses. "*Actually*—" she starts, then breaks off, seeming to change her mind about something. She knocks back the rest of her wine. "You guys wanna go see the village?" she asks. "We can pick up some stuff for dinner?"

The five of us ramble down the winding road to the town's one diminutive grocery, a narrow, dimly lit storefront packed full from the water-stained drop ceiling to the gritty linoleum floors. Domed cake stands stacked with homemade baked goods line a cheerful front table. An immaculate butcher counter gleams at the back.

Imogen puts me in charge of a salad and I wander the perimeter of the shop for a while, picking out baby lettuce and fat summer tomatoes, a red onion and a hunk of blue cheese. I'm peering down the cramped aisles looking for dressing when I catch sight of Gabe and Sadie leaning up against a shelf full of digestive biscuits, their tall, narrow bodies angled close together. Sadie giggles, reaching up to flick his earlobe playfully. Gabe rubs a casual hand across her side.

I take a step back, irrationally startled; I scurry away and pretend to be really interested in the label of some Irish butter, my jealous heart thumping useless adrenaline all through my limbs. I'm being stupid—*they're a couple, Molly*, I remind myself; *of course they touch*—but I'm also freshly stung. I thought it was real, what Gabe and I had last summer. But seeing him with Sadie makes it achingly clear why he didn't call me back in the fall.

I found out I was pregnant my second full week of classes in Boston, squatting over the toilet in the handicapped bathroom in my dorm, the taste of my own heart hot and metallic at the back of my mouth. I buried the test at the bottom of the garbage can and zipped my jeans up with shaking hands, pushing my hair out of my suddenly sweaty face as I stumbled out into the brightly lit hallway. I remember there were two guys tossing a Nerf football back and forth, an RA yelling at them to cut it out before they hit the sprinklers, and I remember thinking it didn't matter. I remember thinking that nothing did.

I stood there for a moment watching dumbly, a sound like a hundred-story skyscraper collapsing deep inside my head. Then I did what I always did, faced with a reality too big and terrifying to get my arms around:

I ran.

I wasn't wearing my gym clothes. I had ankle boots on my feet. But I took off at a dead tear anyway, down the stairs and out the door and through the crowd of strangers on the sidewalk, ignoring the dirty looks and quizzical cries in my wake. My hair streamed like a flag behind me. My lungs burned in the still-humid air. I ran as hard and as fast as I could manage with no destination in mind besides the obvious: *Not here. Not now.*

"Hey," Imogen says now, laying a cool, firm hand on my arm and squeezing. When I startle alert I see she's followed my sight line, is looking at me with worried eyes. "You ready?"

"Yup," I promise, swallowing, plucking a tomato out of my basket and waggling it in her direction as evidence. "Let's go."

Back at the house we put the boys in charge of dinner prep while the rest of us open another bottle of wine, Imogen turning Beyoncé up on her little Bluetooth speaker. "What do you want, fiddles?" she asks, when Ian raises his eyebrows in her direction. "Beyoncé is appropriate on all continents."

"Fair enough," Ian says, holding his hands up and grinning. "I know when I'm outnumbered."

Imogen and I take our wineglasses out to the tiny covered porch off the side of the cottage, which houses a rickety wicker love seat and a few scraggly plants in chipped terracotta pots. "It's my plant hospital," Imogen explains. "I take the ones the ag kids think are too far gone to save."

I smile. "Of course you do." Imogen loves broken things, projects and fixer-uppers. It's probably why she's stayed friends with me all these years.

"So what is going *on* with you, Boston girl?" she asks me, propping her feet up on the wobbly coffee table and lifting her chin in my direction. "You're looking very Bostonian these days, actually."

I glance down at my jeans and simple black tank top, the long gray cardigan I brought to wear over everything. "What does that mean?" I ask.

Imogen shrugs. "It's not an insult," she says. "It's just not how you normally dress, that's all."

She's not wrong, I guess. Back in high school I was always drawn to brighter colors: flowy purple tank tops or neon-yellow jeans, a pair of bright-red cork-heeled sandals I found while trailing her through a questionable secondhand shop outside of Star Lake. Sometime last fall, though, my entire wardrobe started to feel slightly ridiculous. I don't know how much of that is just a function of growing up and how much of it is more pointed—a line of sartorial demarcation between the old me and the new one. I guess I hadn't really thought about it. "It's faster to get ready," I tell her, trying to sound casual. "If all my clothes match all my other clothes."

"It's very Steve Jobs," Imogen teases. "Very business school." Then, off my wide-eyed expression: "What? It's a compliment!"

I snort. "I'm sorry, how is 'you look like Steve Jobs' a compliment, exactly?"

"Oh, shut up." Imogen shakes her head. "You look good. And, speaking of compliments, can I just say that I'm really glad you decided to come on this trip?"

"Oh yeah?" I ask teasingly. "You missed me that badly, huh?"

"I mean, obviously." She shrugs. "But even beyond that, I don't know. I just feel like maybe it's good, a chance for you to get out of your normal routine or whatever. It seemed like maybe there wasn't a whole lot of room in your life for, like, *whimsy*, after everything that happened last year."

I bristle at that a little bit, I can't help it, even though I know she's only trying to look out for me. "I mean, I don't think it's that there's not room for whimsy," I tell her. "I just kind of like things more planned and organized now, that's all." Then I grin. "You know, like Steve Jobs."

It's good to catch up in person after months of texts and Gchats, both of us talking as fast as we can: about the on-campus apartment I'm going to live in this fall with my roommate, Roisin, and a bunch of other girls we know;

about her mom's yearly cancer scan, which—thankfully—came back clean; about Sabrina Hudson, who just posted an expletive-laden Instagram update excoriating the paparazzi camped outside her DJ boyfriend's house.

"That girl should read a book," Imogen says with a sigh, and I shrug noncommittally. I don't know why I feel weirdly defensive of Sabrina—after all, she's a millionaire celebrity with every advantage in the world and, in all likelihood, nobody to blame for this ugly circus but herself. Still, I guess I know what it's like to have outsiders speculating smugly about how you'll next manage to embarrass yourself with your own bad behavior. I know what it's like to have people rooting for you to fail.

"What's *your* boy situation, PS?" I ask, sitting back and pulling one leg up onto the tottery love seat, wrapping my arms around my knee to ward off the damp Irish chill. Imogen broke up with Jay, her boyfriend from Star Lake, halfway through this year; back in the spring she declared a dating sabbatical, but I'm not sure if it stuck or not. "Is that what you were being cagey about before, when you were saying how much you like it here? I thought I got a distinct whiff of, like, Saint Paddy's–type sexytimes."

"Oh my God, stop!" Imogen exclaims, then claps a hand over her freckly alabaster face. "We've been dating all summer," she admits, peeking at me from between two fingers. "His name is Seamus."

"Oh my God, naturally." I laugh. "What's he like?"

He's a mechanic, Imogen tells me; he lives with his family on the other side of the village, in a house with three elegant setters. "He feels older than us, does that make sense?" she asks, face alight with a rosy flush. "I mean, he *is* a little older than us, he's twenty-two, but it's also more than that. I don't know." She shrugs. "He's serious. He makes me want to be serious, too."

"Well, don't get too serious," I tease. "I like you the way you are."

"Uh-huh." Imogen makes a face. "Anyway, you're definitely going to meet him while you're here, and I have a bunch more stuff to tell you about him, but first you go," she says. "Please tell me all the things about Handsome Ian, but also more importantly please tell me what British drugs you were smoking that made you think it was a good idea to invite—"

She breaks off as the back door creaks open and Sadie pokes her head out, then startles a bit—probably at our abrupt, wide-eyed silence. "I'm sorry," she says, holding a half-empty wine bottle up like an offering. "I don't want to interrupt anything. I was just looking for some fresh air."

"You're not interrupting anything," I promise, scooting over to make room for her on the love seat and somehow managing not to fling myself to the floor and writhe in agony at the idea of Ian and Gabe now alone in the kitchen together, cooking dinner. "Come sit."

"You sure?" Sadie hesitates another moment, and

immediately I feel like a bitch for not having invited her out here in the first place. Imogen must, too, because she motions Sadie closer.

"Yes! Come!" she says. "And bring that wine."

I keep expecting it to be awkward around Sadie, but Imogen is the most gracious of hostesses, and the truth is the conversation feels easy: we cover Sadie's terrifying org chem professor and Imogen's fellowship portfolio and the internship I had over the summer, as a glorified errand girl at a social media startup in a high-rise at the Seaport in Boston. I got coffee and made copies, but they also let me sit in on strategy meetings and help proof presentations to investors.

"It was really cool," I confess, thinking of the buzzing, frenetic energy in the clean white offices, the tall windows looking out over the harbor. "They offered to keep me on for the fall so that maybe I could get a few credits, but I need to see if I can make it work once classes start again."

Sadie nods. "You're a business major, right?"

"She is," Imogen answers for me. "After graduation she's going to make a trillion dollars founding all-female tech startups and selling them to Google."

I snort. "Oh, is that what I'm going to do?"

Imogen shrugs. "Just a suggestion. I'm calling it into the universe. Power of manifesting, et cetera."

Sadie smiles a little uncertainly, but that's just Imogen: all crystals and smudge sticks, an altar to the Goddess set up at her mom's house back in Star Lake. "Do you like it?" Sadie asks me. "The major, I mean."

"I do," I tell her truthfully. I like the math and the logic and the strategy, the orderliness of it all. "I mean, my classes are all kind of bro central, but other than that."

"Ugh, you're probably sitting there surrounded by every boat shoe in Boston," Imogen says ruefully. "Is there any kind of women's organization?"

I raise my eyebrows. "What, like a support group?"

"I mean, I guess you could call it that, if you're trying to make it sound silly," Imogen says, rolling her eyes. "But more just like a place for you all to talk stuff out and come up with strategies so you're not getting steamrolled all the time. Some girls at Harvard did it; I read about it in *Rookie*."

"Is it like that in premed?" I ask Sadie, wanting to include her in the conversation. "It's gotta be, right? Total sausage fest?"

Sadie frowns. "Sort of, maybe," she says, considering. "But I guess I don't really spend a lot of time thinking about that stuff, you know? I feel like people make too big a deal about it sometimes. Like, as long as you're doing good work, I don't see why it matters if you're a girl or a guy."

Imogen tilts her head to the side, an expression on her face that I recognize immediately as the one she wears right before she's about to take someone to school about feminism. "Well, the thing is," she begins calmly, but Gabe opens the back door just then, a dish towel slung over one shoulder.

His gaze darts back and forth between Sadie and me, and I wonder briefly if he wants to writhe on the floor in agony, too. "What are you guys talking about?" he asks.

"Starting an all-girl metal band," I answer immediately.

Gabe nods. "Sounds awesome," he says without missing a step. "You're great on the tambourine. You guys wanna eat?"

Inside, the boys have put together a pretty decent pasta dinner, pesto made with basil from the convent's overflowing garden and hunks of chewy bread from the bakery counter at the shop. Imogen lights a couple of fat vanilla candles and plunks them on the table, and the whole effect is kind of intimate and cozy, the smell of garlic and the sound of the rain pattering quietly against the rooftop, spaghetti heaped into piles on mismatched plates. As I pass Sadie a mixing bowl full of salad greens studded with tiny red radishes it occurs to me that maybe this wasn't actually such a catastrophic idea after all. Maybe it really is ancient history, what happened between me and Gabe on the other side of the ocean. Maybe we really have moved on.

After dinner we drift off in different directions, Sadie slipping outside to call her mom back in Omaha and Ian wandering over to examine the bookshelves, which are full of yellowing C. S. Lewis paperbacks and what look like catechism books from the seventies. I stack a bunch of plates and bring them into the kitchen only to find Gabe already in there, sleeves of his thermal pushed up to the elbows and the stainless-steel sink full of soapy water. "You don't have to wash those," I tell him, nodding at the pile of dirty pots waiting on the drainboard. "You guys cooked."

"It's fine," Gabe says, shaking his head. "I like having a job."

"Well," I say, hesitating for a moment, a precarious load of dishes listing dangerously in my arms. I set them down on the counter, careful to leave a wide berth between us. It's the first time we've been alone since last night at the bar in London. Already that seems like a lifetime ago. "I can dry, at least."

Gabe doesn't say anything either way, but he shifts to make room for me, and for a few minutes we work in a silence that isn't exactly companionable. He was quiet through dinner, too, I realize, and the more I think about it the stupider I feel. Just because I felt like this was going okay—was enjoying myself, even—doesn't mean anything has changed between us. He's probably counting the minutes until he can grab his new girlfriend and escape back to his peacefully Barlow-free life.

"Look," I begin, twisting the thin dish towel between my nervous hands. "I'm sorry about all this. I know you kind of got dragged here against your will."

Gabe huffs a sound that isn't quite a laugh. "Don't worry about it," he tells me. "I made my own bed. The whole thing just kind of got away from me, you know? I was so surprised to see you last night at the bar that I didn't know how to explain—"

"I know," I say quickly. "Me either."

Gabe nods, both hands submerged in the soapy, lemon-scented water. "So I'm taking it you haven't talked to Ian about—"

"No," I say, rubbing hard at a spot on a water glass and not looking at him. "Have you told—?"

"I haven't," he admits. "I mean, not that there's any reason to keep it from her or anything like that, I just—"

"No, I get it," I interrupt. "Totally. It's complicated."

Gabe hums a sound that might or might not be agreement, smiling wryly. "That's one word for it," he says.

We're quiet for another moment then, just the hiss of the running water and the clink of dishes as Gabe pulls them from the sink and hands them to me to dry; I can hear Imogen's muffled voice from the living room, Ian's full-throated laugh.

"He seems like a good dude," Gabe says. "Ian, I mean."

"He is," I agree, standing on my tiptoes and setting a plate in the narrow cupboard. "Sadie, too."

Gabe nods. "Yeah," he agrees, mouth quirking. "She's a good dude."

"So how's things?" I ask as we finish up, wiping my hands on the threadbare dish towel and then on the back of my jeans for good measure. "How's school, how's everybody at home, how's Pilot?" Pilot is the Donnellys' hound mix, a loyal rescue with soulful eyes and terrible breath; he used to rest his head in my lap while I did homework at the kitchen table in the farmhouse, leaving damp spots of drool on my thigh.

"Everything's good," Gabe replies, though he's angling his body slightly away from mine so I can't get a real look at his face as he says it. "Same as always. Not a ton to report." He hesitates for a minute, draping a dish towel over the edge of the sink to dry. "The shop had kind of a slow summer, I guess, but other than that."

"Really?" I'm surprised—when I think of his family's pizza place it's always packed, old Motown on the jukebox and pies coming out of the brick oven at breakneck speed, little kids and their tired-looking parents lined up on the bench outside the front window to wait. "What's going on?"

Gabe shrugs almost violently, all shoulders and elbows. "Who knows?" he says. "It's fine, it's not a big deal or anything. We'll bounce back."

I nod cautiously. There's something about his delivery I don't entirely buy—it's a reasonable facsimile of breezy coolness, maybe, but not the real thing. Still, I keep my mouth shut. After all, he isn't mine to press.

"So how you doing, Molly Barlow?" he asks, leaning back against the orange laminate countertop and crossing his arms. He always used to call me by my first and last names when we were dating, paradoxically intimate, and the nickname combined with the fact that he hasn't bolted from the room at his first available opportunity does something to the inside of my body, wringing all my organs out like a sponge.

"You taking the business world by storm up in Boston?"

"I mean, I don't know about *that*," I say carefully. "But I really, really love it there."

Gabe's smile falls then—just a little bit, around the eyes, and nothing you'd notice if you hadn't spent your whole life getting intimately acquainted with the finer details of his face—and I wonder if he's thinking of his own brush with Boston life. Last summer while we were dating he got pretty far along in the interview process for an undergrad program at Mass General, which would have put him just down the road from my dorm near Kenmore Square. He and I were already broken up by the time he found out he didn't get in, but for a while at least, Boston was a thing Gabe and I were going to do together. "Yeah," he says now, "I can tell."

It doesn't sound precisely like a compliment, and I raise my eyebrows. "What?" I ask. "How do you mean?"

"I don't know," Gabe says. "You're different, is all."

I shake my head, suddenly self-conscious, lifting a hand to the back of my neck as I remember what Imogen said outside in the plant hospital. "It's just a haircut," I protest, trying not to sound defensive. "Some new clothes."

"I don't mean your haircut." Gabe picks the dish towel up again, wipes at the already clean countertop. "So what," he asks, not quite looking at me, "you did the whole college reinvention thing? New year, new you?"

His tone riles me—like he thinks it's stupid or immature, something I read about in *Cosmo*. "It has nothing to do with college," I tell him, although of course it does, a little—after all, when else was I going to get the chance to start so entirely over? The chance to be someone so perfectly new? But that's not the only reason why. "Maybe I just didn't like who I was back in Star Lake."

Gabe shrugs. "Seems like kind of a big transformation, is all."

"Does it?" I ask, prickly. "Well, next time I'll check with you before I make any significant lifestyle changes, how about."

Gabe rolls his eyes. "I'm not trying to pick a fight with you," he says, although actually it feels like that's exactly what he's doing. "I'm just saying, I never thought you were so bad to begin with."

I laugh out loud, I can't help it, a mean witchy cackle that doesn't sound anything like my normal laugh. "Oh, *really?*" I demand, emboldened by the naked nerve of him. "'Cause I'll be honest, you could have fooled me."

Gabe opens his mouth, closes it again. "I—" He breaks off. "Look, Molly," he tries. "What happened last summer was—"

"Hurry up in here!" comes Imogen's voice from behind me. When I turn she's standing in the doorway with her arms crossed, a skeptical look on her face like she suspects she's saving me from myself. *It's not like that,* I want to tell her, except for the part where maybe it actually is. "Everything okay?"

I nod, pushing my hair behind my ears and smiling sunnily, turning purposefully away from Gabe. "Everything's super," I tell her, wrapping an arm around her waist and squeezing. "Just catching up. Is there more wine?"

"There sure is," Imogen says, picking the bottle up by the neck and waving it in my direction. "Come on."

Out in the living room Beyoncé has given way to Amy Winehouse, moody and mournful; I plunk down next to Ian on the carpet, breathing in his whiskey-skin smell. "Hi," I say, more enthusiastically than I mean to. It occurs to me that I'm really glad to see his face.

"Come sit," Sadie calls to Gabe, who's still skulking in the kitchen doorway. She scoots over on the sofa to make room for him, tucking her bare, callused feet underneath her. "We're playing Never Have I Ever."

"We're playing *what*?" I all but squawk. Oh, that does not feel like a good idea at *all*. Back at school I made it my mission to avoid getting-to-know-you games of any stripe, up to and including the throwback rum-soaked rounds of Truth or Dare Roisin and her sorority sisters liked to play after their meetings on Monday nights. I liked those girls, the gaggle of them huddled on Roisin's bed in a cloud of perfectly drapey Madewell sweaters, but I always smiled and shook my head when they asked me to come play. "Really?"

"I was pushing for Quarters," Imogen tells me, topping off my wineglass by way of apology. "But we don't have enough beer."

"Can you not play Quarters with wine?" I ask hopefully.

"How sophisticated," Ian teases. "Very French."

I'm about to suggest a list of more desirable alternatives—a late-night nature walk, a game of charades, ritual blood sacrifice—when Gabe speaks up. "I think it sounds fun," he says as he crosses the living room and settles down beside Sadie, slinging one ropy arm around her shoulders and putting his feet up on Imogen's rickety coffee table. "I'll play."

That throws me: after all, I'd have expected him to be at least as unwilling to go dredging up the past as I am. For a second I wonder what he's after, if maybe he's only agreeing for the sake of giving me a hard time—but that's something Patrick would have done, not Gabe. *Not every decision he makes is about you,* I remind myself firmly. If he doesn't think it's a big deal, then neither do I. I can't live the rest of my life desperate to control every single social interaction, can I? Maybe I really do just need to loosen up.

"I mean, if everybody's doing it," I say, taking a generous gulp of my wine. "I'm in."

"Really?" Ian looks over at me, surprise written all over his face.

"Sure," I say, a little too forcefully. "Why not?"

"Just surprised, that's all." Ian shrugs. "It's not usually your kind of thing."

"Well," I reply with a smile, trying to keep my voice light. "I guess tonight it is. Kuddelmuddel, right?"

Ian smiles back at that, easy. "Fair enough," he agrees,

reaching behind me and running a finger over the small of my back inside my tank top.

"Okay, I'm starting," Imogen announces, then grins wickedly. "Never have I ever been to London this morning."

All of us groan. "Oh, come on!" I shout in mock outrage. "*That's* how it's going to be?"

"That is exactly how it's going to be," Imogen says primly. "Now drink, all of you."

Forty-five minutes later we've polished off the rest of the wine, plus some Jameson and an ancient, dust-furred bottle of Sambuca Ian found at the back of a kitchen cabinet. Imogen is warm and giggly, lying on her back with her head propped up on a stack of throw pillows. There's a humming looseness in my limbs. Only Sadie, who has apparently never so much as jaywalked, is still resolutely sober, sitting with her tan fingers wrapped around the bowl of her wineglass as the rest of us confess to cheating on finals (Gabe and Imogen), shoplifting (me and Imogen together, plus Ian in an incident involving a plastic dinosaur when he was six), and having sex in a public place (Imogen again). I know that shouldn't irritate me—the fact that I'm even registering it makes me feel like a mean girl in a nineties movie, judging some fresh-faced ingenue for her lack of debaucherous behavior—but the longer we sit here the clearer it becomes that Gabe has chosen someone as unlike me as humanly possible, like she and I are a study in chiaroscuro out of one of Imogen's art books.

"Really?" Imogen asks, looking at Sadie incredulously as

the rest of us raise our glasses yet again. "You've never broken curfew?"

Sadie shrugs. "I never had a curfew to break!" she says, smiling a helpless, *what can you do* kind of smile. "My parents just trusted me, I guess."

"Oh, you're one of *those*," Ian says, grinning; he's enjoying himself, his cheeks flushed a ruddy pink under his beard. "Okay, my turn. Never have I ever . . ." He trails off, thinking a moment. "Never have I ever cheated on anybody."

Oh, for God's sake. It was inevitable, I guess, from the moment we started playing; still, just like that, the game is done. Suddenly I'm furious—at Sadie for her cheerful guilelessness, at Gabe for saying any of this sounded like fun to begin with, at myself most of all for the million and one bad decisions that led up to this point. The rules of the game are clear: I need to pick up my glass, take a sip, and own up to my past indiscretions.

But I don't.

Instead I hold my drink resolutely in my lap, silently daring Gabe to call me out in front of everyone and gambling on the notion I still know him well enough that he won't. After all, we've both moved on, haven't we? What could he possibly have to gain?

My bet pays off: the room goes quiet, save the low croon of Imogen's speakers, Amy Winehouse wondering who'll still love her tomorrow. "Nobody, huh?" Ian asks, looking around the silent circle with interest. "What upright emotional citizens we all are."

"Seriously," Imogen says, then—and God, have I ever loved anyone like I love Imogen?—lets out a big, exaggerated yawn. "Probably best to quit while we're ahead," she says. "Time for bed, yeah? Which means the rest of you need to clear out of here so I can put sheets on the pullout for these two." She motions to Sadie and Gabe, stopping to think for a minute. "Assuming I *have* sheets for the pullout. Huh."

"I'll help you look," Sadie says, climbing to her feet with an easy, athletic grace and following Imogen in the direction of a tiny front closet. I escape down the hallway to the bedroom I'm sharing with Ian, and I don't look back as I go.

DAY 4

Ireland in the early morning reminds me of Star Lake at the very end of winter when the ground has just thawed, everything damp and fresh and green-smelling. I dig my sneakers out of the bottom of my suitcase and do a few loops around the grounds of the convent, taking deep sips of the cool morning air. I ran competitively in high school, but now it's just a thing I like to do to shake the cobwebs out, a way to clear my head; in Boston I went every morning even in the dead of winter, icy pavement slippery under my feet and the cold wind rattling deep inside my chest cavity. Roisin thought I was a maniac. "Who's chasing you?" she liked to joke.

"Myself," I always told her, and jammed my headphones into my ears.

This morning it's more of a shuffle than a sprint, jet lag

coupled with the sticky residue of last night's wine fog; still, I'm pink-cheeked and puffing when I make it back, stopping to stretch for a minute before heading inside. I stumble into the bathroom, bumping the door open with my hip as I untangle my headphones—and find Gabe standing in front of the ancient enamel sink wearing a pair of gray boxer briefs and nothing else.

"Oh my God!" I yelp, louder than is probably necessary, holding my hands up in raw, shocked panic. "Sorry sorry sorry, I didn't know anybody was in here."

"Um, yeah," Gabe says quickly, sounding a bit rattled himself. "I am."

"I . . . see that," I agree. My eyes flick around the green-tiled bathroom for a second, desperately trying to find somewhere safe to land, but it's like everywhere I look there's Gabe and his mostly naked body, his chest and his collarbones and the faint trail of dark hair between his navel and his waistband. "Sorry. I'll—" I motion toward the door so enthusiastically that one of my headphones flies out of my hand and lassoes itself around the doorknob. I grimace.

"No, it's cool," Gabe says as I'm desperately trying to set myself free. "I'm just finishing up. You can—"

"Oh, no, that's fine, I—" I shake my head, finally getting the cord untangled with a brutal yank and straightening up again. He and I dance an awkward two-step, both of us moving from side to side in tandem to try and get out of each other's way. He smells like toothpaste and like sleep, his body radiating that just-woke warmness. "Sorry," I say again. He shared a bed with Sadie last night, I remind myself. "Hangover brain, or something."

Gabe smiles at that, just faintly. "Yeah," he admits, "I guess everybody hit it kind of hard last night."

Well, not everybody, I think, then immediately feel ashamed of myself. God, I have no chill at all. I remember how riled I got last night during our argument in the kitchen, remind myself to get a grip. "Yeah," I echo, then lower my voice. "Um, about that. Sorry about the whole Never Have I Ever thing."

Gabe waves a hand to stop me. "Don't worry about it," he says. "I had fun, for a while at least. And it's a complicated situation, right? Bound to get a little awkward now and then."

Well, that's an understatement. "Yeah," I finally agree. "I guess you're right."

We stand there for a moment, neither one of us talking. Gabe rubs at his bare, freckly shoulder, self-conscious; it occurs to me that I'm definitely not the only person aware of just how small this space is. Still, I can't help but notice he isn't moving anymore. In fact, neither one of us is.

"So I'm going to go," I blurt, even though he literally just said he was finished. "Um. Sorry again. Bye!" I turn around and bail out of the tiny bathroom before I can catch sight of the expression on his face—or, I think guiltily, before he can read anything into the expression on mine.

I find Imogen in the kitchen. "I just walked in on Gabe in the bathroom," I announce, compelled to unburden myself. Then I turn around and see Sadie standing at the table with a mixing bowl and wooden spoon.

"Um," I amend immediately, "I didn't see anything." I smile at Sadie, looking at her with wide, interested eyes and changing the subject. "What are you making?"

"They're trail mix muffins," she says, scraping down the sides of the bowl. "I went down into town this morning to get the ingredients. It felt like the least I could do to say thank you to Imogen for letting us crash here."

"I keep telling her it's nothing," Imogen says, hopping up on the counter, her bare heels bumping lightly along the cabinets. "But I've also never turned down a baked good in my life, so. Trail mix muffins for everybody."

"We used to make them at base camp and eat them on hikes," Sadie says. She sets the bowl down on the table and reaches for an ancient-looking muffin tin that Imogen must have scrounged up from the back of some dusty cabinet. "The kids couldn't get enough of them."

"Gabe wasn't a camp counselor too, was he?" Imogen asks, sneaking a chocolate chip out of the open bag on the counter. "I can't really picture him out there on the mountain starting fires with, like, a piece of string and one safety pin."

Sadie shakes her head. "He was back at home with his

family this summer," she says, voice quiet. She pauses for a moment, eyes cast down as she spoons the batter into the greased tins. "So hey, can I ask you two something?" she begins, still not looking at us. "You've known Gabe a long time, right?"

I feel Imogen's dark gaze flick in my direction; I nearly swallow my tongue. "Um, yeah," I manage, a flush that's got nothing to do with my run creeping up my back underneath my T-shirt. "Both of us have, since we were little kids."

Sadie nods. She wipes a smear of batter from the back of her hand with a dish towel, not licking it off like I would have. "Does he seem—" She stops, seeming to reconsider. "I don't know. Never mind."

My brow furrows; I think, very clearly, *leave it*. Still, "Does he seem what?" I hear myself ask.

Sadie sighs. "He's just so *unhappy*," she says, setting her spoon down. "It started at the end of the school year—he was just such a bear all the time. And I thought it was finals stress or whatever, but we were apart all summer and now we're on this amazing trip together and he's so—" She shrugs. "I don't know."

"Really?" I ask. That doesn't sound like Gabe at all. Back in Star Lake he was everybody's favorite person, easygoing and sure of himself and happy to get along. Yeah, he's seemed out of sorts the last couple of days, but I just assumed it was my fault for barreling back into his life like a bull charging the streets of Pamplona. It's startling—and a little embarrassing—to realize that of course he has more on his mind than me.

"Have you talked to him about it?" Imogen asks, the voice of reason from her perch on the counter.

"I've tried," Sadie says. "And he keeps saying everything is fine. But then I'll say something about Indiana or our program or the future, and he gets all weird and cranky again."

"So is it school-related?" Imogen asks, sounding intrigued in spite of herself. "Does he not want to be a doctor anymore?"

"I don't know," Sadie says, the oven door creaking loudly as she slides the muffin tin inside. "Sometimes to hear him talk I don't know why he ever wanted to be one to begin with."

I do, although I don't say it out loud. Gabe's dad died of a heart attack right in front of him and both his siblings, collapsing at the dinner table halfway through a plate of spaghetti Bolognese the summer Gabe was sixteen. Of course he knows in his head that he can't bring Chuck back by becoming a doctor. But I don't always know if he knows it in his gut.

"Look," I say finally, my chest aching with time and memory. God, what do I think I'm doing, listening to the private details of Gabe's new relationship? I've been down this road before, last summer with Patrick's girlfriend Tess, and I know exactly where it leads. "It's been ages since I spent any real time with Gabe. But he's the greatest. I'm sure it'll all sort itself out with a little time, won't it?"

As romantic advice goes, it's about as dumb and useless as *just be yourself* or *follow your heart*, but it seems to do the trick for Sadie: "Yeah, no, definitely," she says, nodding gratefully. It occurs to me that maybe the reassurance was all she wanted to begin with. "I'm sure you're right."

Imogen hops down off the counter then, eyeing me like maybe she's the one in medical school and she suspects there's something here to diagnose. "I'm going to make coffee," she announces cheerily. "Sadie-lady, do you want coffee?"

"Sure," Sadie says. She sets the oven timer, turns around, and smiles at us. "You guys are great, you know that?" she asks. "I'll be honest, I don't have a ton of girlfriends. There's always just so much drama, you know? But you guys are chill."

Immediately my eyes cut to Imogen; sure enough, she's looking at Sadie skeptically, head tilted to the side and lips pursed. "Well," she begins. "I don't really know if that's—"

"If dudes have a problem, they just punch each other in the face and move on," Sadie continues, oblivious. "But with girls it's always like, 'well, she said this to this person, so then I did this, and—'"

"Coffee!" I blurt inelegantly, before Imogen's head pops off her head entirely and flies around the room like a deflating balloon. "Hey, Sadie, want to help me grind the beans?"

Gabe and Sadie borrow Imogen's car to try to find the house where his grandfather grew up, and Imogen's got some work to finish up on her fellowship project, so I find Ian reading his book out in the plant hospital and ask him if he wants to go for a walk into the village. He takes my hand as we stroll down the winding byways, passing carefully tended gardens and a dog snoozing under a mountain ash tree and a truly staggering number of churches. This part of the country looks like something out of a storybook, as if we got off the bus and traveled through time like characters on my apparently silly Highlander show. Even the cars look charming to me, with their steering wheels all on the opposite side.

"Did you know," Ian says as we walk, "that when pensions became a thing in Ireland in the nineteenth century, there was no uniform system for recording birthdates and ages and stuff, so to prove you were old you had to be able to remember 'the night of the big wind' in 1839?"

"That's not true," I say immediately. "What?"

"It is!" Ian laughs.

"How do you even *know* that?"

He shrugs cheerfully. "I read a lot."

"Yeah, you've mentioned," I tease, but I'm smiling. We pass another church, a repair shop, a post office that from the look of things is only open on Wednesdays. I let go of his hand, excavate my phone from my pocket. "Okay," I tell him, "so there's a shop that does all different kinds of meat pies up here that I want to check out, and then there's a super-old graveyard on the edge of town that could be cool if you're in the mood to creep on some dead people who *were* probably around for the night of the big wind."

Ian's eyes widen, exaggerated. "Do you seriously have an itinerary for this part of the trip too?" he asks. "How is that even possible? There are literally more cows here than people."

"I'm just trying to make the most of our vacation!" I defend myself. Then I frown. "Wait, do you not like my app?"

"No no no, it has nothing to do with not liking your app," Ian promises. "I know you love your app. I would never impugn your app." He hesitates. "It's just—sometimes having everything so planned out kind of limits the opportunity for . . ."

"Kuddelmuddel?" I supply.

"See, when you say it in that voice it sounds ridiculous," Ian says, "but yes, basically. Don't you ever want to just . . . wander?"

Truthfully, the addition of Gabe and Sadie into our traveling party is kind of all the kuddelmuddel I can handle for one trip, but I can't exactly tell Ian that. "I'm sorry," I say, a little abashed. "I know I'm probably not the easiest person to travel with."

Ian shakes his head. "You're okay," he promises, smiling. "I'll keep you. I mean, at the very least I'll never accidentally wind up at a place with inconsistent Yelp reviews."

We get the meat pies and a couple of iced teas from the shop in town—which is, for the record, adorable, with big windows and an old-fashioned slide-letter menu above the counter, a girl with two long braids like Pippi Longstocking running the register—and walk about halfway back to the cottage before we find a low stone wall to sit on while we eat. We perch there in one of our comfortable silences for a while, just the sound of two birds chattering somewhere off in the distance.

"So, speaking of kuddelmuddel," I say finally, picking at the flaky crust of my meat pie. "Sorry for being such a weirdo yesterday morning, about Gabe and Sadie coming with us. I know you were just being friendly. And it can't be exactly how you wanted to spend your European vacation either."

Ian raises his eyebrows. "What, hanging out with your home friends?" he asks, looking at me uncertainly. "I always wanted to meet them, Molly. You know that."

"No, I know you did." I nod uneasily. "You're right." It's the only real fight Ian and I have ever had, actually, the week before the end of spring semester; I was sitting at my desk writing a final research paper on workplace diversity policies when Ian showed up at my dorm and announced his mom had canceled the trip to the Galápagos his family had scheduled for once school let out.

I frowned, squinting at my bibliography for a second before looking up from my laptop. "Seriously?" I asked. "That sucks."

Ian nodded. "She's gotta go to Toronto for a client thing," he said, toeing his boots off and hopping up onto my bed with its fluffy white duvet, the flannel-covered throw pillows all arranged in perfect order. The dorm room I shared with Roisin was a cinder-block shoe box with a window that opened three inches and overlooked an air duct; still, I'd decorated it with as much care and precision as if I were outfitting a ten-thousand-square-foot mansion. My books were organized by color on the bookshelf; a rag rug in varying shades of blue covered the industrial stain-resistant carpet on the floor. Above the desk was an art poster Imogen had sent me with graphic renderings of vintage running shoes, and over on the windowsill a tiny cactus sucked up what little springtime sunlight trickled through the glass. It was neat and tidy and organized. There was no space in here for a mess.

"So are you gonna go home anyway?" I asked Ian, pushing my chair away from the desk and turning to look at him. He was wearing a BU T-shirt and a worn-in pair of khakis; his hair was sticking up a little, like it always did when he'd been studying. "See your dad and sister? Or just hang around your apartment until summer classes start?"

"I dunno." Ian looked at me a moment. "You're still heading home for a few days, right? Before your internship?"

I raised my eyebrows; he knew I was. "Unfortunately," I said.

Ian smiled. "You always make your hometown sound like a total nightmare, do you know that?"

"It's fine," I hedged, curling the toes of one socked foot

around the wooden bed frame and not looking directly at him. If I'd given him that impression it was a miscalculation on my part; truthfully, I didn't want to draw any attention to Star Lake, or the person I'd been there, either way.

"*It's fine*," Ian mimicked in an Eeyore voice. Then he sat back against the throw pillows, looked at me for a moment. "I could always come with you," he said.

I laughed out loud before I realized, with no small amount of horror, that he was serious. "Wait," I said. "You want to come to Star Lake?"

"I mean, maybe not with that tone in your voice, I don't," Ian said pointedly. Then he shrugged. "I dunno," he continued. "Is it such a ridiculous idea?"

"I mean, no," I said, already scanning my mind for any possible way to dissuade him. "Of course it's not ridiculous. It's just—*why?*"

Ian laughed. "Because you're my girlfriend?" he suggested mildly. "Because I want to see your house and make fun of your dorky middle school pictures? Because I want to meet your friends?"

"I'll have my mom send you my middle school pictures," I promised, smiling a little. "I had braces and a bowl cut, it was a whole thing."

But Ian shook his head. "I'm serious," he said quietly.

"No, I know." My whole body felt hot and prickly; I shifted uncomfortably in the hard wooden chair. "I get it, I just—" I broke off, wishing Roisin would come back from class to interrupt us. Wishing a meteor would whiz past the building. Anything to cut this conversation short. "I don't think it's a good idea, is all."

"Why?" Ian asked, sitting up a little straighter. "Who are you embarrassed of?" He was trying to sound like he was joking but not hitting it, exactly; there was an underlying sharpness at the back of his voice that gave him away. "Them or me?"

"Neither!" I said, louder than I meant to.

Ian looked at me blankly. "Then *what?*"

I didn't say anything for a moment, the silence stretching out between us gray and cold as the Neponset River in January. The answer, of course, was that I was embarrassed of myself, of the person I was back in Star Lake. I could feel it now, the nauseating green horror of walking down Main Street and running into Julia; the drink knocked into my lap at a restaurant, the unexpected backhand of a whispered insult as we wandered through the bookstore or strolled around the lake. The confusion—and then, inevitably, the disgust—on Ian's face.

"Look," he said finally, sighing a little. "Are you not serious enough about this to bring me home? Is that what it is? And you just don't want to tell me?"

"No," I said, reaching forward and taking his hands. "Hey, come on. That's not it, I promise."

"Are you sure?"

"Yes!" I insisted.

"Well then why are you being so cagey about this?"

"Ian," I snapped, letting go of him abruptly, "can you please just drop it?"

"Why?"

"Because it's not going to *happen*!"

Ian looked startled; I'd never raised my voice at him before. I scrubbed both hands over my face, shaking my head hard like I could rattle all the knots loose that way. "I'm sorry," I said. "I'm just stressed out with finals and stuff. I didn't mean . . ." I trailed off, mortified by my own outburst and trying to reel myself back in as quickly as I could manage. But what could I possibly tell him? How could I possibly explain?

"Look," Ian said again, sliding off the bed and jamming his socked feet into his boots, not bothering with the laces. "I've got a hundred pages to read for tomorrow. I should go."

"No, wait." I stood up too, reached an arm out. "Come on, Ian—"

"I'll text you later, okay?"

I looked at him for a moment, resenting him for putting the pressure on me. Resenting myself for not being able to give him what he wanted. "Yeah," I said finally. "Okay."

Once he was gone I sprawled on the mattress and stared out the window at the air shaft, trapped and pissed and guilty. I picked at my essay for a while. I ate a stale dining-hall cookie I wasn't hungry for. Finally I rolled over and picked up my phone. That was horrible, I texted. Can you meet me?

It took him a long time to text back. Sure, he said. Coffee?

I jumped into my flats and jean jacket, hurrying down the sidewalk with my hands shoved into my pockets. Boston in May is all promise, warm sunshine and pale-green leaves on the trees; still, I found myself shivering like it was the middle of winter, like there was an icicle dripping right down the back of my shirt.

Ian was sitting at a table by the window at our usual coffee shop, one hand wrapped around the back of his neck while he paged through a lit theory textbook. I gazed at him through the window, at his wavy hair and serious expression. For a second it felt like he was a stranger. And that was what I'd wanted back when we started dating, right? Somebody who didn't know me. Someone completely new. Somehow I'd never calculated for how complicated that might get down the road.

"Hi," I said cautiously, touching his shoulder. The café smelled like pastries and freshly ground coffee; Edison bulbs glowed dimly above the counter, and the long tendrils of a hanging pothos plant trailed nearly to the floor.

"Hi yourself," Ian said quietly. He didn't smile.

I sat down across from him, tucked my hands under my thighs to warm them. "Are you breaking up with me?" I asked.

Ian sat up straight. "Am I breaking up with—*no*, Molly." He sighed. "I'm just frustrated, you know? Sometimes it feels like you're purposely keeping me from getting close to you. Like you have this whole other life that I'm just never going to get to see."

"That's not true," I protested, reaching for his arm across the table; a girl in glasses at the table next to ours peered over curiously. "This is my only life, Ian. That's the whole point, you know?" I shrugged and let go of him, picking a paper napkin up off the table and twisting it into a rope. "I told you when we first got together that there was stuff I didn't want to talk about. And you said yourself that it didn't matter. So now—"

"Were you with, like, a ton of dudes? Is that it?"

My eyes widened; I shoved my chair back hard enough that it screeched. "Are you serious right now?" I hissed, glancing at the girl one table over; she was fussing with her phone, probably live-tweeting the couple embarrassing themselves in front of a dozen strangers at a coffee shop. "No! Jesus Christ, Ian."

"I'm sorry," he said immediately, cheeks coloring underneath his beard. "That was out of line."

"Yeah," I snapped, "it was." Out of line or not, the question cut way too close to the bone; I was surprised by the heat of my own outrage, the instinct to defend myself with claws and teeth. I hadn't felt anything like it since last summer, when Julia's ground campaign of social misery finally became too much to tolerate even for me. "First of all," I said, channeling every *Jezebel* article Imogen had ever emailed to me, "even if I'd been with the whole United States Army, that wouldn't be something I had to apologize to you for. Second of all—"

"No, of course." Ian held his hands up. "I'm sorry. I just—what exactly is it that you don't want me to know?" He was smiling at me now, abashed, trying to turn the whole thing into a joke. "Are you on the run from the law? Do you have multiple personalities? Is there a crazy wife locked in your attic?"

I huffed a breath out, leaning back and carding my hands through my hair. "I don't think the wife in *Jane Eyre* is crazy," I finally said.

Ian tilted his head to the side, interested. "You don't?" he asked.

"No, actually," I said, "I don't. I think Mr. Rochester got tired of her, locked her away, and told everybody she was a nutbar so he could have sex with the babysitter."

Ian grinned at me, our fight momentarily forgotten. "You're something else, you know that?" he asked.

I rolled my eyes a little and tried not to smile, not totally ready to give it up yet. "I have been told that in the past, yes."

"Yeah," he said softly. "I bet."

We were quiet then, just the hiss of the espresso machine behind the counter and the occasional jangle of the bells above the door as people walked into the shop; Sam Smith piped mournfully through the speakers overhead. This was my chance, I knew. I could be honest with him. I could tell him about Gabe and about Patrick, about getting picked on and then about getting pregnant. But then what? Once he knew the truth about me, there was no way he was going to want to deal with it. All of this hard work—this whole year—would be for nothing.

Instead I reached for his hand across the table, laced my fingers through his. "I hate this," I told him, squeezing. "I'm sorry. Let's just be nice to each other again, okay?"

Ian looked at me for a long moment. Then he sighed. "Okay," he said finally. "Let's be nice."

In the end his mom had a conscience crisis and canceled her work trip instead of their family vacation, so Ian and his sister spent the week off the coast of Ecuador, swimming with giant tortoises in immaculately clear, blue-green water. As for me, I managed to avoid Star Lake altogether: my mom scheduled a meeting with her publisher in New York, and I took the train from Boston and met her at Penn Station, the two of us haunting museums and theaters and eating roughly six meals a day. It was a neat and tidy solution. It all worked out very well. Still, it wasn't lost on me that Ian and I hadn't actually solved anything, not really—it hung between us all summer, a question that hadn't been properly answered. Coming to visit Imogen was a compromise, in a way.

Of course, I wasn't counting on Gabe.

I don't like thinking about fighting with Ian; it opens up

a gulf deep inside me, a chasm I'm afraid of falling through. "Kiss me," I order now, bumping his ankle with mine as we sit side by side on the wall.

Ian raises his eyebrows, grinning. "Twist my arm," he says, and ducks his head.

He slides down off the wall to do it properly, standing between my knees and nudging them wider. "I'm really glad you're here with me," I tell him quietly, slipping my fingertips into the collar of his button-down; Ian smiles, pleased and maybe a tiny bit baffled, then closes his eyes and kisses me again.

My mom calls as we're getting back to the cottage. "Hey, world traveler," she greets me. I hear the grumble of the ice machine in the background, can picture her standing barefoot in front of the fridge back in Star Lake. "You drinking wine and eating cheese?"

"Some of both," I assure her, stepping out into the plant hospital for privacy. "Just like you made me promise."

"Good girl," she says, sounding satisfied. "I give pretty solid advice, I think."

"Yeah," I agree, looking out at the gray horizon line; thunder rumbles in the distance, and I shiver. "You really do."

The night after I took my pregnancy test I shut myself in the stairwell in my dorm building, made myself as small as humanly possible, and dialed Gabe's number, listening to the echo of the unanswered ring on the other end of the line.

I waited a week for him to call me back, steadfast.

On night eight, I called my mom.

I was terrified to tell her what was going on, terrified that she'd be furious at me—or worse, that she'd turn around and write a book about what I'd done. Instead she stayed very, very calm. "It's all right," she said, once I'd finally finished crying. "That's where we are, then. What do you want to do?"

"I know you probably want me to think about giving it up for adoption," I began, trying to keep my voice steady. After all, my mom would never have been my mom to begin with if some other couple hadn't taken exactly that route eighteen years before. But for everything I'd ever been taught—everything I'd ever *believed*—about a woman's right to choose, nothing about this felt like a choice to me, not really. It wasn't something I'd consciously decided. I was a freshman in college, and Gabe hadn't even returned my phone call. There was no way I was ready to have a kid. It occurred to me, not for the first time and definitely not for the last, how lucky I was that I had the option not to. "But I just—"

"I want you to do whatever's right for you," my mom interrupted quietly. "And that's all."

She came to Boston the following morning, took me to the clinic the day after that; once the procedure was over she brought me back to her hotel in Copley Square, a tall old-fashioned building with a view of the park and a fireplace in the lobby, cookies frosted with the Red Sox logo in little cellophane bags on the pillows.

"I don't deserve this," I said when she brought me a hot toddy from the cozy Irish pub downstairs, setting it on the bedside table and flipping the channels on the hotel TV until she found a bright, soothing rerun. "Mom, really. After everything—I just don't."

My mom's face got very tight then, her lips disappearing and her shoulders going sharp. She grabbed the remote again and clicked the TV off, plunging the room into silence; I thought she was upset with me for being ungrateful until I realized her eyes were full of tears.

"I never want to hear you say that again," she told me, her voice low and urgent. It was the only time I saw her cry all weekend; it was the first time I'd seen her cry in my entire life. "You deserve everything, do you hear me? You are smart and you are kind and you are hardworking, and this doesn't change any of that." She sniffled once and gazed at me for a moment, waiting. "Do you understand?"

I fisted my hands in the clean white sheets, nodded. "Yes," I said quietly. I didn't believe her, not really, but I wanted—in this small way, at least—to be obedient and good. "I understand."

My mom nodded back like the matter was settled—the terms agreed on, the contract signed. "All right," she said. "Now drink your toddy and get some rest."

Almost a full year later I look out at the garden behind

Imogen's cottage, shivering a bit in the late-morning breeze. "So tell me about it," my mom says cheerfully. "How's the trip?"

"Interesting so far," I begin, tucking the phone between my ear and my shoulder and wrapping my cardigan around me like a blanket. "You have time for the long version?"

The sky opens up as I'm saying good-bye to my mom, sheets of rain sluicing off the sagging roof of Imogen's cottage and the fields gone soaked and squelching, the goats clustered up behind the convent and puddles half as wide as Star Lake covering the grass outside. The whole house smells like an aquarium. The couch cushions are damp to the touch. We hole up watching game shows while the boys play some weird variation on euchre with a waterlogged deck of cards and Sadie flips through an Irish tabloid, a bowl of salty stovetop popcorn on the coffee table between us. It ought to be cozy and relaxing, but instead it makes me claustrophobic to be trapped inside like this, like the forced proximity invites disaster. My eyes flick from Gabe to Ian and back again.

"Hey, is your mom's name Diana?" Sadie asks suddenly, tilting her head back onto the couch cushions to look at me; she's finished with her magazine and is holding her phone aloft, cross-legged on the rag rug with an unraveling afghan piled in her lap. "I went on Amazon to look for that defor-estation book Ian was talking about, but *Driftwood* by Diana Barlow is, like, right there on the homepage."

"Oh!" I blink, my heart dropping like the cables have snapped. "Ha. Yeah, that's her. They must be running some kind of deal or something."

"Is it good?" Sadie asks, grinning. "Should I buy it?"

"Um." I panic. "I mean, if you don't like girly-type stuff, then you probably wouldn't really be into—"

"You know, the internet is actually super spotty here," Imogen jumps in, hopping up off the couch like her underwear is on fire. "You're probably better off waiting till you get to the airport to try and buy anything."

"Really?" Sadie asks, squinting at the screen. "It was working fine a second ago."

"Yeah, it goes in and out." Imogen waves her hand vaguely. "Hey, you wanna come help me make more popcorn?"

She takes Sadie's hand, pulling her into the kitchen before she can answer; when I look up Gabe is watching me, the barest hint of a secret smirk visible on his face. *Oh, this is funny to you?* I want to ask—*would* ask, if Ian weren't sitting beside him, calmly shuffling the cards for their next hand.

I think of what Sadie said this morning, how unhappy Gabe's been lately. I think of what he said last night about the shop. I hate to think of the Donnellys struggling, even though it's a pretty fair bet that the last thing any of them want is my pity. Still, a part of me wants to force Gabe to tell me what's really going on.

I think of the hundred thousand slices I've eaten in my

lifetime. I think about the birthday party I had there in second grade. I think of the picture of Chuck hung up in the kitchen, all beefy forearms and thick dark hair, his head thrown back laughing, and wish for the hundred thousandth time he was still around to tell us all what to do.

Twenty minutes later I find Gabe setting out a game of solitaire on the kitchen table just like Connie, his mom, used to do after dinner when we were kids, the cards making a crisp, quiet snapping sound as he lays them down on the Formica. "What happened to Ian?" I ask.

Gabe shrugs. "Shower, I think?"

"Got it." I watch his hands move as he shuffles, his long competent fingers casual and deliberate. For no good reason at all—at least, not one I'd ever be able to say out loud—my entire body goes prickly and alert. "So hey," I announce, reminding myself firmly to stop being such an enormous creep about everything, "I was thinking about the shop."

That gets his attention: Gabe raises his eyebrows as he turns around to look at me, equal parts skeptical and amused. "You were, huh?" He bangs the deck lightly against the edge of the table to even it out.

"Um, yeah," I say, blushing. The house is quiet. Sadie's asleep on the love seat out in the plant hospital, her long limbs splayed out every which way; Imogen's in her room talking to Seamus on the phone. The rain has mostly stopped by now, a trickle instead of a deluge. I can hear it dripping off the rooftop, a steady, near-musical *plink*. "I have some ideas."

"Molly—" Gabe blows a breath out. "I don't know if that's really—"

"Just hear me out, okay?" Off his dubious expression, I sigh. "Look, I know you didn't ask me to do this. And clearly I'm not Warren Buffett. You guys have been running a business for a long time, and I'm sure you've already thought of a lot of this stuff. But on the off chance you haven't, maybe I can help." I look at him. "I *want* to help, okay?"

Gabe looks at me. Then finally he shrugs, leaning back in the rickety kitchen chair and crossing his arms inside his hoodie. "Okay," he says after a moment, chin tucked like a boxer's. "Go ahead."

So I launch into my pitch for a new, improved Donnelly's Pizza: early-bird happy hours with half-price cheese pies for families on vacation and an old-fashioned late-night speakeasy with beer specials and local bands. "You could even set up space outside in the back, like they did at the bar we were at back in London," I suggest brightly. "Put a bunch of Christmas lights up, drag some picnic tables out there, and bam, you got yourselves a patio."

Gabe raises his eyebrows, smirking a bit. "Bam, huh?"

"Yeah!" I insist, laughing a little. "Bam! Come on, these are good ideas."

"They are good ideas," Gabe admits, his smile turning into something real. "You're smart about this stuff, you always have been." Then, presumably off my surprised expression: "What, you wanna fist-bump again?"

"Okay, you know what?" I make a face at him. "Do *you* wanna fist-bump again?"

I'm expecting a joke in return, but Gabe just gazes at me evenly. "No, Molly Barlow," he says, and the skin on the back of my neck prickles. "That's not what I want."

Imogen's bedroom door opens then, the sound of her laughter ringing out like a school bell; I swallow my own swollen, aching heart back down where it belongs. "Anyway," I say, wiping my suddenly sweaty palms on my jeans. "It's worth a shot."

"Yeah," Gabe says, getting up from the table with no preamble, looking everywhere in the world but at me. "Maybe it is."

Imogen reads my cards after lunch, the two of us sprawled on her bed with her battered, beloved tarot deck spread between us. She's been reading for me—and almost everybody else back in Star Lake—since we were in middle school, and her cards have been handled so many times that the edges have gone furry and frayed. It's still drizzling, but barely; out the window Gabe and Ian are kicking a grimy-looking soccer ball around the yard like two little kids after school. "Where's Sadie?" Imogen asks me, following my gaze through the glass as she sets the final card down.

"Who knows?" I ask distractedly, peering down at the Queen of Swords with her fall of raven-black hair; Imogen's deck is beautiful and intricate, the images all drawn in chalk pastel by an artist from California that she loves. "Building a lean-to in the woods, probably, where she can commune with the mountains and get away from bitchy drama queens." I clap my hand over my mouth and look up at Imogen, wide-eyed. "Oh my God, I didn't mean that. It just came right out!"

"Uh-huh." Imogen laughs. "Not a fan of the new girl-friend?"

"No, that's horrible of me," I protest quickly, shaking my head. "That's gross. I like her! She's lovely. She's so nice."

"You sound like Rizzo talking about Sandy," Imogen informs me, smirking.

"Ugh, I do, right?" I sigh, digging the heels of my hands into my eyes. "It's not even that I think she's too pure to be Pink—although, okay, she does kind of seem that way some-times, right? But it's more that she's, like . . ."

"One of those girls who thinks she's better than other girls because she doesn't wear eyeliner?" Imogen supplies.

"Kind of!" The truth is there's a part of me that feels better for admitting it out loud, like the moment of shameful satisfaction after popping a pimple. Still. "I hate feeling like this. It's so boring to not like your ex-boyfriend's new girl-friend. It makes me feel like a terrible feminist."

"Being a feminist doesn't mean you have to personally like every woman," Imogen points out reasonably. "Espe-cially one who is, like, a human slice of Ezekiel bread." Then she grins. "Just don't have sex with her boyfriend, and you're good."

My jaw drops. "Mean!" I exclaim, sitting upright.

"I'm kidding," Imogen says. Then she makes a face. "I mean, kind of. Seriously though, don't."

"Is that really what you think I'm going to do?" I ask, stung. "Because it's not. I'm not *like* that anymore, Imogen. I don't—" I break off, weirdly afraid I might be about to cry all of a sudden. It feels very, very important that she believes me.

Imogen can tell. "No no no," she amends quickly, "hey, I'm just playing. I'm sorry." She reaches and puts a hand on my shoulder, squeezing; I can tell by the stricken look on her face that she really was just kidding around. "Some things aren't for joking, I'm sorry."

I shake my head again, pulling it together. "No, you're fine," I promise, tucking my hair neatly back behind my ears. "Clearly I'm wound a little tight about the whole thing, is all."

"All of us being cooped up in my fucking dollhouse isn't helping, probably," Imogen says. She looks out the window: it's stopped raining, clouds breaking up and buttery-yellow sunlight spilling through. "You know," she says thoughtfully, twisting a strand of her hair around two pale fingers, "There is actually *one* thing to do here, if you're looking to blow off some steam."

"Oh yeah?" I raise my eyebrows with some trepidation,

thinking of last night's game of Never Have I Ever. "What's that?"

Imogen grins. "How do you feel about skydiving?"

"You guys are ridiculous," Sadie says an hour later, standing in the tiny front office of the County Kerry Parachute Club with her arms crossed inside her Outward Bound hoodie. "I'm just saying, if you've got a death wish, I'm sure there are easier ways to go about it."

Gabe is grinning at her. "So I take it you're not going to go up, then?" he teases.

Sadie shakes her head. "I'll stay down here and hold purses, thanks. And call your moms to tell them we had to scrape your flattened bodies out of a field somewhere."

"Oh, I don't think it will come to that," says Ralph, one of the instructors, slightly built with friendly blue eyes and a sandy-blond beard, oddly normal-looking for a person who makes his living plummeting through the atmosphere at breakneck speed. "We hardly ever have two calamities in one week." Then, off Sadie's horrified expression, "I'm joking, love."

"Uh-huh." Sadie nods, profoundly unamused. "Right."

"I'm surprised this isn't your kind of thing, actually," Ian tells her. "Outdoor girl, all of that."

Sadie waves her hand, dismissive. "Hiking is totally different," she points out. "No matter how high you're climbing, you're still technically on the ground. Give me a dozen kids to take out on trail, I'm good. *This* nonsense, on the other hand . . ." She shakes her head ominously.

"I've actually always wanted to try it," Gabe puts in, skimming the release form before signing his name with a flourish and handing it over to Ralph. "My brother did a smoke-jumping thing last year in Colorado. Well, he started doing a smoke-jumping thing, I guess. Then he punched a kid in the nose and got kicked out of the program."

"Can we all go up together?" I ask Ralph, blurting it out before Gabe can say anything else about whatever physical altercations he or his brother might have gotten into last summer—or my involvement therein. "I mean, can you take all of us at once?"

Ian looks at me with interest as he hands his credit card over to the woman behind the counter. "You're in?" he asks, sounding surprised.

I hesitate. I don't know if I'm in, actually; I was undecided on the drive over here, close to an hour in Imogen's ancient clunker. "Um," I hedge, "potentially?"

"Oh, come on," Gabe says. "You love an adrenaline rush."

Ian laughs out loud. *"Molly?"* he asks, incredulous. "Molly—and I say this with love—is probably the least adrenaline-seeking person I've ever met in my life."

Gabe looks confused. "I mean, fair enough," he says after a moment. "I guess you'd know better than me."

I cringe. There's something in Gabe's tone I don't like—a

faint whiff of goading, maybe. But I also get why he thinks of me as someone who'd be up for something like this. There was a time I was game for anything, skinny-dipping in Star Lake or a middle-of-the-night road trip or a clandestine make-out in the woods behind the Lodge. But I learned my lesson. All too often *adrenaline* really meant bad decisions, fire-breathing dragons woken from slumber. All too often adrenaline meant me left holding the bag.

But that's over now.

Isn't it?

I take a deep breath, looking at the various warnings posted on the walls of the office. *You may not skydive if you have a heart condition. You may not skydive if you are under the age of sixteen, or under the age of eighteen without the consent of a parent or guardian. You may not skydive if you are pregnant.*

"Yeah," I say, lifting my chin in quiet defiance. "I think I want to go."

Which is how we wind up nine thousand feet in the air in matching gray jumpsuits like something out of an action movie, the roar of the engines all around us, physical as a cloud. I'm strapped to a cheerful green-eyed instructor named Rose who calls me *love* and promises we're in this together—literally, in fact. "You nervous?" she asks as the airplane climbs.

I wave my hand to say so-so, though the reality is it's taking every particle of self-control in my body not to start shrieking and demand the pilot turn around immediately.

"Um, it's not the heights, really," I yell over the cacophony. "It's more the whole, like, surrendering all control and putting my life into the hands of the universe thing!"

Rose grins at that. "Not the universe!" she promises. "Just me."

Gabe and his instructor jump first, there one second and gone a heartbeat later; they're followed by Ian and Ralph, Ian blowing me a kiss before he goes. By the time it's Imogen's turn I can barely beat back the panic: God, what made me think I could do this? There are too many unknowns here. There are too many risks. Once upon a time, this might have been a thrill for me, an adventure, a lark. But not anymore.

Finally it's just Rose and me left in the hold, Rose looking at me carefully; I think she can tell that I'm about to chicken out. "You with me, love?" she asks.

I hesitate. Jumping out of this airplane feels impossible. But so does turning around now. I swallow. "I'm with you," I promise.

"That's a girl," she says, smiling like maybe I've done something to be proud of. "Then let's go."

So. We jump.

At first all I can register is the racket, the rush of the air speeding by as we plummet through nothingness like the worst kind of dream: it's too loud and terrifying to think of anything, my mind white with panic in the long moments before Rose pulls the ripcord and the parachute thumps open. I gasp at the snapback, then again at the endless view: suddenly it is so, so quiet.

"You okay?" Rose asks, grinning like it's just another day at the office—which, for her, I guess, it is.

I manage a nod, then a hoarse, croaking "yes" that barely travels the distance between us, but the truth is I'm better than okay. I'm windburned and shaky but I'm not afraid anymore, I realize abruptly; I feel peaceful and euphoric and calm. For the first time in a year I'm not frantically calculating for every possible outcome. For the first time in a year I feel free.

I stretch my arms out as we slip through the deep, endless blueness, keep my eyes wide open as we float down toward earth.

That night Imogen wants to take us out in the village; she and I cram into the cottage's tiny bathroom for hair and makeup, cranking some ancient Dixie Chicks up on her phone. It's been a long time since we got ready together, filling in each other's eyebrows and picking out each other's clothes: "Here," she instructs, pulling a screaming red dress with a low neckline and a short, flouncy skirt off a wire hanger and tossing it in my direction. "Wear this."

"Imogen . . ." I shake my head. "That's, like, a little much for a night at your local, no?"

Imogen makes a face. "It's just a dress, Molly. And it's going to look amazing on you." She plugs a curling iron into the outlet above the sink, waves at me with it. "Now put it on and come here so I can give you party hair."

"You know, somehow I can't picture you talking to Steve Jobs that way," I grumble, but I do what she tells me, pulling the dress over my head before sitting down on the toilet seat and holding still as she gently separates my hair into thin sections, pinning them back with claw clips. "My mom sent me one of these at school," I tell her, nodding up at the curling wand, "but every time I try to use it I wind up looking like a poodle."

"How is dear Diana Barlow these days?" Imogen asks, a hint of a smile in her voice. "Cannibalized the romantic histories of any close family members lately?"

"Not that I know of," I report. "She's good, though. She's finishing up revisions for her new book, the one about the carnival family with all the incest. And actually, now that I say that out loud, I *really* hope it isn't about anyone we know." I pause. "Also, I think she might have a girlfriend."

Imogen almost yanks a hank of my hair clean out. *"What?"* she squawks. "Shit, sorry. But since when does your mom have girlfriends?"

"I don't know for sure!" I say. "I've never known her to date anybody, honestly, man or woman. I mean, I'm sure she did. But when I went and stayed with her in New York back in May after school ended somebody had sent flowers to her hotel room, and I know it wasn't her publisher because of how she grabbed the card and put it in her jeans pocket like a big secretive weirdo. And then we had dinner with this woman Corina, who's a publicist, who kept calling her Di and touched her on the back while we were walking to the table. And *then* when my mom was peeing, Corina told me like fifty times how dynamite she is."

"Wow," Imogen says thoughtfully. "Get it, Diana." She pauses for a moment. "I'll be honest with you, Mols, if anybody's mom was going to turn out to be a late-in-life lesbian, my money would have been on mine."

I think of Imogen's mom, with her tarot cards and crystals and *The Future Is Female* tote bag, and laugh. "I don't even know if it's late in life, though!" I point out. "Once I started thinking about it, it actually occurred to me that she might have been dating that woman Joanne who was her assistant when we were in middle school."

"Joanne with the nose ring?" Imogen asks, twisting a few last pieces of hair around the iron. "She was hot."

She was, kind of, I remember now; she always smelled like juniper and secretly taught me how to put on mascara even though I was only in fourth grade. "We never really talked before this year," I point out. "Me and my mom, I mean. Like, I don't think that's necessarily a thing I would have known about her."

Imogen considers that—she and her mom are preternaturally close, the kind of mother and daughter who know each other's every thought and bodily function. It's always seemed foreign to me, though lately it isn't as unimaginable as it used to be. "Does it feel weird?" she asks.

"Not really," I tell her honestly. "I mean, probably it would feel way stranger if I'd actually grown up with a dad. But mostly I just want her to have somebody, you know? It's gotta be kind of lonely, living out there all by herself."

"That's a good point," Imogen concedes, nudging at my back until I flip my head over and reaching for the can of hairspray on the shelf above the toilet; the massive cloud she aims in my direction smells chemical and sweet. "I guess maybe that's one good thing that came out of this year, huh?" she asks. "You guys, like, actually have a mother-daughter relationship now."

I smile as I stand upright, thinking of it. "Yeah," I say. "I think we kind of do."

Imogen nods, fluffing my hair a bit and turning me by my shoulders until I'm facing the mirror. "There you are," she says, sounding satisfied. I stick my tongue out, hide a grin.

I make Imogen wear a sparkly top and sky-high heels so I'm not the only one dressed up for what I'm assuming is going to be a dive bar; still, Ian's eyes widen when we come out into the living room. "Wow," he says quietly. *"Hi."*

"Good wow or bad wow?" I ask, smoothing the dress down. I don't remember the last time I wore something this bright.

"No no, good wow," Ian says quickly. "Great wow, even. You just look . . . you know. Different."

"Yeah." I *feel* different too, truthfully, exposed and eye-catching in a way that's a little scary but not entirely bad. Still, I grab my cardigan before we leave the cottage, ignoring the face Imogen shoots in my direction.

We're headed to the one pub in the village—or at least, I think that's where we're going until we stop halfway down the main street, directly in front of what looks for all the world to be a functioning hardware store.

"Imogen," I say carefully, the cluster of us standing on the sidewalk like sheep in the twilight. The streets are blue and quiet, the shops all closed down for the night. "Like, clearly I'm not an expert on the drinking customs in Ireland, but—"

Imogen laughs. "Yeah, yeah," she says, pulling the door to the hardware store open. "Come on."

We follow her into the bright, empty shop, past a sleepy cat lounging on the counter beside an antique cash register; he eyes us imperiously as we edge down a narrow, crowded aisle full of flathead screws and garden hoses and socket wrenches. When we reach the very back of the store Imogen pulls open what I think is the door to the stockroom, but which actually reveals the tiny foyer of—

"What *is* this place?" Ian asks, looking around in naked delight. The space is small and wood-paneled and dimly lit, black-and-white photos of Irish folk heroes covering the walls alongside a giant banner emblazoned with the green and gold of Kerry's Gaelic football team. It's packed to the rafters with what must be everyone in town, old men in caps alongside young couples, clumps of local girls in low-cut sweaters flicking through the glowing touchscreens of the jukebox and noisy dudes in jerseys clustered around the dartboard in the back. It's hot inside, a narrow door propped open at the end of the hallway that leads to the restrooms and a damp, slightly fetid breeze coming through every now and then. "Is it like a speakeasy?"

"Nope," Imogen reports, "the store is totally real. Two brothers inherited the building like twenty years ago, and they couldn't agree on what to do with it, and it was breaking up the whole family and causing all this drama at Sunday dinner every week. So finally they decided to do both."

I glance at Gabe, I can't help it—*two brothers* and *breaking up the family* feels achingly familiar—but he's peering up at the intricate woodwork on the ceiling, expression inscrutable. *He's not your responsibility anymore*, I remind myself, turning purposefully away as he and Sadie get swallowed up by the crowd in the pub, his dark head just visible over the broad shoulder of a middle-aged woman in a Fair Isle cardigan.

"What are you all drinking, hm?" Ian asks, one hand splayed low on my back as he cranes his neck to see the taps behind the bar. "I'll get the first round."

"Whatever you're having," I tell him. He looks at Imogen, who asks for a cider, then catches the bartender's attention with a subtle lift of his chin.

"He's very gentlemanly," Imogen says, once Ian is out of earshot.

I smile at her. "He is, right?" A thing I've always loved about Imogen is how generous she is with new people, how quick she is to like them. She is, unequivocally, the kind of friend to whom you can say, *I am bringing two extra people to your Irish cottage, please say it's okay*, and when she says it's okay she actually means it. Not everybody is like that.

"He is," Imogen agrees. Then, looking at me more closely, "What?"

"What?" I echo. "Nothing." A red-faced guy in his forties lumbers down off his barstool beside us, and I nudge Imogen into the empty space. "Here, sit."

Imogen does, but she's frowning. "Not nothing," she announces. "That's your *I'm not telling you the whole story* face. Is there something secretly weird about him?"

"About Ian? No! Ian is perfect." I glance around to make sure nobody's listening, but we're protected by the clang and clatter all around us, the din of the crowded bar. Bass from the jukebox thuds in my brain stem; I'm expecting something stereotypically Irish, or at the very least Mumford and Sons, but I think this is actually the Weeknd. I can see Ian gabbing happily away with the bartender, the guy handing him a tasting glass of some dark beer to try. I love watching Ian in bars and restaurants; he always seems older than other people our age, no self-consciousness to him at all. "I just . . . okay. Do you think it's strange that he and I still haven't . . ." I trail off. "I mean, you know what I mean."

Imogen makes a face at me like, *use your words, Molly.*

"Boned?" she supplies when I completely fail to fill in the blank myself.

"Imogen!" I laugh, but it comes out more like a barking cough, as if I'm trying to force the panicky embarrassment out of my lungs like a ball of phlegm. "Yes. I mean, no, we haven't. We've fooled around and stuff, but like—" I wave my hand vaguely. "Is that weird?"

"I don't think it's weird at all," Imogen assures me, sitting back on her barstool. "You've only been dating a few months, right? Why would that be weird?"

"I don't know." I sigh. "I'm being stupid. I always figured how it worked was, like, once you did it with one of your boyfriends then you did it with all your boyfriends, right?"

"I mean, that definitely doesn't *have* to be how it works," Imogen points out. "You aren't actually required to have sex with anybody, no matter how many people you've dated."

"No, of course not." I shake my head quickly. "I know that. But I didn't think it would be this huge deal to me, either." I shrug. "I'm just waiting for the perfect moment, you know? I want to make sure I don't screw everything up like I did last time."

"I mean, sure," Imogen agrees, though she doesn't actually sound convinced. "I get that. But I also think if you're with the right person then the whole perfection thing doesn't really matter, right? Like, you can just be yourself, past screw-ups and all."

"No, that's not what I meant," I counter immediately. "I

can be myself with Ian, I just—"

"Can you?" Imogen interrupts. "I'm not saying that as a dig, I'm just asking sincerely."

"*Yes*," I insist. "I just—"

I break off abruptly as Ian reappears with our drinks, edging through the crowd with three pint glasses balanced in his clever hands. "You guys okay?" he asks, eyes cutting back and forth between us like he suspects he just missed some kind of punch line.

I smile. "We're great," I promise, popping up on tiptoes to peck him on the jaw.

Imogen takes my lead, launching into a story about the night she and a bunch of the ag students living in the convent sang karaoke here all night regardless of the fact that karaoke is not one of this bar's offerings, and the next hour speeds by in a warm, colorful blur. We feed euros into the jukebox and order every variation of fried potato on the menu; I keep waiting for Gabe and Sadie to wander back over and join us, but they never do.

Soon Imogen's boyfriend Seamus shows up, though, an all-smiles Irish boy who looks like he might possibly be a long-lost Weasley brother: "Molly from America!" he says, enveloping me in a bear hug that smells like cigarettes and whiskey. "My girl's been talking about you nonstop since she found out you were coming."

That makes me smile, and I bump my shoulder against Imogen's. "I mean, the feeling is pretty mutual," I tell him.

She nudges me with her hip in return.

Eventually I sneak through the crowd and run to the bathroom; it's pretty disgusting in there, two dingy stalls and grimy tile, a sink not much bigger than a souvenir postcard. I'm just washing my hands when I hear a wet, familiar-sounding sniffle from the stall next to mine. "Sadie?" I ask, tilting my head to the side.

"Um," comes Sadie's voice, then another snotty inhale. "Yeah. Hey, Molly."

I frown. "You okay in there?"

"Yeah!" she replies, voice fake as a wax model in Madame Tussauds and just about that convincing. "I'm great."

"You sure?" I tap my fingernails lightly against the scarred-up stall door, listening a moment. I wait. Finally the lock snicks open.

"Hi," Sadie says thickly. In the greenish glow of the fluorescent light above the sink I can see she's been crying, her clear skin blotchy and red.

"Hi," I say, offering her a hesitant smile. On one hand, I was literally just complaining about how annoying I find this person. On the other, I am certainly no stranger to the secret public cry. "You wanna talk about it?"

"I just said I'm *fine*, Molly."

Her voice is harsh and irritated, and I blink in surprise. This isn't a side of her I've seen before, sunny, crunchy Sadie with her unflappable wilderness-guide cheer, and it must register on my face because she sighs loudly. "I'm sorry," she amends, finger-combing the tangles out of her long yellow hair, twisting it into a rope over one shoulder. "You're trying to be nice to me, I shouldn't snap at you like that. I just had another stupid fight with Gabe, is all. It's not a big deal."

My heart does something complicated inside my chest, painful. "Another?" I ask cautiously. "You guys fight a lot?"

"Constantly," Sadie says. She hops up on the edge of the minuscule sink, apparently unconcerned by the general filth all around us. She's wearing a pair of loose jeans cuffed to her ankles; her feet are tan and unpainted inside her Birkenstocks. "I mean, we didn't use to. But the last few months, all the time."

I'm quiet for a beat, trying to picture it. Gabe and I annoyed each other sometimes when we were together, sure, but we never really argued; he was always way too affable for that. Of course, Patrick liked to point out that it was easy to be everyone's best friend as long as you were getting your way all the time, if life presqueezed your lemonade for you. I wonder if that's the difference now.

"It's like I was telling you guys this morning," Sadie explains, resting the back of her head against the smudgy mirror. "He's just so *unhappy*. He doesn't know what he wants to do and he won't admit it and it's making him so frustrated. And, to be honest, kind of a dick."

God, I do not want to be the trustee of this information. I *shouldn't* be. But I don't know how to stop her without revealing more than what's actually mine to give away. "That really sucks," I finally say. I shift my weight on the gritty tile, trying to figure out how to best make my escape without totally blowing her off.

Sadie sighs. "You know that story we told you guys, about meeting in an English class?" she asks me. "I mean, it's technically true. But I'd had a crush on him literally all of sophomore year and never got up the courage to say anything to him. I transferred into that class after somebody told me he was in it." Her lips twist. "I know, it's stalkery."

I shake my head. "Only in a benign way." It makes me like her a little bit more, weirdly, to know she's got it in her. "I've totally done stuff like that."

Sadie looks surprised. "Really?" she asks. "You don't seem like the type at all."

"I'm a good faker, I guess."

Sadie smiles. "Anyway, it's like the Gabe I noticed around campus was this awesome, confident, self-possessed guy, you know? He was so sure of himself, and it made him so friendly and easygoing. And now he's just . . . not. I don't even know if we're going to last, honestly."

I flinch without knowing I'm going to do it, crossing my arms to cover. "No?"

She shrugs. "I'm about to apply to med school, you know? I love the guy, I want to help him, but I also don't want to get bogged down in somebody else's problems if they can't even admit how miserable they are. I thought this trip was going to be the answer to everything, but instead it's like—" She stops short. "Anyway. I'm sorry. You're a good listener, you know that?"

It's all I can do not to laugh. Roisin used to say the same thing, how easy it was to tell me stuff. What she didn't realize is that the art of asking well-timed questions keeps people from noticing you haven't told them much of anything in return.

"Gabe doesn't even have *that*," Sadie tells me, getting a second wind. "Somebody to talk to who isn't me, I mean. He's pulling away from all his school friends. He has some weird thing with his brother where they don't get along. And he won't listen to me at all at this point." She sits up a little straighter on the sink. "Actually," she says, "would you try talking to him, maybe?"

I gape at her. "Me?"

"Not about, like, our relationship or anything," she clarifies quickly, looking the faintest bit embarrassed. "But about school stuff? I just feel like he needs somebody besides me to tell him to get his shit together." Sadie shrugs again. "He's gotta trust you, doesn't he? I mean, the way he tells it, you basically grew up at his house."

I wonder what else Gabe has told her about our history; if she thinks I'm even remotely the kind of person he'll trust or listen to, I know it can't have been the whole truth. I'm about to explain in the vaguest terms possible that I don't think it's such a good idea when the bathroom door swings open.

"Here you are!" Imogen crows. "I was looking all over the place." Her gaze darts back and forth between us, curious and quick. "God, you guys, it is disgusting in here. Everything okay?"

I glance over at Sadie, let her take the lead. "Everything's good," she promises, and to her credit she does look better, her eyes less puffy and her cheeks less red.

The curiosity is radiating off Imogen like scent lines in an old cartoon, but all she does is smile. "Good." She loops an arm around my shoulders, steers me toward the doorway. "Can we get out of here now, please?"

"How's your cute Irish boyfriend doing out there?" I ask her as we follow Sadie back down the narrow hallway into the pub; it seems like it got louder while we were in there, more people crammed into the tiny space.

Imogen grins. "The cutest," she says. "He's great, right?"

"He's really great," I promise, although an hour of shouted conversation in a roiling bar doesn't actually seem like enough information to go on. But he's ass over teakettle for her, that much is obvious, and I like the air of mischief about him, his easy grin. "Have you guys talked about what you're going to do after you go back to RISD?" I ask. "School's gotta be starting for you soon too, right?"

Imogen hesitates then, her thick, dark eyebrows quirking a bit like they always do when she's about to share a secret. "So here's the thing," she begins. "This is what I was starting to tell you yesterday, but it's been so crazy with everybody around it never seemed like the right time to do it." She's stopped in the middle of the hallway, leaning against the dark wood wainscoting and crossing her ankles. "I'm thinking about staying."

I blink at her. "Staying where?"

"Staying here," she says, like it ought to be obvious. "In Kerry."

"Wait, what?" My chin drops. "Really? For how long?"

"I think indefinitely." She smiles a mysterious, catlike smile. "Seamus wants us to get a place."

I laugh out loud, a tickled sleepover-party giggle, in the second before I realize Imogen isn't kidding around. "Wait," I say again, "*what*?" It's like the floor has tipped underneath me, like an earthquake just cleaved the floor in half and I'm the only one who felt it. "You're serious? You're going to *move* here?"

"Why not, right?" Imogen's grinning for real now. "YOLO, et cetera."

"I mean, school, to start with," I say stupidly. "You kind of have to finish it, don't you?" I shake my head, baffled. "I mean—oh, Imogen, *no*."

Her smile pales. "What do you mean, Imogen no?"

"I just—" I break off, my wits dulled by the shock and the noise and the alcohol, at a loss for how to best communicate the obvious terribleness of this plan. "What are you going to do, drop out of school and be a mechanic too?"

Imogen's whole face goes cold then, snapping closed like

the storm shutters on the cottage to keep out bad weather. "Wow," she says, her tone clipped. "Okay then."

"I'm sorry," I say immediately, shaking my head. "That was super bitchy. I didn't mean there's anything wrong with—"

"You just said you liked Seamus!"

"I do like Seamus!" I protest. It's like we're doing some kind of farcical European comedy routine, all slamming doors and misunderstandings. "Seamus seems lovely! It's just that I met him like twenty minutes ago, and you met him like twenty minutes before *that*, so—"

"So *what*?" Imogen interrupts.

"So I just think maybe you should think about it for a little while longer before you throw your whole life a—"

"I'm not throwing my life away, Molly!" She rolls her eyes. "You sound like someone's grandma when you say that, first of all. On top of which, how do you know I haven't thought about it?"

"Because—" I break off, baffled. It's like I'm drowning, like I can't get enough air to put a coherent thought together. "Well, you definitely haven't *said* anything" is the best I can come up with. "I've been here two full days, Imogen. Like, if you're honestly thinking about moving across the Atlantic Ocean forever, I wish you'd thought to mention it before now."

"Seriously?" Imogen makes a face. "You've got so much going on I don't even know when I would have had the chance."

My back prickles with unpleasant recognition. "What does *that* mean?"

"Come on, Molly. We're literally in Europe, we are three thousand miles away from Star Lake, and yet somehow your Donnelly drama has managed to creep all the way to my house in Ireland."

"That's not true!" My jaw drops at the unfairness of it. "If you didn't want them here, you should have said something," I defend myself. "And Gabe and I have barely even talked the whole time we've been here."

"Which is weird!" Imogen points out. "This whole situation is *so weird*! And you want to act like it isn't, and I've been taking your lead on that because I'm a good friend and I know you and Gabe have unfinished business or whatever, but seriously. Who invites their ex-boyfriend on vacation with her and her new boyfriend? Especially when he totally dropped off the face of the planet after you broke up, and *especially* when he doesn't even know—"

"I'm not even the one who invited them!" I interrupt.

"It's me, Molly," Imogen says, more gently. "And you know as well as I do that there is no way that boy would have tagged along unless the both of you not so secretly wanted him to."

My whole body goes hot and sick-feeling, cornered and caught-out. I've been careful to think of this whole outlandish situation as mostly out of my control—a series of bizarre, unlikely events I was powerless to stop or alter. I told myself what was happening here was one giant, exaggerated kuddelmuddel, but of course that isn't actually true. Now that Imogen has named it out loud it seems undeniable, but I try anyway: "First of all," I begin clumsily, "that's not—"

"I don't actually care, Molly!" Imogen cuts me off. "That's what I'm trying to tell you. I'm saying I've been patient because I love you and I know you have a lot going on, but now I'm asking you to let this conversation be about me for once."

I open my mouth and close it again, momentarily speechless. It's not the first time we've had this fight. I tricked Roisin and Sadie into thinking I was a good listener, maybe. But Imogen has always known the real me.

"I'm sorry," she says now, leaning back against the wall and knocking her skull lightly against a picture of a bunch of IRA rebels, frame rattling off the plaster. "I've been drinking. I'm being an asshole."

"No," I say quietly, "you're right. I'm sorry." I shrug. "I just want you to be careful, Imogen. It's your whole life. It's *college*. Don't you think you ought to go back for a little while at least, so—"

"So I can look at more slides of Renaissance paintings?" Imogen interrupts. "I'm living in Europe right now, Molly. I'm looking at art. I'm *making* art. I can make it just as easily—more easily, even—here, where I'm happy, and I'm with somebody that I love." She sighs. "Look," she tells me, "I know your whole thing right now is that you're never going to make another mistake—or even, like, another decision where you haven't considered every possible outcome—in your entire life. But that's not me, okay?"

"What?" My mouth drops open. "I'm not—" I begin, then break off. "That's not why—"

"Imogen!" Seamus's deep, cheerful brogue rises over the din of the crowd; when I look up he's waving his beefy arms from across the bar, exaggerated. "You ladies fancy another pint?"

Imogen nods. "On our way!" she calls brightly, then looks at me and shakes her head. "I don't want to fight anymore, okay?" she asks, though it doesn't actually sound like a question. "Let's just pick this up later." Before I can reply, she's walking away.

I think I'm probably supposed to follow, to rejoin the group and have another beer and stop being such a colossal drama queen about everything, but for the first time in a year I'm completely unable to snap back into enthusiastic fineness. You could land a transatlantic 747 in the light of the shame radiating off my skin. I stand there for a moment, shocked and stupid. Then I push through the crowd and head for the door.

It takes a long time to navigate an exit, the dense trapping crush of bodies all around me and the music louder all of a sudden, an ocean-liner roar inside my brain. I sneak by Sadie at the bar and Ian in deep conversation with a local in a Pogues T-shirt, then edge through the narrow aisles of the hardware store and burst out into the cool blue night. It's a dramatic escape for sure, the front door banging wide open and the bells above it jangling wildly; I whip around at the sound of a low snort of laughter and spy Gabe leaning against the front window with his arms crossed, bottle of Heineken dangling lazily from one hand.

"Whoa," he says, smile falling a bit as he catches sight of my presumably wild expression. "You okay?"

"Imogen wants to *stay* here," I blurt before I can stop myself, though of course that's actually the least of my problems at this particular moment. "She's dropping out of school so that she and Seamus can move *in* together."

"What the fuck?" Gabe's eyes widen, surprise and not a little bit of amusement. "Seriously?"

"Thank you! That's what I said!"

"Wow," he says, rubbing at the back of his neck with his free hand like he's got a muscle cramp. "That is . . . something."

"I have to figure out how to talk her out of it," I tell him, my voice pitched high and a little hysterical. "I have no idea how to do that at this moment, I just tried and it *emphatically* did not work, I think we actually had a huge fight about it? But like." I shake my head. "It's ridiculous."

"Hey," Gabe says, holding his hands up, "easy over there. She'll be okay."

"How is she going to be *okay*?" I demand shrilly. I swallow hard, realizing abruptly that I'm shouting. "I'm sorry,"

I tell him, scraping my hands through my hair and trying to reel myself in. "I'm, like, really overwhelmed all of a sudden, obviously."

"Yeah," Gabe says, "I know the feeling." He hands me his beer bottle, which is still about half full. "Here," he says, "finish this."

I reach out and take it, trying not to think about what Imogen said back inside the bar about Gabe and I both wanting something, telling myself that the two of us sharing a drink doesn't mean she was right. I drain the bottle in two long gulps and we stand there for a moment, neither one of us saying anything. We breathe.

"Do you think I suck all the air out of the room?" I ask finally, setting the empty bottle down carefully on the edge of the store's front windowsill and crossing my arms.

"Why?" Gabe asks, looking at me sidelong. "Is that what your fight was actually about?"

I whip my head around to stare at him. "Shut up," I scold, startled by the sensation of being known both so well and so casually. "No. I mean, yes, obviously, of course it was, but shut up."

He raises his eyebrows, holding his hands up and pressing his lips together like he's physically trying to hold back a smile. I roll my eyes.

"I didn't mean *actually* shut up," I clarify, as if he doesn't already know that. "I want you to answer the question. Do you think I make every single situation about me?" I gesture at myself, keyed up. "Like, actually, am I making this situation about me right now?"

Gabe smiles for real then, a flash of straight white teeth. He thinks for a long moment. "I think controversy sort of follows you sometimes, maybe," he says finally.

"What? It does not!" I defend myself, faintly outraged. "Or, like, it used to, maybe, but it doesn't anymore."

"Okay," Gabe says, shrugging agreeably in a way that reminds me of what he was like last summer, a person so confident that he didn't always need to be right. "Fair enough. I wouldn't know, I guess. But what I mean is, and I'm not saying it was your fault or deserved or anything like that, but you were kind of at the center of a lot of drama back at home, weren't you?"

My mouth drops open. "Excuse you!"

"I said it wasn't your fault!" Gabe laughs then, fond and familiar; for a second it's like he's forgotten he doesn't care about me anymore. "It was my fault, a lot of it; I know that. What I mean is that you've always been this big personality, really fearless and fun and charismatic and stuff like that. Maybe a little bit impulsive. And that's what made people want to be around you all the time—present company included, obviously—but it also made you kind of a magnet for trouble."

It's the nicest thing he's said to me since last summer; the words are like hot stones tucked into my pockets, like I could curl my hands around them to keep warm. "Thanks," I say quietly.

"It's true." Gabe clears his throat then, a little too forcefully; when I glance over his cheeks have gone faintly pink in the light from the store. "Anyway, all of that is to say that no, I don't think you take up all the air. But I can kind of see how Imogen might feel that way sometimes." He shrugs. "It's not like you're some silly drama queen," he adds. "You're tough. All the stuff that happened last year, plenty of people wouldn't have been able to get through it at all. But you just soldiered right on through."

"Yeah, well." I wave my hand vaguely, like I can swat all of last summer away along with my own guilt at not having told him the whole story and my own bafflement at where to begin. "It was a long time ago." I lean my head back against the cool glass of the window, looking out at the empty street. "I wish I smoked," I announce, wanting to change the subject. "That's what you do outside bars in Europe, right? Smoke and look cool?"

"Is it?" Gabe asks, glancing around. "I'm the wrong person to ask, probably. It's my first time out of the country."

"Mine too," I admit, although I bet he already knows that. I haven't actually mentioned it to Ian, secreting my brand-new passport away inside my purse before he could catch sight of its empty pages. "Is it what you thought it was going to be?"

141

"Some of it is," Gabe says slowly. "Other parts . . . maybe not so much."

That makes me smile. "Present company included," I echo, teasing.

Gabe chuffs a laugh. "I mean, to start with, yeah."

We stand there side by side for another long minute. Probably I should go back inside. From out here the noise of the bar is completely inaudible, like we're the only two people left in town; a cat—the mean-looking creature who was sitting on the counter earlier or another one altogether, I'm not sure—darts underneath a streetlight half a block away. Finally I clear my throat. "Anyway," I say, too loudly. "How are you? How's school stuff?"

"You asked me that already," Gabe says, lips twisting in the pale light from inside the store. "It's good."

"No," I say, embarrassed, "I know." Still, I think of Sadie in the bathroom earlier, press him. "You still think surgery is what you want to do?"

I'm trying to keep my voice casual, but Gabe's eyes narrow, his whole body straightening up the slightest bit. "Did Sadie ask you to talk to me?" he asks.

"What?" I bluster, shaking my head. "No, not at all. I'm just making conversation."

Gabe doesn't buy it. "She did," he accuses. "I can't believe her."

"I think she's worried about you," I tell him, wanting

badly to change the subject. This was a stupid gambit. "That's all."

Gabe sighs noisily. "What else do you imagine me doing, exactly?" he asks me. "Should I drop out and go play the guitar on street corners, trying to find myself? I'm literally tone-deaf. Or maybe I could take a sabbatical in Florence and write romantic poetry or, like, try out for the NBA."

"Eh," I joke, trying to lighten the mood again, "would never work. You're not tall enough."

Gabe smiles at that, just faintly. "I'm pretty fucking tall," he points out. "The point is, somebody in my family needs to keep it together and think about a long-term plan." He shrugs. "Julia's the baby. Patrick is—" He breaks off. "I mean, you know how Patrick is."

I do know, actually, but it's not going to help either one of us to get into it. "And your mom?" I ask instead. "She's the grown-up, remember? I don't think she'd be wanting you to put all this stuff on yourself."

Gabe shakes his head. "My mom isn't great, Molly. Like I told you, the shop is in the crapper. She's weird lately. She forgets stuff. She's not holding up like she was right after my dad died."

My heart seizes at the thought of it, Connie, who taught herself to fix their ancient station wagon by watching a You-Tube video and bought me my first box of tampons and mommed me when my own mom didn't always know how.

"I'm sure it's not as bad as you think," I try, then immediately wish I could take the words back. "I just mean, maybe if you guys try some of that stuff we were talking about this afternoon—"

"Can you stop?" Gabe interrupts, sounding suddenly tired. "It *is* that bad, Molly. We're hanging on by our fingernails." He shakes his head again, irritable, and then he tells me. "We're probably going to have to close the shop."

I blink. "Seriously?"

"Yeah, Molly, *seriously.*" Gabe laughs bitterly. He shoves his hands into his pockets, goes quiet for a moment. "Star Lake is coming back, right? That's what everybody says. We were in *Travel and Leisure* this year, did your mom tell you that? We made some BuzzFeed list about the hippest summer getaways in the Northeast. There's all kinds of shit opening up all down Main Street, yoga studios and a green juice place and this home-goods store that sells, like, nine-hundred-dollar blankets. We don't fit there anymore. All the rents are going way up. We'll be lucky if we're even open in a year."

I close my eyes for the briefest of seconds, breathing in the tomato-garlic memory of the shop—the checkered oilcloths covering the tables, the ancient register clanging its noisy hellos. Chuck taught us how to throw pizza dough in the kitchen, all four of us—Julia, Patrick, Gabe, and me—turning it on our tiny knuckles as fast as we possibly could. I grew up back there. All of us did. The thought of it shutting down is unbearable.

"I'm sorry," I tell him quietly. I feel like an idiot, parachuting in with my cheery suggestions and my Susie Sunshine optimism. *Have you tried theme nights,* Jesus Christ. "I had no idea it was that bad."

"Of course you didn't," Gabe snaps. "You don't actually know what it's like to be in my family, okay, Molly?"

I recoil, taking an actual step away from him, the impact as physical as a slap. I made my peace with not being part of the Donnelly family anymore a long time ago—or at least, I tried to. But every once in a while it hits me: passing a woman in Boston who wears Connie's perfume, or hearing a joke I know would make Julia laugh. They were my home, once upon a time. But I wrecked it, and kept on wrecking, and that's my burden to bear.

"I'm sorry," Gabe says, digging the heels of his hands into his eyes. "I'm being an asshole, I'm sorry. You didn't deserve that."

I shrug, don't answer. Gabe leans against the glass. We're quiet for a long time, the sound of a car passing by a few blocks over and the blue-night breeze tickling the back of my neck. I keep expecting him to make an excuse and go inside, but he doesn't. Finally he sighs. "Pilot died," he says.

"Wait," I say, my heart like a capsized ship inside my chest. "*What?* When?"

"My mom put him down a few days after the Fourth of July party this year," Gabe says, clearing his throat and not looking directly at me. "He was full of cancer."

"Oh no," I say, leaning back against the window and hugging myself a little, thinking of Pilot's silky ears. He was old last summer, using a stool to hop up on the bed and the couch for his daily snuggles, though in my head he's still the lean, long-limbed puppy who pooped on the presents at Julia's seventh birthday party and was afraid of his own reflection in the mirror. "Oh, Gabe." Before I know it's going to happen my eyes fill with tears—for Pilot, for all the Donnellys, for Gabe most of all.

"I'm sorry." Gabe swipes a hand over his face in the darkness. "This was a fucked-up way to tell you. I don't know why I didn't say something last night when you asked about him. I just, like, didn't have the heart." He rolls his eyes, like he thinks he's being maudlin. "I know it's stupid to be so upset about it. It just feels like—" He breaks off. "Forget it."

"No," I say—reaching a hand out to touch him, then thinking better and jamming it into my pocket instead. "Tell me."

Gabe sighs so loudly it's almost a cough, like he's trying to clear something foreign from his lungs. "I just mean—like, clearly, this dog dying doesn't mean my family is falling apart. My family fell apart a long time ago, and that's fine. That's what it is."

I shake my head, denial my first and fiercest instinct. "Your family didn't fall apart, Gabe."

"Really?" Gabe asks, his eyes flashing in the darkness. "Because I'll tell you, Molly: my dad's dead, my mom's losing her mind, my brother's a lost cause, and our damn restaurant is going to be a Panera Bread by the time I graduate college. So I guess the point I am trying to make here is that me quitting school isn't really an option."

His voice cracks on that last sentence, ragged. For one heart-stopping, heartbreaking second, I'm pretty sure he's close to tears.

"Gabe," I say quietly. There is, in this moment, nothing I wouldn't do to make things okay. I would fight with claws and teeth and knuckles. I would eat someone's heart. "Hey."

He clears his throat. "I gotta go," he says. "I'll see you inside, okay?"

"No," I say, and this time I do touch him, grabbing his arm so he can't run away from me. "Can you wait for a second?" I ask him. "I'm your friend, okay? Whatever else happened between us, we were friends first."

"That's not true," Gabe says immediately. "You were friends first with my brother, maybe. But you and me? We were never friends. So you can stop—" He inhales damply, the sound of it thick and painful in his throat. "You can just stop."

I let go of his arm like I'm freeing a trapped animal, opening my mouth to contradict him and coming up blank. After all, it's not like he's wrong. Patrick was my forever human, my closest heart, the person I could tell whole stories to just by catching his eye across the room. Gabe and I never quite had that—we've known each other since we were kids, sure, but growing up he always seemed a little too cool for Patrick and me, perpetually gamboling off to a party or a canoe trip or his coronation for prom king. I had no idea he'd ever even noticed me either way until the moment I suddenly realized that maybe I was the one who'd been too distracted to pay proper attention.

We made up for lost time last summer: we saw old movies at the theater in Silverton and went to noisy parties with his friends down at the dock and rode the Ferris wheel at the Knights of Columbus carnival, all of Star Lake spread out in front of us as bright as a quilt. I lost my virginity to Gabe, for Pete's sake: I *loved* him. And I thought—no, I was *sure*—he loved me, too.

It wasn't until the fall that I started to worry that none of it had actually been real.

"Gabe," I say now, and it sounds like I'm begging him. "Hey."

"*Fuck.*" He scrubs savagely at his eyes with the back of his hand, sniffles once, then shakes his head hard enough to rattle his brain loose. "Fuck. I'm fine. This is embarrassing. I'm good, seriously. I'm drunk, is all."

He's lying; I've seen him drunk, and that's not what this is. "Why is it embarrassing?" I ask. "It's just me. I'm the last person you need to be embarrassed in front of."

Gabe doesn't answer. We stand there. We wait. The door to the hardware store opens then, bright light slicing across the pavement and two drunk, giggling girls ambling out, squawking as loud as chickens; I reach for Gabe like an instinct, pulling him around the corner into a darkened alley along the side of the building to give him some privacy. It's darker back here, deep shadows and a pale sliver of moonlight. It smells like old beer and pavement and trash.

"Look," I say finally. "It's a lot of problems to solve, I'm not going to lie to you. But what I don't understand is how it helps anything to stay in a program you hate to learn how to do a job you don't want to do."

"Who says I don't want to do it?" Gabe asks, but he's arguing for the sake of arguing; almost immediately, he exhales. "Now isn't the time for me to chuck my whole major just because I decided it's not, like, following my bliss."

"And going off down a road that's going to leave you with a million dollars in med school loans and a gig you hate just because you're too stubborn to change course isn't the way to help them, either."

"It's not *about* me," he insists. "It's about seeing things through. It's about being a person other people can count on."

"You are, though," I promise him. "You always have been."

Gabe shakes his head, smiling wryly. "You're saying that because you're worried I'm about to fill my pockets with rocks and walk into the fucking ocean."

"I'm not, actually," I tell him, taking a step closer before I quite know I'm going to do it; he smells like the detergent

Connie buys way back home in Star Lake. "I'm saying that because I know you. Like, everything else that ever happened between us, if you put all that aside, don't I know you?"

Gabe looks at me for a moment. "Yeah," he admits finally, and his voice is so, so quiet; he doesn't say it like it's a good thing at all. "I guess you do."

The air changes between us then, heavy and crackling like this morning before the storm rolled in behind Imogen's cottage; it's end-of-summer cool out here, and I shiver inside my clothes. I didn't notice Gabe move, but he must have, because all of a sudden we're standing closer than is probably a smart idea.

"I miss the hell out of you, you know that?" he tells me, and it doesn't sound like that's a good thing either. In fact, he sounds downright annoyed. "I try not to. Like, fuck knows I've tried not to. But I do."

"Gabe." I startle. Our hands brush with the motion, just barely, and it's like every nerve ending in my body is concentrated in the tips of my fingers; the shot of desire is shocking, a surgical jolt to my heart. I should tell him he's being ridiculous—I should tell him I need to go back inside—but all I can come up with is the truth. "I miss you too."

Everything seems to slow down then, the last year unspooling between us. Gabe tilts his head to the side. I want to put my thumb on his clavicle, to feel the tick of the blood beating deep inside his body. I want to catch his collarbone between my teeth.

"We can't," I tell him, swallowing thickly.

Gabe doesn't move—or he *does* move, but closer, so his warm forehead presses against mine. "We can't what, exactly?" he murmurs.

"You know what," I say, straightening up with no small amount of effort, stepping back and putting both hands on my flushed cheeks. "And we can't. Or like—*I* can't. I'm not that person anymore. I have worked so, *so* hard to not be that person."

"Can you stop saying that?" Gabe complains, and just like that he's irritated again; he steps back too, his whole body all angles, like a coat hanger or a cage. "Like, who is this other person you supposedly were?"

"A person who kissed other people's boyfriends," I remind him immediately. My voice is rising again, creeping up along some invisible seawall. "A person who never learned. A person who—" I break off, take a deep breath. "Okay. Gabe, there's something I have to—"

I'm cut off by a crash of biblical proportions down at the back end of the alley; Gabe and I spring apart like we're on fire, even though we aren't even standing that close. When I whip around I see it's just a busboy flinging a bag of trash into the Dumpster, but the stupidity of us standing out here like this together is sickeningly, immediately apparent.

Gabe clears his throat and the moment is over, his narrow body angled away from me and his hands shoved deep into his pockets. I think suddenly of Imogen's artist nun from yesterday, all her deepest secrets catching up with her in the end. "You look really pretty in that dress," Gabe says to the mouth of the alley. Then he walks away without looking back.

I wait a few moments before I follow in a sad, sneaky attempt to stagger our reentrances; I have no idea how I'm going to explain our absence to Ian, but he seems to have barely noticed we were gone. "Come meet these guys!" he says, swinging one heavy arm around my shoulder and introducing me to a crowd of Seamus's newly arrived friends from rugby. Imogen is watching me warily from behind her pint glass, and I do my best to pretend not to see.

Instead I tuck myself into the safe, familiar circle of Ian's arm and take the bottle of cider he offers, trying without much success to follow a complicated story one of Seamus's buddies is telling about a prank involving a jar of orange marmalade and someone else's broken-down car. I want to relax, to enjoy myself like everyone else seems to be able to, but everything that was charming about this place an hour ago is suddenly grim and claustrophobic to me: empty beer bottles litter the tiny tables. There's a mousetrap on the floor behind the bar. I'm achy and empty and guiltily out of sorts, unable to settle. I've had enough of the traveling life for one night.

"I'm exhausted," I tell Ian finally, popping up on my tiptoes to murmur in his ear. "I'm just gonna head back and go to bed, okay?"

Ian frowns. "Hang on," he says, "I'll come with you." He holds up his mostly full pint glass. "Just let me kill this first."

But I shake my head. "It's like thirty feet from here to Imogen's," I remind him, mustering a smile I hope is convincing. "You stay, finish your beer. I'll be fine."

"Okay," Ian says after a moment. "But text me when you're safe."

Outside the air is cool and crisp and head-clearing, like gulping a deep drink of water after a particularly long run. I take big breaths as I head up the deserted lane toward Imogen's, holding them in my lungs for a moment before I exhale. You can see every single star here, bright clusters of them like someone has tossed a generous handful of glitter, and for a moment I'm hit with a wave of homesickness so strong it almost takes me out by the knees.

I let myself in through the back door of Imogen's silent cottage, not bothering to flick any lights on as I slip my muddy shoes off and pad through the kitchen. I'm about to turn down the short hallway that leads to the bedroom I'm sharing with Ian when I hear a quiet sound from the living room, a moan or a whimper; I glance in that direction before I can think better of it, my whole body getting ferociously hot all at once. In the glow of the twinkle lights strung up along the ceiling I can see two bodies moving together on the pull-out: a corona of messy blond hair that is definitely Sadie's, and a pale, narrow back that's unmistakably Gabe's.

I dart down the hallway quick and quiet as a cockroach

before either one of them notices me, shutting the door with a barely audible click and pressing my back against the jamb. I want to climb out the window and run all the way to Dublin. I want to jump in the ocean and swim all the way home. More than that I want to hit rewind on the last two days, back to that night outside the pub in London: *Let's keep our reservation*, I wish I'd said to Ian. *Let's stick to the plan.*

Now I lie awake for what seems like hours, marinating in my own self-loathing and loneliness. Every breath sounds loud enough for Gabe and Sadie to hear all the way down the hall. Eventually the back door opens, Ian's laugh and Seamus's deep murmur filling the hallway, Imogen hissing at them to pipe down. A moment later a sliver of hallway light slices the bed in half as Ian stumbles across the rag rug; he slips under the covers beside me, warm and solid and beer-smelling. "We had the best time," he tells me, exhausted and happy as a little kid after a day at Disneyland. "You should have stayed out."

"Yeah," I say, taking a breath so my voice will be even and trying for all the world not to let him see I'm crying. "I wish I had."

He's out cold in less than a minute, one heavy arm slung over my hip bone. I don't fall asleep for a long time.

DAY 5

I wake up in the blackest of moods, a headache thumping dully at the base of my brain stem and my jaw on fire from clenching it all night long. I know I'm being completely irrational—after all, Gabe and I have been broken up since *last summer*—but I can't stop picturing Sadie and him tangled together on the pullout, can't stop hearing their quiet private sounds. It's compulsive, like poking at an abscessed tooth.

"Are you okay?" Ian asks, and I startle; I didn't even realize he was awake. I look over at his sweet, sleepy face and abruptly feel like the Loch Ness Monster: why the hell am I obsessing over Gabe and his girlfriend when I'm lying next to Ian? Enough is enough.

"Just hung over," I say, even though between all my ridiculous, farcical encounters I hardly had time to drink anything last night at all. Then, pulling him toward me on an impulse: "Come here."

I slide my hands up under Ian's T-shirt, bite lightly at his bottom lip. Then, a second later, I wrinkle my nose and push him gently away. "Okay," I say, laughing a little. "Wait, maybe not. Your mouth tastes like ass."

"I just woke up two seconds ago!" Ian protests. "And you're the one kissing me! You think you taste like a fucking Shamrock Shake right now?" Then he grins, pulling me back under the covers. "Don't stop."

That makes me laugh, warm and pleased-feeling; I'm settling in closer when Imogen's voice rings out.

"Hey, travelers!" she calls from the kitchen, banging what sounds like a wooden spoon on the underside of a pot. "Get out here! I'm making Irish breakfast before you go!"

Ian groans low and quiet against my mouth. "Is she serious right now?" he asks, knocking our foreheads lightly together.

"Imogen doesn't kid about breakfast foods," I say, nudging him off me and swinging my bare feet down onto the rag rug. We get dressed and pad out to the crowded kitchen, where Imogen is standing at the stove in front of a hissing frying pan full of sausages, flipping them onto their backs with a wooden spoon.

"Morning," she says, shooting me a look that I immediately recognize as meaning *I'm sorry* and *we'll talk later* and *you're my best friend* all at the same time. I nod and offer her a small smile, pressing my fingertips against her shoulder in return.

"You guys took off early," Ian says, nodding at Gabe and then Sadie, who's slicing tomatoes at the kitchen table, rosy-cheeked and satisfied like a person who unequivocally spent the night having super-romantic makeup sex. Just looking at her makes me want to howl.

"Yeah. Just tired, I guess." Gabe is standing at the counter pouring coffee out of the ancient metal percolator. "Here," he says, handing me a chipped mugful. I muster a mumbled thanks and turn away, ignoring the quizzical look I can feel him shooting at my back. I don't want anything to do with him this morning. I don't want anything to do with him for the rest of my life.

In the meantime, though, we're due at the airport in Shannon by ten thirty for our flight to Paris; just a few more hours, I promise myself, and Gabe and I will finally be able to go our separate ways. We cram our stuff into our suit-cases, strip the beds, and pile into Imogen's tiny car, where she cranks the eighties rock station too loud for any of us to talk. Sadie sits in the middle of the backseat, Gabe on one side and me on the other; I stare out the window at the gray Irish morning, arms crossed and cardigan wrapped tightly around me.

Imogen drops us off curbside, hugging everybody good-bye and grabbing me by the arm. "Can I talk to you?" she asks quietly.

"I was going to ask you the same thing," I blurt, relieved. Then, calling to Ian: "I'll meet you guys in there!" I turn back to Imogen, shake my head. "I'm really sorry about last night."

Imogen waves me off. "No," she says, "I am."

"No, me," I say, and smile. "You've been so amazing— you are *always* so amazing. I didn't mean to come all the way here and pull all my same old Molly shit."

Imogen sighs, raking her fingers through her dark, shiny hair. "I shouldn't have said that. That's not what you were doing. And honestly, even if you were, I was so happy to see you I don't even care." She leans back against the car door, settling in like we're back in the kitchen at the cottage and not in the airport drop-off lane under the watchful eye of a security guard who's already motioning at her to hurry up. "I get why it sounds like a bad idea," she admits. "Me and Seamus. I would probably think it was a bad idea, if somebody was saying it to me. But I love him, Molly. I really do. And if it turns out to be a disaster, then I'll just . . . get on a plane and come home."

I nod. It occurs to me that maybe this is what friendship is sometimes: saying your piece, then crossing your fingers and hoping for the best. "I'm happy for you," I promise. "I really, really am."

Imogen smiles like the sun coming up over the mountains back at home in Star Lake. "Thank you," she says quietly. "I'm happy, too." Then her lips twist. "My mom is going to fucking *murder* me."

"Yup," I say, and laugh, and then suddenly the two of us are cackling, obnoxious hysterical giggles, like we used to when we stayed up too late watching rom-coms in middle school. I double over, my purse thudding to the pavement; Imogen holds on to the rearview mirror on the side of the car. The security guard scowls wildly, though he stays where he is.

"Okay," she says finally, wiping tears from her eyes with the heels of her hands, smiling. "I'm so glad you came, dummy. And I love you." She hugs me tight then, the smell of hyacinths and oil-based paint. "Travel safe. And remember what I said, okay? You should never have to be afraid to be who you really are."

"Yeah," I say, swallowing down that precry tightness in my throat and face. Not for the first time, I wonder what exactly I did to deserve a friend as true as her. "I know. You're right."

"I mean it," Imogen says firmly.

"Ladies!" Now the security guard is marching in our direction, pointing to his watch. "You cannot be having your afternoon tea in my—"

"I'm going!" Imogen promises, flashing him a dazzling grin.

I'm smiling as I walk through the sliding door into the airport, though the warmness in my chest vanishes at the sight of Gabe and Sadie holding hands near security, her chin resting on his shoulder as she peers at their boarding passes. Well, good for them, then, I think snottily, hooking my hand in the strap of Ian's backpack and tugging gently as we head for the checkpoint. "I love you," I murmur in his ear.

It should get better once we've boarded the plane. Gabe and Sadie are sitting a few rows in front of us on the opposite side of the aisle, too far away for me to be able to see them. But it turns out imagining them is even worse: napping with their heads on each other's shoulders or talking about their plans for the fall back in Indiana or tucked together under a fleecy airline blanket watching a movie, Gabe's hand wrapped around the inside of her thigh.

I curl up next to the window and spend the trip staring out at cloudy gray nothingness with my cardigan on backward and tucked over my knees, arms crossed so I can make myself as small as humanly possible. I want to pull myself out of my own bad mood, but I don't know how to: It's like I've twisted the rusty top off some tightly sealed container, and now I can't screw it back on.

"How you doing?" Ian asks me finally, nudging my arm as the flight attendant passes by with a cart full of snacks I have no interest in eating. He's been absorbed in a book on his phone, seemingly unbothered by my inability to quit sulking.

He clicks out of the app now, opens up a game of Scrabble. "Want to play?"

I don't, really, and he beats me literally every single time, but it's not like I have a better idea. "Sure," I tell him. Anything to help get this flight over with. We're booked at a sweet little rooming house I've been looking forward to since I found it online back in the spring, antique cast-iron tubs and tulips on all the bedside tables and a tiny café on the ground floor famous for their *croque madame*. Best of all: it's clear across town from Gabe and Sadie's hostel. "Why not?"

The two of them are waiting for us when we get through the jet bridge and into the terminal. "Hey dudes," Gabe says, sounding downright cheerful. It makes me want to punch him in his face. "How'd it go?"

"Great," I say brightly, breezing straight past him. "Let's move."

It takes forever to get through customs, all of us shuffling along like a herd of drowsy cattle. It smells like sweat and McDonalds and old-lady perfume. By the time we finally get our passports stamped my stomach is rumbling and my mood is subterranean; all I want to do is drop our stuff and go to lunch. "Come on," I say, looping my arm through Ian's and rubbing my face against the shoulder of his T-shirt. "I'm about to get hangry."

"Just let me pee really fast?" Sadie pipes up, although I'm not really sure why that has anything to do with Ian and me. We've made it to Paris, after all; there is absolutely no reason for us to still be traveling as some kind of weird, fraught foursome. Still, I find myself stopping as she wriggles out of her backpack, dropping it gently on the tile floor at Gabe's feet. "I've had to go since we got off the plane."

"Me too, actually," says Ian, dropping his own backpack into the pile; I park my bag beside it, my shoulders bunched and aching. "I'll be right back." Sadie passes me her purse and Ian hands off his passport, which I rest on top of Gabe's beat-up L.L.Bean duffel for safekeeping. It's monogrammed, I notice for the first time, with Chuck's initials.

Once they're gone Gabe and I stand there for a moment looking anywhere but at each other, his hands shoved in his pockets and me picking at my fingernails with enough intensity to rip them clean off. He feels like a completely different person than the one who almost kissed me in the alley outside the hardware-store bar twelve hours ago. He feels like someone I've never even met.

"I'm going to grab a bottle of water," he says finally, clearly looking for any flimsy excuse to get away from me. I can't blame him, though it makes me hate him even more. "You okay to wait here with the stuff?"

I shrug. "Do whatever you want," I can't resist muttering. "I mean, you probably will anyway."

Gabe stops half a dozen steps away, face darkening. "Okay, can I ask you something?" he says. "What is your problem with me today?"

"I don't have a problem with you," I snap.

"Really?" Gabe raises his eyebrows. "'Cause you're doing a pretty good job of acting like you do."

"Oh, *am I*?" I all but shout, whirling in his direction like I think I'm going to shove him with both hands; suddenly I am so monstrously, ferociously angry. I'm angry that he tried to kiss me last night. I'm angry that I kind of wish I'd let him. I'm angry that since the very beginning, the consequences of whatever he and I have been to each other have always fallen squarely on me, whether that meant girls tucking condoms into my work locker or me lying on my back on an exam table at a clinic in Boston, imagining myself into a cloud. It's not even a hostile act on his part. It's just how it works. Gabe gets away with things. I pay for them. Gabe moves on. I get stuck.

But I can't say that in the middle of the airport in Paris while our significant others use the bathrooms less than fifty feet away. I can't say that *ever*, probably, but especially not now. So I sigh, tucking my hair behind my ears and trying one more time to zip myself up, taking a few steps closer and lowering my voice to an acceptable pitch. "Nothing," I tell him. "Just forget it, okay?"

"I don't want to forget it," he argues. "Come on. It's me."

I shake my head, debating. We're about to go our separate ways, after all. Who knows when I'll see him again? Finally I just say it: "I saw you and Sadie last night, okay?"

Gabe looks at me blankly. "You saw Sadie and me . . . ?"

"The two of you." I grimace. "On the pullout. When I came back to Imogen's after the bar."

Just for a moment, Gabe looks completely and utterly stricken. Then his eyes narrow. "What the hell were you doing?" he demands.

"I wasn't *spying* on you," I snap, immediately defensive.

"It wasn't some creepy, tawdry thing. I just walked in minding my own business and there you were."

"Okay." Gabe shrugs, and the cavalier ease of it takes my breath away. "Well, I'm sorry you saw."

I gape at him. "That's *it?*" I can't keep from saying. "Sorry I *saw?*"

Gabe sighs. "Sadie and I are together, Molly. What did you think we did?"

I open my mouth, shut it again. He's right, of course. Even as their relationship has been going on right in front of my face for the last three days—even though we've been broken up for a year—it occurs to me I'm still thinking of him as on loan to her, like a sweater she'll eventually give back. "You realize you tried to kiss me two seconds before that," I sputter.

Gabe nods. "And I think we can both agree that was a giant mistake."

"Uh, yup." I huff a noisy breath out. "That's a fact."

We face off like that for a moment, glaring at each other, the hassled crowd like schools of fish bobbing and weaving all around us. I know I should leave it alone, that there's nothing to be gained here, but something small and stubborn in me isn't quite ready to concede the point: "So what?" I can't resist pressing. "You guys are all made up now? Everything is fine? You're just going to add last night to the list of things you're not going to talk to her about and move on with your lives in perfect artificial happiness?"

"Perfect artificial—" Gabe's eyes widen. "First of all," he says, "you're not exactly one to talk about keeping secrets."

I know he's right, which doesn't stop me from bristling. "This isn't about me."

"It's always about you, Molly!" Gabe explodes, loud enough that a teenage girl in a Bruno Mars T-shirt whips her head around in alarm. "That's the fucking point!"

I stare at him for a moment, taken aback. It's an uncomfortable echo of what Imogen said last night, although something about the way Gabe is looking at me makes me think that's not exactly how he means it. If he hadn't spent the last year ignoring me completely, I'd almost think—

"You know what?" Gabe continues before I can ask him what exactly he's getting at, scrubbing a frustrated hand over his face. "This is ridiculous. This whole trip was a terrible idea. I don't know what I thought was going to happen here."

"It was," I agree hotly. In fact, it seems absurd to me that I ever thought it could work. I convinced myself it could because I missed him; I convinced myself it could because I didn't want to say good-bye. I couldn't let go of everything that happened a year ago on the other side of the ocean, and now I've gone and risked everything I've worked for in the here and now. "We should have called it that first night back in London."

"It's good we're splitting up, then."

"It's *great* we're splitting up!" It sounds dangerously close to a wail, and for one horrifying second I think I might be about to cry. I swallow hard, biting my tongue until I taste metal and blinking as fast as I possibly can.

That's when Ian and Sadie come strolling across the terminal.

"Hey, pals," Sadie says cheerfully; she's wearing last night's jeans and a T-shirt top with the names of all the US national parks printed on it in a pattern that makes the shape of a tree. "You ready?"

I swallow. "Yup," I manage, trying to keep my voice steady. I glance at Gabe. "Let's just—"

"Where's our stuff?"

My stomach drops, the sensation of tumbling out a window just before you fall asleep. I whip around, though I know it deep in my body even before I turn and look: the pile of bags Sadie and Ian charged us with watching is nowhere to be found. In fact, nearly everything is gone, nothing left behind but my gauzy cardigan sitting in a cotton puddle on the floor.

"Um, you guys," Sadie says, sounding oddly, preternaturally calm. "What happ—"

Gabe cuts her off: "Who had the passports?" he demands.

Holy shit, I realize with a fresh wave of horror, the *passports*. Part of me can recognize that this is funny in an eighties-comedy kind of way, all of us frantically patting our pockets like we did anything with them—and our *wallets*, I realize belatedly—besides what we all know we did. The other part is blinded by dumb, scalding panic.

"This isn't happening," I mutter, my heart like a trapped bird at the back of my mouth, something I need to cough up or spit out. But of course it's happening: the truth is, this all makes a sick kind of sense. I got tangled up with Gabe again and it led to calamity. Just like it always does. "I can't believe I let this happen, I—"

"Did you guys walk away?" Ian asks me. "Is that why—"

"We were right here!" Gabe snaps. "We just—" He breaks off. "Did *you* see anybody?" he demands, looking at me urgently.

"Of *course* I didn't see anybody!" I nearly shout. "Did *you* see anybody? If I had seen anybody, don't you think I would have said something? Like: *hey, don't steal our fucking luggage?*"

"Okay," Sadie says, in a voice like she's talking to a bunch of panicked children. "Let's all take a breath. Maybe it just got lost somehow."

I whirl on her. "All our stuff?" I counter. Suddenly I've had it with her, her guilelessness and her waterfall of hair and her can-do, wilderness-survival-guide, not-like-other-girls superiority like a battering ram against the back of my skull. "Maybe *all our stuff* just somehow got—"

"Easy," Ian cuts in, holding his hands up. "Hey hey hey, Molly, easy, you're okay. This is totally solvable."

"Is it?" Gabe growls. He is so, so pissed: at me, at the situation—and at himself most of all, if I know him as well as I think I do. "Because I'll tell you, dude, from where I'm standing it looks like a pretty colossal clusterfuck."

Ian nods. "No, it's bad, I'm not saying it's not bad. But we'll go to the embassy, we'll sort it out." Through the haze of panic in my own mind it occurs to me to be shocked he's not losing his shit at this. How is he not losing his shit at this? "We should find the airport police, first of all. You got your phone still?"

I slap at my back pocket, nodding numbly when I feel its familiar outline through the denim. Can my mom wire us money, I wonder? How does wiring money even *work*? I'm imagining us sleeping under a bridge somewhere, begging for change at the train station and stealing half-eaten bread-baskets off people's tables at cafés.

"How are we even going to check into the hostel?" Sadie asks, sounding significantly less calm than she did a moment ago. "My credit card was in there, all my money—"

"I still have my wallet," Ian says, digging it out of his back pocket and holding it up as evidence.

"Well, good for you, man," Gabe snaps. "But I don't. And—"

"It's fine," Ian says in that same collected, easy voice. "We can stay at my parents' place while we get it figured out."

For a second I think I've misheard him, that he's naming some French shelter for teenage idiots from America. Then my brain makes the connection.

"Your parents' place?" Gabe and Sadie ask in unison.

"Your *parents'* place?" I echo.

Ian smiles sheepishly.

It's not in Paris, not exactly, but in a quiet residential suburb on the outskirts called Saint-Cloud that's full of lush green parks and expensive-looking houses. Ian uses my phone to get us an Uber from the airport, keying in the address off the top of his head and speaking quiet, capable French to the driver; I sneak incredulous glances in his direction before giving up and openly staring at him, wide-eyed. He looks over, shrugging in a good-natured, slightly embarrassed way, like I caught him picking his nose.

Finally I shrug and lean my head back against the seat, wrung out and exhausted as a used-up travel tube of tooth-paste. We spent close to an hour with the airport police, who took our statements and my cell phone number and instructed all four of us to stay together in case they found our stuff and caught the guys who'd taken it, while also somehow managing to communicate—without ever actually saying it—that we ought not hold our collective breath. "You have a place to stay, yes?" the officer asked us, clearly hoping we weren't planning to camp out in his terminal for the foreseeable future. When Ian nodded hastily, his entire body relaxed.

The house itself is tall and narrow, a stone and stucco situation with a high, peaked roof and fat yellow rosebushes on either side of the bright-red door. From the wide leaded front window I can see straight through to the back of the property, where a small courtyard holds a sunken swimming pool lined with painted Spanish tile. "They rent it out sometimes," Ian explains, keying a four-digit code into the pad above the doorknob. "But there's nobody here right now."

"This is *amazing*," Sadie is saying, clearly taking the entire situation in stride like it's just one more neat backpacking adventure. Gabe still looks like he wants to die. As we step inside the cool, dark house I turn in a circle, gazing around at the wood and marble, the antique chandelier hanging above the steep staircase that leads to the second floor. I can't help thinking of Ian's dowdy Bay State parents, who I met for dinner at a Legal Sea Foods in Boston back in April: his dad was wearing Tevas and a golf shirt. His mom carried a Museum of Fine Arts tote bag instead of a purse. Both of them were friendly and engaging, but neither of them seemed like the kind of person who secretly owned vacation property in France. Not to mention Ian himself, with his flannel button-downs and job shelving books at the library and nose for the cheapest noodle bowls in Chinatown. How the hell did he forget to mention this place the whole time we were planning our vacation?

Never mind how—*why?*

"Ian, seriously," I start, then snap my jaws shut as I catch sight of Gabe and Sadie still standing in the front hall, empty-handed as two paupers straight out of a fairy tale. I don't know what I want to say to him, exactly, but whatever it is, I know that I don't want to say it in front of this particular audience. "Um, is this okay with your mom and dad?"

"Oh, yeah, for sure," Ian says. "I mean, I'll call them from your phone in a bit, but they're definitely not going to mind." He turns to Gabe and Sadie, motioning down a long, wide hallway beside the staircase. "You guys can camp out in the guest room through there." He sounds completely unbothered by the whole situation—happy for a chance to play the host, even, like having our luggage and passports stolen in a foreign country is just another kuddelmuddel to tell stories about later. For the first time his competence kind of annoys me: I've spent the last few days—I've spent our whole *relationship*—admiring his talent at getting around in unfamiliar places, how unflappable and open to the unexpected he is. But now I can't help feeling like it's probably easy to seem sophisticated if you've already secretly been everywhere with your rich parents, eating snails and strolling through galleries and sneaking sips of wine across the table.

Gabe and Sadie and I follow him into the kitchen, which is like something out of a magazine: all marble tile and wide-planked floors and an old-fashioned enamel sink with a big white drainboard. Schoolhouse lights hang above a butcher-block island. "I don't think there's a ton here to eat," Ian says, opening the stainless-steel fridge and peering skeptically inside, "but there's a grocery store like two blocks down that way if you guys want to get some snacks and wine and stuff?" He motions toward the side of the house, back in the direction we came from.

Gabe nods. "We'll go," he says, nodding at Sadie. Then, looking suddenly mortified: "But——" He breaks off.

"No no, it's fine." Ian shakes his head. "It's a wicked old-fashioned place, my parents keep an account there. So you can just put it on that." He trails off a little bit as he explains it, as if the absurdity of telling us that his parents have an account at an old-fashioned French grocery and that we can use it to pay for our lunch is suddenly dawning on him. He has the decency to look embarrassed.

"We'll pay you back," Gabe says firmly, and for a second I forget how angry I've been all day and feel a little bit bad for him—I know he's already feeling sensitive about money, on account of everything that's going on at home with the pizza place. There's no way this isn't humiliating.

Once the door snicks shut behind them Ian takes a breath, then turns to look at me. "So, okay," he says, rubbing a wary hand over his beard. "About this place."

"Yeah." I brush past him, opening various cabinet doors open until I find the one housing a cache of pristine glassware flecked with tiny bubbles, heavy and handmade. I fill a cup at the sink, gulp it down like I've been wandering the desert for forty years. "About this place."

Ian sighs like I'm being dramatic. "Molly——"

"No, Ian. I have no clue what's going on here, and actually I'm kind of pissed." Now that the initial bafflement has

172

passed, I'm angry for some reason, and I don't even know how to explain exactly why. There's the obvious, of course: that he's been holding this back, that he's flat-out lied to me about who he is and where he comes from. But there's also the sting of looking like an idiot in front of Sadie and Gabe, and the shameful shock of realizing I'm not the only one in this relationship with secrets. If I'm being honest with myself, I'm not sure which part upsets me most. "I'm trying to figure out how we've spent the last five days tooling around Europe—never mind the eight months we've known each other—and you somehow neglected to mention your parents have a fucking palace in Paris, France."

Ian leans back against the counter with his arms crossed, like I'm someone's irascible toddler. "First of all," he begins, "I didn't neglect to mention it."

"Yeah," I snap, "no kidding. You didn't tell me on purpose. What were you worried about, that I was some kind of manky gold digger?"

"Of course not," Ian says. "Come on."

"Then what?" I demand. "You let me pick out hotels and search for bargain flights and print us all a freaking Groupon for skydiving yesterday—you let me plan *this whole trip*—and meanwhile the entire time you're sitting on this place? You grew *up* in places like this place." That's a part of it too, I realize suddenly. Admitting it even to myself is gross and unflattering, but the truth is I've spent the last eight months walking around with this made-up version of Ian in my mind: a sweet, unassuming book nerd who'd somehow managed to pick up all this knowledge and insight about the world just by exercising his library card. I was so sure he was inventing me, back at the beginning. But I did exactly the same thing to him.

"I feel like an idiot," I tell him finally.

"I'm sorry. I don't want you to feel that way." Ian shakes his head, reaching a hand out in my direction; I jerk away, and he sighs. "Molly. Come on. You were so excited about this trip. I didn't want to take away from that. I would have sounded like a huge douche."

"Okay," I say. "What about the however many months we knew each other before I started planning it, then? You just never found a moment to drop it into conversation that your parents are gajillionaires?"

He shrugs. "They're not gajillionaires, first of all. And it never came up while we were at school."

"At school you have three roommates, one of whom is a mouse." I blow out a frustrated breath. In Boston one of our favorite things to do was to meet halfway between my dorm and his apartment, then see how far we could get on ten bucks. I tried dollar oysters that way; we wandered up to the top of the Green Monster in the middle of a rain delay at Fenway. Suddenly I'm wondering if those things were pretend, some kind of disingenuous experiment in slumming it. "I don't understand," I finally say. "Like—you *work*."

Ian snorts a laugh. "Yeah, Molly," he says. "I work."

"Why?"

"Because I like the library?" Ian asks, holding his hands out, palms up. "Because my parents think it's important not to have things handed to you? Because having things handed to you makes you an asshole? I don't know. I just do."

"Do you guys have other houses?" I can't resist asking. It's crass, but less crass than what I actually want to ask, which is *how rich are you, exactly?* "Like, besides your regular house?"

Ian shrugs, uneasy. "A place in Aspen, yeah," he admits. "And one near Lake Como, but we never go to that one, they just bought it as an investment."

"Oh my God." I shake my head. "Seriously? *Seriously.*"

Ian makes a face at that. "Okay. Enough over there, please, tiger. It's not like you grew up on the mean streets. Your mom was literally on the homepage of Amazon the other day."

"That's not the point," I say, though of course I know he's got one. My righteous anger is breaking a little, the knowledge that I'm being slightly ridiculous beginning to seep through the cracks. It's *not* actually that different from how my mom lives, after all, padding barefoot around her quiet house in Star Lake instead of dressing up for publishing parties down in Manhattan; still, there's no way I'm going to admit that out loud. "And anyway, we've never had an investment property next door to George Clooney."

"Would it have made a difference?" Ian asks. "If I told you

that my parents had a bunch of money? Would you have, like, liked me more, or wanted to get more serious faster, or—"

My eyes widen. "You *do* think I'm a gold digger!"

"*No*," Ian says, "I'm just saying it makes people weird sometimes." He sighs, leaning back against the massive butcher-block island. "I don't know what to tell you, Molly. There are things about yourself you don't like to talk about, right? I mean, I think you've been pretty clear about that."

It's the winning shot, a three-pointer from midcourt, and both of us know it. Still, I dig my heels in. "That's different," I insist.

Ian raises his eyebrows. "Really?" he asks. "How?"

"Because—" I start, then break off in frustration. I don't have an answer, not really. By now I'm fully aware I'm being a complete dingbat—quite seriously, what kind of spoiled brat throws a tantrum at the prospect of three unexpected cost-free days at a giant house in the Parisian suburbs?—but the truth is I just feel so *foolish*. I want Ian to feel foolish, too.

"Look," he says, when all I can come up with is a belligerent shrug of my shoulders. "You told me at the very beginning of our relationship that there were limits on what you were willing to tell me about yourself—limits on how close you'd let me get to you."

That stings. "It's not about not wanting to be close," I promise for the hundredth time. "It's just—"

"But I don't push you, do I?" Ian cuts me off. "I assume you'll tell me what I need to know, when I need to know it. I respect the fact that your life is yours to share or not."

I cross my arms, staring at the complicated tile work on the backsplash. The worst part is how I know he's right. The things I've chosen to keep from him—the fallout from my mom's book, getting pregnant, the fact that Gabe and I were together at all—are way more significant than something as ultimately meaningless as money. And deep down in the smallest, darkest caverns of my heart, I know that's the real reason I'm so upset. "You're right," I finally say. The words taste like ash on the back of my tongue. "I'm sorry."

Ian shakes his head. "I don't want you to apologize."

"What *do* you want, then?"

"I don't know." He breaks off then, stays quiet for a long, loaded minute. Through the window I can hear a bird singing something lonely, the faint hum of the pool filter out in the courtyard. Finally he lifts his head. "You want to hear a story?"

"Um," I say, not sure what he's getting at. "Sure."

"Okay." Ian lets a breath out, boosting himself up onto the island before he begins. "Look," he says again, "I'm sure this is going to be shocking to you, but I wasn't the coolest, most popular dude in high school. I didn't get, like, shoved into lockers or anything, and I had some friends, but mostly I just kind of . . . faded into the wallpaper. Does that make sense?"

It's hard to picture, actually—Ian is such a magnet around campus, with friends from all different social groups—but I nod. "Sure," I say again. "Keep going."

Ian nods. "Anyway, there was this girl Alyssa I'd liked basically since middle school. She was a math genius and on the dance team and she had exactly zero time for me, which wasn't her fault since mostly I was, like, sitting at the bus stop reading *Lord of the Rings* for the fiftieth time." He looks down for a moment, picking at the skin around his thumb. "But junior year I got this car. And it was my dad's old car, he'd gotten a new one, but it was still probably a nicer car than a sixteen-year-old kid had any business driving."

"Aha." Suddenly I think I might know where this story is going. "And out of the blue Alyssa was like, *hey boy how you doing?*"

Ian smiles. "Not just Alyssa," he admits. "Also all of Alyssa's dance friends. But it was less *hey boy how you doing* and more like, *hey boy can you take us to Starbucks, and since you're in the driver's seat would you mind paying?*"

I wince. "Ouch."

"I mean, it was my own fault," Ian says with a shrug. "I'm the one who kept saying yes. And she was always kind of different when it was just the two of us, you know? She was funny and smart and cool, and she always had great music on her phone. So I kind of didn't mind buying her lunch, or spotting her cash at the juice place or wherever." He makes a face. "It wasn't until she asked if I'd mind driving her boyfriend home too that I figured out she *probably* wasn't sitting up every night waiting for me to make my move."

I clap a hand over my face. "Oh noooooo."

"The worst part is I didn't even say no," Ian continues, smiling a little ruefully. "I drove them both home like every day of senior year."

"Oh, *Ian*," I say, wanting to travel back in time and protect his vulnerable high school heart. "That's miserable. I'm sorry."

Ian shrugs again, easy; it's the gesture of a person who has learned his lesson the hard way. "I'm not telling you this so you'll feel bad for me, or think my life is so tough or whatever. Clearly I know my life isn't tough. And I should have told you the truth from the beginning. But once I got to Boston I decided that I was going to be absolutely sure that anybody who liked me was in it for my sparkling personality, and not 'cause I drove a stupid nice car or whatever."

I nod slowly. It makes perfect sense: he wanted to be a new version of himself, free from his old blunders and baggage. How can I possibly blame him for that when it's exactly what I wanted, too? "I get it," I tell him. "I really do."

"I thought you might," Ian says. He reaches out and nudges my knee with the toe of his sneaker; I loop my finger through the laces, yanking once.

"So," I tease, looking up at him and smiling a little. "What kind of car *was* it, exactly?"

"Jerk," Ian says, but he's smiling back.

The four of us lay low that afternoon, Sadie floating on her back in the swimming pool and Gabe taking off on a walk around the leafy green neighborhood, a pair of borrowed headphones jammed into his ears. My book was in my suitcase, so I find a battered paperback copy of *The Tempest* on one of Ian's parents' bookshelves and post up in a lounge chair, struggling through the old English with my brow furrowed and my jaw clenched in determined consternation. I feel guilty for not rushing out to see the Eiffel Tower and the gardens at the Rodin Museum—both of which were on the itinerary for today, I remember grimly, cringing at the idea of all those boxes left unchecked—but in the end I'm too wrung out to care.

"You hungry?" Ian asks in the early evening, appearing at the back door as the sun sinks behind the olive trees and the air takes on a cool dampness that tempts fall. He called the airport police about an hour ago for an update: Gabe and I were standing in a security-camera blind spot, he reported when he hung up, though they said they were going over footage from other parts of the terminal and wanted us to stay together for the rest of the night in case they found anything. "There's a neighborhood place my parents like not too far from here—we could ask those guys if they want to go."

I drop the book on my chest, eyes cutting in Sadie's direction. *Do we have to?* I almost ask. "That sounds great," I say instead, holding my hand up so he can pull me to my feet. "Just let me wash my face first."

The restaurant is tucked at the end of an alley off the main drag in town, a tiny bistro with white penny tile on the floor and flaking gold-leaf lettering on the windows. A long marble bar runs along one side of the room. Tea lights flicker inside tiny glass jars on the tables, casting the room in yellow and rose and amber; there's a giant chalkboard on one wall covered with a map of the wine regions of France.

"A neighborhood place, sure," Gabe mutters as the maître d' leads us to a small table near the window. "It's basically a TGI Fridays, no big deal."

I've been thinking the same thing—*what kind of life do you have to live for this to be the kind of place you come for a casual dinner?*—but something about hearing Gabe say it pisses me off. After all, if it wasn't for Ian, where would the rest of us be right now? Not here, that's for sure. "You know what?" I snap, quietly enough so only Gabe can hear me. "Chill out, how about."

He startles at that, all eyebrows and cheekbones. "Jesus," he says. "Sorry."

I brush past him, sitting down next to Ian and picking up the menu—which is, of course, entirely in French. "You order," I say, setting it down again. "I trust you."

It's the best meal I've ever eaten, no question: crusty bread and ramekins of bright-yellow butter flecked with coarse salt and herbs; chicken cooked in wine until it falls apart at the gentlest nudge of my fork. For dessert are tiny dark-chocolate cakes topped with perfect dollops of thick sour cream, and I snap a picture to send to Imogen, who loves a well-executed baked good more than anyone I have ever met. Made it to

Paris, I type, thumbs moving quickly under the table. Sort of. More soon.

The whole scene is idyllic, exactly the kind of night I might have pictured when I was planning this trip in my summer dorm room in Boston back in June—except, maybe, for the part where Gabe is sitting sullenly across the table beside his new girlfriend, swallowing wine like he's downing a wax-coated cup of Dr Pepper at the shop in Star Lake.

Sadie raises her wineglass and smiles at Ian, her tan face luminous in the candlelight. "To our super-fancy rescuer," she pronounces. "Thanks so much again, Ian." Then, turning to me and Gabe: "And to you two crabs. I know you're both still upset about the passports and everything. But this worked out kind of magically, didn't it?"

"That's one word for it," Gabe mutters, and I roll my eyes at him. *There's no reason to be a dick*, I nearly say. Instead I make myself smile back at Sadie and lift my glass in her direction, the four of us clinking in some dark parody of that very first night at the pub in London.

"Cheers," I murmur, and swallow down the rest of my wine.

I'm exhausted and overfull by the time we head back to Ian's parents'; I can't believe it was just this morning that we woke up in Imogen's cottage. It feels like this day has somehow lasted an age. As we're ambling up the street we pass an open *tabac* with magazines fanned out on a rack in the window:

Sabrina Hudson grimaces out from half a dozen covers, hair mussed and eyes glazed. *Sabs Goes Knickerless*, screams one of the few English headlines, across a censored photo of Sabrina climbing out of a limousine.

"Gross," Sadie says, shaking her head. "I'm sorry, but how hard is it to put on a pair of underwear before you leave your house in the morning? She's so tacky."

"Oh my God, can everybody please stop shitting on Sabrina Hudson?" I snap before I know it's going to come out of my mouth, my voice echoing sharply down the empty sidewalk.

There's a stunned silence then, just the sound of a car rumbling by somewhere in the distance; Ian raises his eyebrows. Sadie looks downright shocked. "Whoa there," Gabe says mildly. "I didn't know you were such a Sabrina fan."

"I'm not," I reply, irritable and embarrassed at my own outburst. "I just think it's boring to pick on her all the time. I mean, accidents happen, don't they? I think our current situation is a pretty good example of that."

"Well, sure," Sadie says, still pretty obviously unconvinced. "But having your luggage stolen isn't exactly the same as showing your lady bits to the entire world. I just think some people make things more difficult for themselves. If she would stay home for once in her life, eventually everybody would leave her alone like she says she wants them to." She shrugs. "I don't know. I just think she invites it."

"Well, so what if she does?" Even though I'm regretting

starting this conversation, I'm in it now, and I'm not about to back down. "It still doesn't make it right for the rest of us to use it as entertainment." I'm surprised to hear myself arguing this side of it—after all, hasn't my MO for the entire year been not to cause trouble, not to draw attention to myself? But there's something about Sadie's confidence—her own blissful certainty that she herself would never be caught on camera without her proverbial underwear on—that gets under my skin, bruising more deeply than I would have thought was possible at this point. In her voice I can hear the screech of a key against my car door; I hear the echo of *slut* from down the hall. "Like, maybe there is some part of Sabrina Hudson that likes the drama, but you know who I bet likes it way more? All the magazine people who make money off whatever wild thing she's doing, and also every person across the world who gets to feel smug about how much better than her they supposedly are." I look around at the three of them, at their shocked, silent faces. We're still standing in the middle of the road.

"I just think it's sort of mean, is all," I finish weakly, the air and the energy going out of me all at once. "I don't know. I'm tired. Let's just drop it and get back."

"Sure," Ian agrees after a moment, just the one quiet syllable. It's the last thing anyone says the rest of the long walk up the hill.

DAY 6

I wake up early and anxious, clammy with shame over last night's flare-up. Exhausted or not, picking a fight with Sadie—over Sabrina Hudson of all people—was a sloppy move, even by old-Molly standards. Still, I'd be lying if I said there wasn't also a tiny flicker of satisfaction burning steadfastly in my chest: the truth is it felt *good* not to hold my tongue for once, not to worry about what I said before I said it. It's been a long time since I did something like that.

I climb out of bed and spend twenty full minutes trying to figure out how to work the fancy French coffeemaker in Ian's parents' immaculate kitchen, pulling levers and pressing buttons and swearing quietly to no avail; in desperation I dig the instruction manual out of a drawer, but it is, predictably, in French. I consider texting Imogen, who worked three years at the coffee place at home in Star Lake, before finally giving up and slipping outside, rolling the legs of yesterday's jeans up past my ankles and dipping my feet into the chilly, leaf-speckled pool.

I don't know how long I sit there, leaning back on my palms with my face tilted up toward the warm morning sunshine, before I hear the glass door sliding open behind me. When I open my eyes there's Ian in his hoodie holding two cups of coffee, sunglasses perched on top of his sandy head. "Thought you might want this," he says, holding up one of the heavy ceramic mugs.

"Oh my God, I *love* you," I blurt, thrusting my hands out eagerly. Ian smiles back at me, but it doesn't reach the top half of his face. "I do, you know," I promise quietly, reaching up and tugging on his belt loop until he sits down beside me. "I meant that, back in London."

Ian's eyes narrow just a little, like he's trying to decide whether he believes me or not. "Good," he says finally. "I meant it, too."

We sit there for a moment, drinking our coffee and listening to the birds waking up in the trees high above us. Eventually Ian nudges his ankle with mine. "So," he says, sounding cautious. "That was kind of intense last night, huh?"

"What was?" I ask, raising my eyebrows. "Me and Sadie?" I frown. Even though I was literally just regretting the whole embarrassing situation, there's a part of me that bristles at hearing him describe it that way. "Sorry. It just really bothered me."

"You don't have to apologize," Ian says, shrugging. "It just didn't seem like something you'd normally say, that's all."

I hesitate for a moment. He's not wrong, exactly—it's *not* the kind of thing I'd normally say, at least not lately. But at one point it definitely was. I wonder what it would look like to try and be that person in front of Ian—intense and prone to scene-making, maybe, but also a little bit brave. I think of what Imogen said yesterday, about not being afraid to be myself even if it made things messy. I wonder what would happen if I finally let him in.

Once Gabe and Sadie are up Ian leads the way to the embassy so we can get our temporary passports issued in time to fly home in a couple of days. Where Ireland felt like an old-fashioned fairy tale and London reminded me of a movie set, I'm struck by how *real* Paris is, humming and crowded. Cars barrel down the uneven roadways; business-men in sleek gray suits jabber into their phones. Fat pigeons take it all in from their high perches on the narrow win-dowsills of tall stone buildings, periodically letting out their cranky French coos.

On the way to the embassy we stop at the hostel Gabe and Sadie are booked at, where Ian and I wait outside in the white morning sunshine while they try to check in with-out their credit cards. "Do you want me to take a crack at it?" Ian asks when they return empty-handed a few minutes later, looking pissed and dejected. "Sometimes it's easier if you go in there speaking the language."

"I'm sure it is," Gabe says, his voice just this side of testy. I watch his expression darken as he does the calculations in his head, rearranging the figures this way and that and clearly rejecting every answer he comes up with: either he can let Ian help him out of a tight spot now or get stuck taking his charity again later tonight. His eyes tick from Ian to the hostel entrance, caught.

"That would be great," he says finally, and I can actually see him swallowing his pride down. "Thanks a lot."

Ian waves him off like *no problem* and gamely trots inside; even he's back a few moments later, though, shaking his head in defeat. "Sorry, dude," he says to Gabe. "No luck. They won't do anything without credit card and ID, I think especially since we're young. But you guys are welcome to stay with us till it's time to head home."

"Thanks, Ian," Sadie says, reaching out and patting his arm in gratitude. Gabe grumbles his agreement, stuck now with the worst of both possible worlds. I'd feel almost bad for him—normally he's so self-reliant that I know this must chafe—if it felt like he actually wanted my sympathy.

It seems like a full night's sleep should have taken the edge off all our various interpersonal dramas, but somehow by the time we get to the embassy the temperature among the four of us is frostier than it was at last night's dinner. Even

Sadie is uncharacteristically quiet as she sits on a bench next to Gabe in the wood-paneled waiting room, picking nervously at the ends of her long flaxen braid and sweating in yesterday's clothes. Gabe has barely said a word all morning, especially not to me, and the last dregs of our airport argument pulse like a hangover behind my eyeballs. The faster we all can get away from each other, the better.

Once we've finally been belched back out onto the sidewalk I slip my hand into Ian's, squeezing purposefully. "Let's hang out by ourselves today, okay?" I murmur. I want to be alone with him, for things to get back to normal between us; I want the vacation I planned for so carefully back in Boston. "Just you and me."

Ian grins at that, like possibly he was thinking something similar. "Yeah," he agrees quietly. "I'd love that."

We make a plan to meet up with Sadie and Gabe at the house again later, then take the Metro to the Musée de l'Orangerie to see Monet's *Water Lilies*. Afterward we walk along the Seine, where a million stalls are set up to sell battered secondhand books and fruit and tourist tchotchkes, key chains shaped like the Eiffel Tower and tote bags bearing Mona Lisa's lovely, inscrutable face. I lean over the stone wall overlooking the brown, brackish water, hit with a strange pang of homesickness for the Charles back in Boston.

Ian bumps my shoulder with his own, warm and affectionate. "Did you know that Paris has more libraries than any other city in the world?" he asks.

"I didn't, in fact," I tell him, unable to hide a smile. "But if that's true then it's no wonder you love it here so much."

Ian grins back. "So what's next?" he asks, motioning to my phone wedged in my back pocket. "Per the app, I mean."

I open it up, flick through the schedule; I shuffled some things around this morning, trying to make up for lost time. "Top of the Eiffel Tower," I report, and he makes a face.

"What?" I demand, more defensive than I necessarily mean to be. "What's wrong with the Eiffel Tower?"

"I mean, nothing," he clarifies mildly, "if you want to be elbow to elbow with every other tourist in Paris." He shrugs. "We can totally go if you want to. It's just a little . . . you know. Cliché."

"Okay then, fancy," I tell him, sticking my phone back in my pocket. *See?* I want to tell him. *I can go with the flow.* "What do you want to do?"

Ian's about to reply when my stomach lets out a loud, audible growl; he laughs, raising his eyebrows. "I mean, lunch, maybe?" he asks, and I laugh. "Just, like, a wild guess."

He ducks into a shop to pick up provisions: a hunk of soft cheese and a baguette, plus a container of delicate red strawberries and bar of expensive-looking dark chocolate for dessert. We plunk ourselves down on the grass in a small park to eat, watching a gaggle of kids riding a menagerie of intricately painted carousel animals, a cheetah and an elephant and even a dolphin. Hundreds of tiny mirrored tiles catch the sunlight as tinkling, old-fashioned music fills the air.

"Back in Star Lake they do a carnival every summer," I hear myself say, the force of the memory knocking me back a little, like I've lowered some invisible grate: the smell of funnel cake and the noisy hum of the generators, the squeal of kids barreling down the Fun Slide on burlap sacks. "Everybody in town turns out, it's a whole big thing. This was the first year I missed it in . . ." I trail off, thinking about it. "Ever, actually."

Ian raises his eyebrows, spreading cheese onto a hunk of bread with a plastic knife. "So it wasn't *always* bad then," he points out. "Star Lake, I mean."

"I never said it was always bad!" I protest. "It's nice, really. It was in *Travel and Leisure* this year actually, it's one of the hippest getaways in the Northeast." I look at him for a moment, hesitating, all the fear and shame and trepidation from the last couple of years conspiring to keep me from saying anything else about it. Then I take a deep breath and forge ahead.

"All right," I say finally, wiping my suddenly sweaty palms on my thighs. "You really want to know the deal about Star Lake?"

Ian sets his bread down. "Yeah," he tells me. "I really do."

"Okay," I begin, before I can talk myself out of it. "So basically what happened is that I got kind of mean-girled there the last couple of years. Like, bullied, I guess is the word, although that always makes me think of a shrimpy kid getting shoved into a locker or something, like you were saying yesterday. And that's not what it was like."

Ian nods. "What *was* it like?" he asks.

"It was just . . . a few people trying to make sure I knew they didn't like me," I explain with an embarrassed shrug. "And guess what: I definitely knew. I got my car keyed. They egged my mom's house right when I first got back from school."

"Seriously?" He grimaces. "That must have been awful. And also, like, really smelly."

"I mean, it did not smell good, no," I admit, smiling a little. "Don't get me wrong, a lot of it was my fault. I made things way harder for myself in a lot of ways—same as Sadie was saying about Sabrina Hudson last night, which is probably why I got so worked up about it. But it still really, really sucked."

"Yeah," Ian says quietly. "I bet."

I let a breath out, slow and careful: my heart is beating harder even telling him this much, my voice shakier than it normally is. "So anyway," I continue, "all of that is to say that I've just got a lot of bad memories around Star Lake. And every time I thought about going back there, or especially bringing you with me, it just felt, like, complicated and yucky and more trouble than it was worth." I smile cautiously. "I like how I am in Boston, you know? I like how you think of me. I didn't want to ruin that."

"Okay," Ian says, looking puzzled. "I kind of don't get it,

though. You thought I wouldn't like you anymore because you got bullied back in your hometown?"

"No, I thought you wouldn't like me anymore because—" I break off midsentence, adrenaline surging as suddenly as if I'd driven right off the road. Even now—no, *especially* now—there's no way I can tell him the entire truth. As recently as a few days ago I probably could have come all the way clean, could have explained about my past while feeling reasonably confident it would stay there. But I threw that chance away forever the moment I lied to him about Gabe.

"I thought you wouldn't like me because I was a mess," I hedge finally, tearing the end of the baguette into crumbs instead of looking at him. The regret is physical, copper-bitter at the back of my mouth. "The kind of person who made the same mistakes over and over, you know? Who wasn't careful."

He chuckles at that, faintly disbelieving. "I find it extremely hard to believe that you ever weren't careful."

I shrug, lifting my chin up at him. "That's because you didn't know me then."

Ian gazes back at me for a moment, and then he nods. "No," he says slowly. "I guess I didn't."

We're done with lunch now; Ian feeds the last of the strawberries to a mangy French squirrel, and we crumple up our garbage and toss it into the trash. "Thanks for telling me all that," he says, wrapping his arms around me and bumping his forehead against mine. "I know it couldn't have been, you know. A picnic."

That makes me smile. "I mean, you told me about Alyssa from the dance team," I point out, tilting my head back and stamping a kiss against his mouth. "It felt like maybe I owed you one."

"You know, I kind of like this whole emotional honesty thing," he continues as we head for the Metro; there's a famous English-language bookstore he wants to take me to, full of rare first editions. "It's kind of sexy."

"Oh, that's what you're into, huh?" I ask with a laugh.

"I mean, maybe," Ian says thoughtfully. "What else you got?"

I consider that for a moment. "I'm really glad it's just you and me today," I confess, lacing our fingers together and squeezing. "It feels like I've been waiting a really long time to be alone with you."

Ian looks down at our interlocked hands, then back up at me, and smiles. "How about that," he replies. "Me too."

We spend the rest of the afternoon like that, strolling hand in hand through the busy streets of Paris, browsing shops and munching macarons and telling each other stories. I feel closer to him than I have since we got here, find myself talking about things I haven't thought of in years: sitting next to Imogen on the dock beside the lake weaving key chains out of lanyards, the cacti that grew outside the window of my dorm room back in Tempe. Ian, for his part, tells me about learning to behave himself in fancy restaurants when he was a kid and about the parade of weird nannies they never managed to keep on account of his little sister being a holy terror.

"My mom's an environmental consultant for big banks, so she traveled a lot," he explains over a midafternoon snack of crepes purchased from a tiny street cart, butter and sugar dripping down the back of my hand. "We lived in Germany for six months when I was a baby. She was in Stockholm for a lot of the year when I was in middle school. One year we did Christmas in Kyoto."

I nod. I knew this, I guess, or pieces of it. But until now he always talked about it in a different tone of voice, in between stories about family trips to the Hoover Dam and his dad mowing the lawn in a pair of short shorts and all of them getting into a fight while playing Settlers of Catan on Thanksgiving. Normal, slightly dorky stuff—that fit, I realize now, into the normal, slightly dorky narrative I'd created around Ian in my head. It occurs to me, not for the first time, that we see what we're expecting to see when we look at other people.

"It was always really important to them that we knew not everybody was this lucky, though," he says, offering me a bite of his crepe. "My parents, I mean. Like, not letting money make you a monster was always a really big thing for them."

"Well, they succeeded," I say, reaching up and wiping hazelnut spread off the corner of his mouth. "You are emphatically not a monster."

Ian laughs. "Aw, sweetheart, that's the nicest thing you've ever said to me," he teases. I drag him down for a kiss in reply.

Ian says there's one more place he wants to show me after dinner, taking my hand as we amble through a quiet, leafy neighborhood not too far from his parents' house. Cozy yellow lamplight spills from tall apartment windows. A young woman walks a slouchy, grumbly dog. Ian leads me down a winding lane that reminds me of Beacon Hill back in Boston, the two of us bumping across the uneven cobblestones. The sky has turned a soft, lovely navy, like you could reach up and wrap it around you like a shawl.

"Okay, are you taking me somewhere to murder me or what?" I joke as we peel off down a narrow, shoddily paved alley butted up against the backs of the grander buildings one block over; these must have been servants' entrances, once upon a time. "Is this about the app?"

Ian grins. "We're almost there," he promises. "You'll see."

He's as good as his word: a moment later he stops in front of a wrought-iron gate about halfway down the alley, reaching up and pulling open the thick, rust-pocked latch. He lays a gentle palm at the small of my back as he pushes it open, ushering me into a tiny courtyard surrounded by moss-covered walls on three sides and canopied by sinuous, winding grapevines. A massive fountain burbles quietly away in one far corner, a tall, elegant goddess holding court in the center. A waterfall of long marble hair ripples down her back.

"Holy crap," I blurt, looking around in astonished wonder. "Ian. This is *incredible*."

"Yeah?" Ian asks, following me deeper into the courtyard. He's standing behind me, but I can hear the hopefulness in his voice. "Better than the Eiffel Tower?"

"I mean, yes," I admit, a little embarrassed by my own dopiness. "It's better than the Eiffel Tower." I take a few steps closer to the fountain, drawn both by the welcoming gurgle of the water and the statue's warm, intelligent expression.

"It's Aphrodite," Ian tells me.

That makes me smile. "Goddess of love?"

He makes a face. "Too on the nose?"

"Not in a bad way." I turn in a slow circle, taking in the herringbone brick and the flowering shrubs, the recessed lights glowing softly in the basin of the fountain. "This place is public?" I ask in disbelief.

"It's technically a city park, yeah." Ian nods, settling himself on a wooden bench beside the fountain and stretching his long legs out in front of him. "My dad proposed to my mom here a million years ago," he explains, wincing a little bit as he says it, like maybe he's not sure if I'm going to rich-shame him again for having parents who do things like get engaged in France. "So when we used to come as a family they always liked to bring us by and check on it."

"I see why they love it so much," I tell him. "It's romantic as all hell."

Ian grins at me. "That was kind of the idea, yeah."

I gaze at Aphrodite for another long moment. There's something about her that calls me closer: the cool, clean smoothness of the marble, the honesty and self-possession on her face. I look from Ian to the fountain, back to Ian again. "I kind of want to get in," I hear myself confess.

Ian laughs; then, looking at me in surprise: "Wait, really?"

I shrug, suddenly bashful. "I mean, a little bit." I was joking, truthfully, but as soon as it's out of my mouth I realize how badly I actually want to do it. My feet are aching from all the walking we've been doing; my hands and arms feel gritty from the dirty city air. More than that, though, I keep thinking of what Gabe said the other day: *you're always up for an adventure.* That fountain—that *goddess*—is calling, and I want to go. "Why not?"

"Well, because I don't want you to get arrested and wind up in a French prison like Jean Valjean, to start with," he points out.

"Do you see any cops?" I ask, gesturing around the deserted courtyard as I slip out of my sandals, wiggling my blistery toes: no matter how hard I tried to break them in, these shoes never got any comfier. "They're probably all busy looking for our lost luggage."

Ian considers that. He still looks a little nervous—but not, I note with a warm lick of pleasure, entirely put off. In fact he's watching me with interest, head tilted just slightly to one side and a half smile playing across his mouth. Maybe

I've been underestimating him, all these months that I've been so quiet and demure and receding. Maybe he could love the person I really am after all.

"Come on," I tell him now, leaning down and bracing my hands on his shoulders, planting a kiss on his curious mouth before I turn and head for Aphrodite. "It's a kuddelmuddel!"

Ian laughs then, the sound of it warm and rumbling. "I guess you're right," he agrees—or at least, I think that's what he's saying. I can barely hear him over the sound of my own splash as I jump in.

It's full dark by the time we get back to Saint-Cloud that night. The house is quiet save the low hum of the refrigerator, the door to Gabe and Sadie's room shut tight. I wonder what they did today, if they fought, if Gabe was happy to be rid of me. Then I remind myself I don't actually care.

Upstairs in Ian's parents' giant bathroom I spend an extra-long time brushing my teeth and washing my face, anticipation blooming like a climbing vine inside me. Last night I was so exhausted and brattily cranky that I collapsed into bed as soon as we got back from dinner, mumbling a good-night into the pillow when Ian came upstairs a little while later. But now . . .

By the time I make it into the master bedroom my heart is thumping expectantly, my whole body warm and alert. Ian is lying on the bed watching French television, one sturdy arm propped behind his head. "Hey," he says sleepily, his voice the tiniest bit slurred. We split a bottle of wine at a café on the way back from the Metro, though I think he actually drank a lot more of it than me.

"Hey," I say, barely resisting the urge to explode into hysterical giggles. Ugh, why am I so *nervous* all of a sudden? I stand awkwardly at the end of the bed, watching as two Parisians argue on a street corner on-screen, all wild gesticulations and the angry red slash of the actress's lipstick. "So you understand all of this, huh?" I ask.

Ian smiles at me a little crookedly, like he knows I'm making small talk to cover my own anxiousness but finds it charming. "Yeah," he says, nodding, and turns off the TV.

I take a breath. There's nobody to interrupt us now—no alarms going off or friends knocking on the door or marching bands playing "The Entertainer" parading through the room. It's just the two of us, Ian and me.

"Molly," he says quietly. "Come here."

He reaches for me as I climb under the covers; his mouth is warm and eager and wet. I scratch my fingernails through the hair at the nape of his neck, running the bottom of my foot along the back of his calf and trying to relax. After all, it's not like I'm ever going to find a more romantic venue: the moonlight makes patterns on the plush Oriental carpet. The duvet is cumulus-fluffy and soft. If ever there was a perfect moment to have sex with your boyfriend for the first time—if all my hesitation really has been about waiting for one— alone in his parents' French vacation house is probably about as ideal as a reasonable person could hope to get.

Still, as we lie there with our limbs tangled together I'm surprised to find myself wishing for the grungy comfort of Imogen's cottage. I find myself wishing for my mom's place back in Star Lake. The muscles in my shoulders are balled tight as socks underneath my skin, my fight-or-flight instincts all humming; when Ian reaches for the drawstring on my pajama bottoms, I freeze.

I take a steadying breath and kiss him harder, knowing even as I do it that I'm overcompensating, that it feels fake and forced and strange. God, what is my *malfunction* tonight? It's Ian. I love him. We had an amazing day together. Our whole trip has been leading up to this moment—in a lot of ways, our whole relationship has.

In theory the reason is obvious, of course, and for a moment I imagine just sitting up and blurting the whole truth, or at least more of it than I let slip this afternoon: that I got pregnant last year and had an abortion, that I'm gun-shy and terrified to make any more mistakes. But something stops me. Even in my head, that explanation feels like a cop-out: what I'm feeling isn't as simple as worrying I'll get pregnant again. It's not as straightforward as shame or regret for the choices I made. I might not be entirely sure what's going on here, but I know it's broader and deeper and messier than that.

I remember how much I wanted Gabe the other night in the alley outside the bar in Kerry, the force and ferocity of it.

I remember how I could feel it in my teeth. I think again of what Imogen said, about perfection not mattering if you're with the right person, and cringe. There's nothing wrong with Ian, I think, even as he's trailing a neat row of kisses along my stomach. But no matter how much time I've spent the last few days trying to convince myself otherwise, I know something about *this* isn't right.

"Wait," I say, sitting up finally, my feet sliding against the starchy sheets as I push him gently away. "Hang on a sec, I just—"

"Hm?" Ian's voice is a tiny bit slow, distraction, or maybe he's drunker than I thought. He goes for my waistband again, smiling a little like he thinks we're playing a game.

I shake my head. "Easy." Then, more forcefully, wrapping my hand around his wrist: "Hey."

Ian's smile falls. "What?" he asks.

"Just hold up a minute, okay?" I take a deep breath. "I just—I don't—" I break off. "I don't know if tonight should be the night."

"Oh." Ian sits up, scratching at the back of his neck. He exhales, something that might be a normal breath and might be a sigh. "All right."

I wince. "Don't be mad, okay?"

"No, I'm not mad. But, like—this trip is almost over, you know?"

I blink. "Meaning what, exactly?"

Ian shrugs; his T-shirt is in a puddle at the foot of the

mattress, and he makes a fist in it with one hand. "Meaning we've been together a long time, we're exclusive, we're in *France*—"

"Wait a second." I sit bolt upright. "Did you bring me to Europe specifically to have sex with me?"

"No!" Ian says, sounding honestly offended. "Of course not. But—"

"Because I don't actually owe it to you to have sex with you," I inform him, swinging both legs off the mattress and standing up. "You know that, right? We could date for twenty years, we could be *married*, and I do not have to have sex with you if I don't want to."

"Of course I know that," Ian says, shaking his head like I'm being dramatic. "Come on, Molly, don't make it like that."

"Don't make it like what?"

"Like I'm a fucking sex predator!" he all but shouts. He's never sworn at me in anger before, not once in all the time we've been together; I flinch, glancing instinctively at the closed door. The last thing I want is for Gabe and Sadie to overhear us. Ian takes a breath. "You're my girlfriend," he continues, lowering his voice with what seems like some effort. "It doesn't make me a creep to want to have sex with you."

"I'm not saying you're a creep," I protest. "I'm saying it's not cool to put pressure on me when—"

"I'm not putting pressure on you!"

"Then what do you call this?" This time, I'm the one who's yelling; Ian looks startled, then slightly cowed.

"It's not some gross, cheap thing," he says after a moment, raking a hand through his beard roughly enough to yank it right off his face. "I want to be close to you. I want to *know* you. And yeah, sex is a part of that for me." He looks at me for a moment. "Really, in all honesty. Do you even l—"

"Don't you dare," I interrupt him, holding up a hand. "Don't you *dare* ask if I even love you." I'm furious; I'm actually outraged. But I'm also worried that he's right. After all, at what point do I need to admit out loud that this isn't about waiting for some hypothetical perfect moment? At what point do I need to admit that this is just about . . . me?

"Look," Ian says, sounding so calm and logical it makes me want to fling myself on the floor and throw a tantrum, "we're both tired. The last couple of days have been wild. And you haven't really been yourself all week."

That surprises me. "What do you mean, I haven't been myself?"

Ian shrugs. "I don't know," he says, looking uncomfortable. "It's just been little things, you know? Like a vibe I've been getting. But ever since London you've just seemed kind of . . . off."

"I don't know what you're talking about," I lie. The truth is I know exactly what he's talking about; what I *don't* know is how to explain to him that those so-called little things— jumping out of an airplane, wearing a bright-red dress, sticking up for Sabrina Hudson even if it was weird and awkward—were the closest I've felt to myself in a year.

Neither one of us says anything for a moment. I stare miserably down at my hands. Earlier today I thought there was a chance Ian could be into the real me, that it was just a matter of being brave enough to introduce him to her. But suddenly I'm not so sure.

"Okay," I tell him finally; it feels like all of the energy has been drained out of me, like someone's pulled a plug somewhere. "I'm calling it."

Ian startles. "Calling *what?*" he asks, alarmed.

"This fight," I amend quickly. "I'm calling this fight." I tuck my hair behind my ears, trying to figure out how to fix this. "Look," I say finally, sitting down on the very edge of the mattress. "Can we just . . . lie here and not talk about any of this for a while? And can we just agree that that's all it's going to be?"

Ian looks at me warily. After a long moment he nods.

I can't sleep at all that night, lying awake in the darkness listening to Ian's deep, even breathing. Finally I slip out from under the covers, careful not to disturb him, and pad as quietly as I can down the narrow, creaking stairs. I'm going to get a drink of water, maybe sit with my feet in the cool blue pool for a while, but when I turn the corner into the kitchen there's Gabe sitting on the counter, beer in one hand and his phone in the other.

"Jesus Christ," I swear, holding both my hands up. "You scared the shit out of me."

Gabe shrugs. "Sorry," he says, in a voice like he's not, really. "Couldn't sleep."

"Yeah," I say, exhaling, my heart still chattering nervously away. "Me either."

We stay where we are for a moment, looking at each other. I can feel my pulse ticking in my neck. I know I should go back upstairs—the only thing that could turn this night into more of a disaster would be another brawl with Gabe—but sleep seems more foreign and unfamiliar than any country we've been to so far. "You hungry?" I hear myself ask.

Gabe looks surprised at that. "Sure."

I open the cupboards. It's definitely a vacation-house kitchen, full of random half-empty bottles of balsamic vinegar and not so big on staples, but after a couple of minutes I've scrounged mostly everything I need to make pancakes. "Impressive," Gabe says, eyeing the supplies I've lined up on the island.

I shake my head. "This is nothing," I tell him, using a coffee cup to scoop flour into a mixing bowl. "My roommate cooked an entire Thanksgiving dinner on the two-burner stove in the common room of our dorm. She's an actual wizard."

Gabe grins. "You really like it up there, huh?" he asks. "Boston?"

"I do." I thought it was just that I liked the person I was there, shiny new Molly, but now that I've been away I realize that's not totally true. I love the city itself: the tour guides riding the T in their silly tricorn hats and the bros in their Bruins jerseys and the trees bursting into bloom along Marlborough Street on Marathon Monday. I'm so lucky I get to go back there. Somehow, when I wasn't paying attention, it became my home. "You should come visit sometime." Then I hear myself. "Not—" I break off. "I just mean—"

"Yeah, no, totally." Gabe nods quickly. "I know."

I busy myself with the pancakes, wondering if he's also thinking about last summer, how close he came to doing a lot more than just visiting. I can't help but wonder what it would have been like to have him so close by: if we would have been able to make things work between us. If I could have looked him in his face and told him I was pregnant. If I would have needed to reinvent myself quite so hard.

I add milk and baking powder and a teaspoon of cinnamon to the mixing bowl, olive oil when I can't find vegetable. Outside in the courtyard I can hear crickets singing their lonely song, the night air cool through the open window and the faint smell of chlorine from the pool. I drop a pat of butter into the frying pan, listen to it hiss. "So how was your day?" Gabe finally asks.

"It was fine," I say eventually, spooning a silver-dollar-sized amount of batter into the skillet and completely failing to elaborate. "How was yours?"

Gabe's eyebrows flicker, but he doesn't comment. "Good," he says at length. Then, watching me: "You remember when my dad used to make us pancakes after dances?"

I make a face. "First of all, it was only you who ever went to any dances, if you recall." Patrick and I were notorious for keeping to ourselves back in high school, the two of us camped out in the den watching movies or holed up in the collapsing barn behind the Donnellys' house, locked in our own private universe. Still, Chuck could usually coax us out into civilization with the promise of late-night breakfast, the smell of butter browning on the stovetop and the corny yacht rock he loved, Steely Dan or Hall & Oates, playing on the ancient boom box above the fridge. Even Pilot used to get in on the action, all of us dropping bits of pancake onto the floor for him to snarf. "Second of all, do I *remember*? Dude, where do you think I got this recipe?"

Gabe's mouth drops open, surprise and delight. "Seriously?"

"I got your mom to give it to me," I confess, flipping the first batch of tiny pancakes as their edges start to bubble. "Like a hundred years ago, before—you know." I wave the spatula vaguely. "All of it."

Gabe doesn't answer right away and for a moment I think I've ruined it, shattered this careful détente with my tanks and my machine guns, but when I chance a glance in his direction he just looks sort of sad. "I've been thinking about him a lot since we got here," he tells me, opening an overhead cupboard and pulling out a couple of plates. "My dad, I mean."

"Did you guys find his parents' house?" I ask. "I never

even asked you that, I'm sorry."

Gabe shakes his head. "We tried," he says. "We found the right town and street and everything, but not the house. I think maybe it isn't there anymore."

"That's disappointing."

"Yeah," he says, looking rueful. "It kind of was."

I consider him for a moment. "Can I ask you something?" I begin carefully.

Gabe raises his eyebrows, smirking a little. "I mean, you're going to anyway, aren't you?"

"Yes, actually," I say, making a face in return. "Because it's important. I just—" I break off, shake my head. "You know he'd be proud of you, right? Like, whether you go to med school or you don't, or whether the shop folds or it doesn't, or whether you find your grandparents' house or you can't. All Chuck ever wanted for you guys—all three of you—was for you to be good, happy people."

Gabe wrinkles his nose at that, like he thinks I'm being corny—but I notice his shoulders drop a little, like maybe some of the knots there have loosened up just a bit. "No, I know," he says quietly. "You're probably right."

"I am," I say firmly. "Not often, maybe. But about this, for sure."

I nudge the first batch of pancakes onto the plates and we eat in companionable silence, leaning against the island side by side. It should be horrible, the quiet stretching out all around us, wide and black as the Atlantic Ocean itself, but it isn't, really. It's actually kind of nice.

"Well," I say when we're finished, holding my hand out for Gabe's plate and loading it into the futuristic French dishwasher. "I should probably get to bed."

Gabe nods. "Yeah," he says, though he doesn't make any move to go. "Me too."

"Okay," I say, lifting a hand awkwardly. "Good night."

"Night, Molly. And, um. Thanks." He pauses for a moment. "For the pancakes and for what you said."

That makes me smile. "Anytime."

I slip back up the stairs to the room I'm sharing with Ian, careful and quiet. I stare out the window for a long time.

DAY 7

Ian wakes me up in the morning with coffee and fresh, flaky croissants from the bakery down at the bottom of the hill. "I'm sorry," he says, the bulk of his body making a dip on the edge of the mattress. His eyes are red and bleary, his normally ruddy face hangover-gray. "I was drunk. I was a huge asshole."

"Okay," I say uncertainly, drawing my legs up to my chest as I take the coffee cup, arranging the sheet over my knees. "Thank you."

Ian winces. "I mean it," he says, lifting his hand and letting it fall again like he can't decide if he should touch me or not. "Of course I don't want you to do anything you don't feel ready for. And I don't want you to feel like I do."

I shrug. "Okay," I say again, rubbing my thumb around the lip of the mug instead of looking at him. "Because you kind of made me feel like that was what you wanted."

"I know," he says. "And I'm sorry." He shakes his head, and he looks very sincere. "Honestly, Molly, I just want to be around you."

I offer him a watery smile, but the truth is I feel drained and exhausted: my body aches like I've been training for a track meet. My skin is itchy and raw. It occurs to me that I'm tired of traveling, of packing up and moving on and exploring places I've never been before. It occurs to me that I'm almost ready to go home. "I'm sorry too," I tell him finally.

"Eat some of this," he advises, nudging the waxed-paper bag of croissants in my direction. I nod, tearing a pastry in two and handing him half. Both of us chew silently for a moment; then Ian swallows, flopping back onto the bed with such force I lift my coffee into the air to keep it from spilling all over the sheets. "God, I feel like *shit*," he says, shutting his eyes and digging the heels of his hands into them. "I'm never drinking red wine again." He opens his eyes, peers at me guiltily. "You probably want to go out and, like, see stuff today, huh?"

"I do in fact kind of want to go out and see stuff," I confirm, tearing off another piece of croissant and chewing thoughtfully. "But you don't have to come with me, if you don't want to."

Ian hesitates, rolling over to look at me more closely. I can see him trying to figure out if this is a trap or not. "It's fine," I promise. "Look, clearly you've already seen all this stuff, right? There's no reason for you to schlep all over creation with me to go see the *Mona Lisa*."

Ian looks so intensely sheepish I almost smile. "I really, *really* don't want to go see the *Mona Lisa*," he confesses.

"It's okay," I tell him again, and I mean it. I *do* want to see the *Mona Lisa*, actually; I wanted to see the Eiffel Tower, too, but if he thinks it's dumb or boring I'd rather just go on my own. "Seriously, take the day off, chill out. I'll be fine."

I'm planning to say the same thing to Gabe and Sadie—the last thing I want is to wind up spending the day as their third wheel—but once I'm dressed and downstairs I find Sadie still unshowered, drinking coffee on a lounge chair in the courtyard with a set of borrowed headphones in her ears. "You know, I think I'm going to stay here today," she announces, pulling out one earbud and squinting up at me in the whitish morning sunshine.

I blink. "Really?" I ask. "But . . . we're in Paris."

Sadie smiles. "You know, I heard something about that." She shrugs, leaning back against the chaise. "We went to the Louvre yesterday. I ate some Brie. I've been traveling for ten days, and now I want to sit by this pool and listen to TED Talks. That's what vacation is for, right? Going where the trail takes you, guilt-free?"

"I mean, yeah," I agree. I think of my carefully planned itinerary, all the *should*s and *must*s and *ought to*s I packed in my suitcase on the way over here. It's almost like someone else made all those plans. "I guess you're right."

Sadie grins at that, leaning back and stretching as luxuriously as a cat on a windowsill. "I like to think I usually am."

"Well, Ian's begging off too," I tell her, frowning a little bit. "Massive hang-xiety up there. So if you're committed to this chair for the day, that leaves—"

"You and me," Gabe says, appearing at the sliding doors that lead back into the kitchen. He's in the same clothes he's been wearing since we got here, jeans and a soft-looking T-shirt, his short hair wet from the shower.

"You and me," I say, trying not to sound too obviously panicked. I can tell my expression mirrors his, a combination of dread and false equanimity, *don't fight in front of the kids.*

Gabe's gaze cuts from me to Sadie, then back again. "I just gotta grab my stuff, okay? I'll meet you inside."

"Um, yup," I tell him. "I'll be here."

Once he's gone Sadie wrinkles her nose, tipping her head back against her lounge chair. "Anyway, it's probably not the worst thing in the world for us to take a little bit of a break from each other," she admits more quietly. "Yesterday we argued all the way around Montparnasse."

My heart sinks like a penny in a fountain, turns over once on the way down. "Oh, Sadie," I say, and I'm surprised to find I really mean it. I think I could have been a better friend to her while we were here. "I'm sorry."

Sadie shakes her head. "It's okay. It is what it is, right?"

"I guess," I agree. "But it still sucks."

She smirks at that, a sharper, wryer expression than I've

seen on her face until now. "Yeah," she admits. "It totally sucks." She sighs then, determined and resigned as a hiker taking a break before the last long leg of a journey. "Anyway, I have no idea what's going to happen when we get back to Indiana. But for today, I am going to enjoy my own personal Versailles."

I consider her for a moment, Sadie with her quick thinking and indefatigable optimism and midwestern cornfield of yellow hair. Looking at her I can't help but remember Tess, who Patrick dated last summer; she and I could have been real friends, I think, but just like always I let the Donnellys get in the way. "Look, Sadie," I begin cautiously, "I'm really sorry I snapped at you the other night. I was just really tired."

Sadie looks confused. "When did you—what, about Sabrina Hudson?" She shakes her head. "I thought about that, actually. And I think you were right."

I blink at her. "I was?"

Sadie nods. "Yeah. I mean, what do I care if some celebrity wants to show her business to the whole world, right?" She shrugs again then, like it's no skin off her tan, freckled nose. "I know I can be kind of, like, a judger sometimes, especially when it comes to other girls or whatever. But I meant what I said about you and Imogen. You guys make me think it wouldn't be so bad to have more girlfriends."

That makes me smile. It occurs to me that for better or worse Sadie is the only one of us who's been one hundred percent herself the whole time we've been on this trip: who hasn't been hiding secret family money or a paralyzing fear of the future or a messy, shameful past. Even if I haven't always been her biggest fan, I have to respect that much. I hope I can be more like her in that way.

"I'm really glad you came on this trip," I blurt before I can talk myself out of it, decide it's too awkward or forward or out of the blue.

Sadie looks slightly confused, but she grins in return. "Well thanks, Molly," she says. "I'm really glad I did, too."

"I'll bring you back some fancy-ass chocolate," I promise. "You enjoy today."

"Yeah," Sadie says, and smiles like a person who knows herself down to the tiniest particle. "I think I will."

When I get back inside I find Gabe waiting near the front door wearing a hoodie and a dubious expression, arms crossed like he's already annoyed at me. "Hey," he says. "You ready to go?"

"Um," I say, standing awkwardly in place like my limbs aren't working all of a sudden. "Sure."

We shuffle down the front walk in tense, unfriendly silence, all the horrifying awkwardness we somehow managed to avoid last night rushing up at us like a high-speed light rail. "You know, we don't *actually* have to spend today together," I point out as we make it to the sidewalk. "We could just go our separate ways now, meet up with these guys back here later."

Gabe's eyes narrow. "Is that what you want to do?" he asks roughly.

I wasn't expecting an argument; I blink. "I don't know," I say. "I just, I figured—"

"That's kind of depressing, isn't it?"

I raise my eyebrows, surprised. "More depressing than walking around Paris fighting all day?" Then I realize it sounds like I'm talking about him and Sadie. "I'm just saying, you and I haven't exactly been getting along like gangbusters this week."

Gabe smirks at that. "Well, nobody says we're contractually obligated to fight all day," he points out. "It's not, like, a written requirement."

"Oh no?" I look at him for a moment, skeptical. In the first place, I can't actually imagine the two of us making it through a day of sightseeing without destroying each other. And in the second, I don't actually know if getting along is a much better option. I haven't forgotten the other night outside the hardware-store bar—that jolt right down the center of my body, enough white heat to rend me clear in half. He said it himself: we've never been just friends. "You really think that's a good idea?"

Gabe makes a face like I'm being unnecessarily stubborn. "What if we don't talk about it?" he bargains.

I squint as the morning sunlight filters through the trees, making patterns on his arms and chest and catching the coppery brown in his hair. "About what?" I ask, suspicious.

"About anything," Gabe says. "What if we just act like two randos who happen to be traveling together? No personal discussions whatsoever."

"You wanna *role play*?" I blurt.

Gabe blushes faintly, rolls his eyes. "Not in, like, a sexy way, thanks. Just—"

"I'm teasing," I tell him. I don't understand why he's pushing this so hard for someone who doesn't actually seem to like me very much; still, I'm so tired of trying to sort through my own emotions that spending a day pretending they don't exist sounds great. "Let's do it."

Now it's Gabe's turn to look surprised—but not, if I had to guess, disappointed. "Okay," he says, and it sounds like a challenge. "Let's."

Paris without Ian is a completely different experience. Yesterday we slipped seamlessly into the fabric of the city, pulling treasures from its secret pockets and peeling back layer after hidden layer like so many raw-silk petticoats; today, we might as well be wearing tube socks with sandals and Bermuda shorts. Gabe and I fumble through as best we can, pointing to the simplest menu items at a patisserie and mangling the pronunciation of *je suis desolé* over and over. We get lost on the Metro twice.

Still, there's something weirdly relaxing about being so unsophisticated, the two of us traipsing in hopeless circles like a couple of walking, talking Chicken McNuggets. It's almost liberating, to be so bad at this.

"I think we were supposed to turn left back there," I report now, squinting at the map on my phone and then back in the direction we came from, trying to read the street sign we passed half a block ago. We're looking for the Arc de Triomphe, which Ian pronounced overrated and a magnet for bird poop but Gabe promised Julia he'd visit on her behalf. "I'm almost positive we passed this café before."

"How would you even know?" Gabe asks. "All of these cafés are identical. Like, *oh, right, that's the one with a million tiny little tables out front, my favorite.*" He rubs at the back of his head. "It's a huge fucking arch, it's at the end of a giant street, I don't know how we keep missing it." He holds his hand out for my phone. "Let me see?"

I peer over his shoulder while he orients it, our heads tipped close together as we squint against the glare. He smells clean and slightly sweaty, heat from walking around all morning radiating off him; when he turns his face in my direction, suddenly he's close enough to kiss.

"Um," he says, swallowing audibly. I can see the muscles flex in his throat. "You're right, I think. We need to turn around."

"Okay," I agree, not moving. Then I blink and come back to myself. "I—right. Yes. Let's . . . do that."

Gabe coughs. "Let's," he agrees, straightening up.

We head back in the direction we came from, a careful, respectful distance between us. My whole body is humming and hot. "So who are we, then?" Gabe asks, after a seemingly endless stretch of awkward silence. "If we're not being ourselves, I mean?"

"That's a good question." I think for a moment, grateful for the distraction. "A count and countess from a small but prosperous kingdom near Switzerland," I decide. "Brother and sister, of course."

"Of course," Gabe echoes.

"We're here for the summer to stay with our rich and eccentric aunt," I continue, getting into it, "who it turns out was running an illegal pigeon-fighting ring out of the secret subbasement of her mansion, but it was raided by French police off a tip by her jilted ex-lover, so now—" I break off at the sight of Gabe's skeptical expression. "What?" I ask, laughing a little self-consciously. "Too much?"

He shakes his head. "Not *enough*," he counters, grinning. "If we're going to go for it we should really go for it, you know?"

"Oh, *okay*," I tease, surprised and pleased. "You think you can do better?"

"I do, in fact," Gabe tells me grandly. "We're Lars and Heidi von Krinklestein, heirs to the world's largest ball-bearing fortune. We're in Paris as emissaries of our mother, the ball-bearing magnate, but we lost our luggage in a terrible private-jet mix-up—"

"Art imitating life, I see."

"I don't know what you're talking about," Gabe says

smoothly, but the wink he sends in my direction gives him away. "Anyway, the shock of losing her priceless souvenir shot-glass collection, which she never leaves home without, sent Heidi into an amnesiac episode—"

"Actually, I think it was Lars's collection of diamond-encrusted belt buckles that went missing," I cut in. "His favorite is in the shape of a wedge of Swiss cheese."

"Oh, is that what it was?" Gabe asks, stroking his chin thoughtfully. "He must have forgotten."

I burst out laughing. "Oh my God, *corny!*"

Gabe laughs too, his whole face breaking open. "You missed me," he says with a shrug, and in this moment I can't deny that it's true. I'd forgotten over the last few days, in the fog of sour moods and misunderstandings, how happy it used to make me just to goof around with him.

"Come on," I say now, shaking my head and smiling. "Let's find this damn arch once and for all."

We wander the narrow, winding streets for another twenty minutes, dodging bicyclists and peering up at flower-filled window boxes and breathing in the smell of car exhaust mixed with yeast from the open door of a tiny boulangerie. My sandals are giving me blisters again, but somehow today I can't bring myself to mind. When we finally turn the corner onto the Champs-Élysées and the Arc comes into view, the victory has me crowing out loud. "Put 'er there," I order, holding my knuckles out for a fist bump; Gabe, I note with some satisfaction, remembers to explode it this time.

"See?" he says, smiling a little. "It's not so terrible, spending the day with me."

That gets my attention. I hurt his feelings this morning, I realize with a sharp pang underneath my breastbone. It hadn't occurred to me that I still could. "I never said it was going to be terrible!" I protest. Then, reaching out and touching his arm before I can talk myself out of it: "Seriously, Gabe, hey. I never *thought* it was going to be terrible, either."

Gabe makes a face at that, skeptical, but at least he doesn't argue. "Come on," I continue, nodding across the plaza. "I'll take your picture so you can prove to Jules you actually made it."

Turns out he's in the mood to be a ham about it, mugging like a chimp and even turning a cartwheel right there on the concrete like I haven't seen him do since we were little kids horsing around on the lawn of his parents' farmhouse, clusters of fireflies lit up all around us. "Very impressive," I say once he's upright again, pink-cheeked and smiling.

"Lars gives good picture," Gabe agrees, taking his phone back; the tips of our fingers brush as I pass it over, my heart tripping a bit in the moment before I remind myself I'm not noticing things like that. "We should probably take a selfie," he jokes. "You know, to send to our mother, the ball-bearing magnate."

I start to laugh, only then he actually *does* it, leaning in close to me and stretching his arm out. "What—delete that!"

I protest, swatting at his shoulder. "I'm making the world's weirdest face."

"You know, I don't think I will, actually," Gabe says calmly, tucking his phone back into his pocket. "Mummy will love that one, don't you think?"

I snort, I can't help it. "Jerk," I huff, though in the back of my mind it occurs to me I'm not actually all that put out about it.

"So how is she, anyway?" I can't help asking as we move through the crowds in the plaza. "Jules, I mean. Not Mummy the ball-bearing magnate."

"Right," Gabe agrees, laughing. "Jules is good. She's going to Syracuse in the fall. She took Elizabeth to senior prom, which I thought was pretty cool."

"That is cool," I echo, feeling a tiny pang like I always do when I think about Jules my former friend and not Jules my sworn blood enemy. We were circling the world's most fragile armistice last summer before everything came crashing down again, and I'd be lying if I said I didn't have regrets.

"We hung out a lot while I was home, actually," Gabe continues, "at the shop and whatnot. She's mellowed out, if you can believe it. She wants to do business stuff too—she's got all these big ideas, just like you do. I actually think you guys might get along now, hugely improbable as I realize that sounds."

"I will . . . take your word for it," I tell him, unable to hold back a quiet laugh. Still, I'm surprised by how it feels almost normal to talk about her, that apparently enough time has passed for me to hear her name without my hands going clammy and my blood pressure spiking like I'm about to have a stroke. "But I'm glad."

Gabe nods; we're quiet for a moment, strolling under a leafy canopy of trees. "You can ask about my brother, too, you know," he tells me. "I can, like, *feel* you wondering over there."

I raise my eyebrows, not entirely sure what he's getting at. "I mean, definitely not in a romantic way," I say truthfully.

"No, I know," Gabe says quickly. "I get it. I think he's good too, though, in his big-grumbles Patrick way. We're not close or anything, but he seemed happier this summer, he's got a bunch of new friends. Maybe only one of us can have an existential crisis at once, I don't know."

"And you're up at bat right now?" I ask, looking at him sidelong.

"Kind of feels that way." Gabe shrugs. "Anyway, I've been thinking about him a lot on this trip, kind of. He was always complaining that things came easy to me, right? And it's not like I ever thought he was wrong, exactly. But I also never thought that I wouldn't be able to handle it if things got hard."

"You are handling it, though," I tell him reflexively. "Gabe, really. I promise things aren't as bad as you think."

Gabe shakes his head. "Aren't they?"

I frown at that, spying an empty bench beneath a row of

chestnut trees on the plaza; I sit down and after a moment Gabe joins me, tipping his head back to peer up through the leaves. "There must be something you like about being in Indiana, right?" I ask, bumping his shoulder with mine before I can talk myself out of it. "Like, even just one thing."

"I mean, the bars," he reports. Then, off my eye roll, "I'm kidding. I'm kidding." He scratches the back of his head. "I like how quiet it gets at night," he says finally. "Like if I'm walking home across campus from Sadie's or the library or wherever. It's peaceful. And it gets kind of peaceful in my head, too." He shrugs, looking a little bit embarrassed at the revelation, like maybe he said more than he meant to. "What about you?" he asks, stretching his arms out along the back of the bench and changing the subject. "What do you like about Boston?"

"I mean, everything, kind of," I confess. "Like, don't get me wrong, it's cold and miserable a lot of the time, but there's something about it that just feels really . . . homey to me? I can imagine being there a long time, I think."

Gabe's eyebrows flicker at that, I notice, but he doesn't comment. "Your roommate sounds cool" is all he says.

"She's fantastic," I confirm, smiling at the thought of Roisin's preppy button-downs and her love of all things Star Wars. "She reminds me of Imogen, kind of, because she's so open and fun and easy to get to know. She invited me to come visit her in Georgia this summer, even."

"That's awesome," Gabe says. "How was it?"

225

Now it's my turn to realize I've said more than I necessarily meant to. "I mean, it's possible I didn't actually go," I admit.

Gabe looks confused. "Why not?"

"I don't really know," I say slowly. It was an instinctive *no*, a reflex; it wasn't until later that it occurred to me my instincts might have been wrong. "Like, we're really, really good roommates. We're going to live together next year, she's the closest person to me at school—um, except for Ian, obviously—but I guess I still kind of held myself at a distance from her sometimes? I was always afraid of things getting, like . . ." I trail off, waving my hand.

"Messy?" Gabe supplies.

"Yeah." I nod, feeling myself blush. "Like if we got too close inevitably I'd do something to make her realize she didn't actually like me that much." I'm surprised—shocked, even—to hear the words come out of my mouth: this isn't the kind of thing I'd normally say to anybody, let alone him. I didn't even know I was thinking it. "Anyway, I'm going to try and do better at that this year," I resolve. "Not *everybody* who gets to know me can possibly be destined for horrible disappointment, right?"

I'm joking around to cover my own embarrassment, but when I glance over at Gabe he's gazing back at me, even. "There's nothing disappointing about you, Molly Barlow," he says quietly. My heart stutters a bit inside my chest.

"Well," I say, standing so quickly I almost get dizzy, all

the blood rushing out of my head at once. "We'll see, any-way. You wanna go find some lunch? My treat," I add, when he hesitates.

Gabe makes a face. "Ian's treat, you mean."

"I mean, yes, Ian's treat," I admit, sighing a little. "He gave me some cash before we left. But what are you going to do otherwise, starve? I get if you're sensitive about Ian pay-ing for stuff, but it's only because—"

"First of all, can you stop saying that?" Gabe asks me, sounding irritated again for the first time since this morning. "That I'm sensitive about stuff? You said it the other night, too, and it makes me sound like such a fucking pansy."

I roll my eyes. "*First of all*," I mimic, "don't say pansy."

"Now you sound like Imogen," he points out.

"Good," I shoot back. "Imogen is smart."

"I *know* Imogen is smart," Gabe says. "And you know what I mean. It makes me sound like somebody who can't handle himself."

You were just saying you don't think you can, I almost point out, then think better of it. "It makes you sound like somebody who's afraid of emotions and isn't going to let his son play with dolls, actually."

"My son can play with dolls if he wants to, Molly!" Gabe says, but he's laughing, which is something. He tilts his head back, stares up at the trees. "I just want to not feel like my life is spiraling wildly out of control at every moment."

That stops me. "What's spiraling out of control?" I ask,

sitting back down beside him.

"Well, I'm depending on your boyfriend for my pocket money, for starters," Gabe says immediately, ticking off a list on his fingers. "I'm about to apply to a bunch of extremely expensive medical schools I don't even want to go to—and yes, you win, this is me saying it: I don't want to go to medical school. I don't even want to go back to Indiana, honestly. Five will get you ten, my girlfriend is about to break up with me because I can't seem to stop being a dickbag, even when I want to. The other day I spent a hundred dollars I definitely do not have on *skydiving*, for some reason. And then there's y—"

He snaps his jaws shut at the very last, but the look on his face is as clear as if he'd finished the sentence: *and then there's you.*

And then there's me.

I gaze at him for a moment, every bone in my body gone hot and heedful. After all, it's not like he's wrong. *Something* is happening between us, clearly, though whether it's garden-variety muscle memory or a rarer breed of bird altogether I couldn't honestly say. What I do know is that I've been batting it away all week: in the obvious moments, like the other night outside the hardware-store bar, but also every single time I've stared for half a second too long at his sharp wrists or the cliff of his collarbone or remembered what it's like to hold his hand. I miss him, Gabe Donnelly with his swagger and his smile and his heart as big and steady as a steamship.

Not just as a person, but as *mine*.

And if the way he's looking at me now is any indication, he misses me, too.

I shake my head to clear it, tucking my hair behind my ears and staring out across the plaza at the Arc. This is a dangerous road to travel, even if it's only in my mind. No matter what's about to happen between him and Sadie—no matter what's going on with Ian and me—there are a million reasons why Gabe and I are a plane crash waiting to happen. There's so much he still doesn't know.

"You're twenty-one, dude," I remind him finally, nudging his elbow with mine in a way I hope is sufficiently platonic; I feel the ache of it anyway, the dull singing of an overworked muscle. "You don't have to have everything perfectly figured out. You don't have to *be* perfect."

"Don't I?" Gabe asks. Then, angling his chin in my direction like he thinks he's caught me at something: "Don't *you*?"

My skin prickles in irritated recognition; I don't like the implication there. "We're not talking about me," I remind him, chafing a bit. "We're not supposed to be talking about any of this, actually, if you recall."

Gabe looks at me for another long moment. Then he nods. "Fair point, Heidi von Krinklestein," he says, holding his hands up. "What do you want to talk about instead?"

"The history of this arch," I announce, pulling up a guide on my phone and pointing to it. "Did you know, for example, that it honors those who fought and died for France in the

Revolutionary and Napoleonic Wars?"

"That's fascinating," Gabe says, in a voice like he still wants to be talking about the other thing. I shrug, looking away.

Eventually we make it to lunch after all, a tiny falafel place with the softest pitas I've ever eaten, the warm air pungent with the smell of oregano and dill. We sit outside on a tiny patio to eat, the midafternoon sun toasting the back of my neck.

"I emailed my mom about what you said, by the way," Gabe tells me, offering me a napkin and motioning to the smear of tzatziki sauce on my face. "Your ideas for the shop, I mean."

"Really?" I ask, surprised. "I thought you said it was all too serious for any of that stuff to work."

"I'm a cranky ass, remember?" Gabe shakes his head. "That was me being a cranky ass. They were good ideas." He plucks a stray tomato out of his tinfoil wrapper, shrugs. "Anyway, she said to say thank you. She said she always knew you had a head for that stuff."

My eyes widen. "She *did*?" It's hardly an absolution, but still I'm hit with a pang of longing for Connie as physical as if someone had reached into my body and squeezed. "Wow," I say, casting my eyes downward, embarrassed by how much I still ache for her approval. "That's really great, Gabe. I'm glad."

Gabe sits back in his metal chair then, all long limbs and

skepticism. "Yeah, well," he says, lips twisting wryly like looking hopeful makes him weak. "We'll see if we're too far gone."

Just for a second it sounds like maybe he's talking about something besides the pizza shop. I clear my throat, crumpling up my wrapper and rattling the ice in my plastic cup. "Okay," I say, bright and impersonal as a tour guide charged with a bus full of sandaled retirees. "Where to next?"

Gabe scoops our garbage up off the table, holds his hand out for my empty cup. "You're going to make fun of me," he says, tossing it all into a trash can at the corner of the patio, "but there actually was one thing I wanted to do that we didn't get to yesterday."

"Why would I make fun of you?" I glance over my shoulder and make a face at him, teasing. "Is it something really shameful and touristy, like going to the top of the Eiffel Tower?"

Gabe blanches. "Uh," he says.

"Oh my God, is it really?" My jaw drops open, recognition and giddy delight. "Do you really want to go to the top of the Eiffel Tower?"

"Fuck you," Gabe says, but he's smiling. The sight of it is like a warm cup of coffee the morning of the first snow of the year. "Not anymore."

"No, it's just—" I break off. I want to explain about Ian, about what happened yesterday, but I don't know how to phrase it in a way that wouldn't be some kind of betrayal.

Instead I only grin back at him, already keying the destination into my phone. "We're totally doing this."

And that's exactly what we do—though not before we ride the Metro in the wrong direction for two stops and walk a block and a half out of our way like a couple of bozos. "How does this keep *happening?*" Gabe asks, both of us laughing at the ridiculousness of it, annoyed with ourselves but also, I think, not *that* annoyed. "I can literally see the fucking thing!" Eventually we find the ticket booth and take a crowded elevator to the top of the tower, my stomach flipping dizzily as we step out onto the observation deck.

Ian was right, of course—it's packed with a million people speaking a million different languages, all iPhone cameras and ugly sneakers and squabbling families elbowing for the best view. It's also *stunning.* When we finally make it over to the railing I can see for ages in every direction, verdant green parks and tall, filigreed buildings and swaths and swaths of dense blue sky.

"Okay," Gabe says with the kind of quietly delighted astonishment I haven't heard out of him since his dad was alive. It makes me think of being out on Chuck's boat in the summertime, of fat fish pulled from murky brown lake water. "You can call me whatever you want, like maybe I really am a filthy American or whatever, but. This is *awesome.*"

I laugh, his excitement contagious. "It is, right?"

"Yeah!" He's grinning openly now, gesturing out at the view with no trace of the briny skepticism he's been marinating in all week long. "Like, look at that, Molly Barlow. That's *special*."

"Yeah," I agree, letting myself wonder for a moment at the tremendous improbability of us winding up here together. In the west the sun is just starting to sink, Gabe's skin going golden in the warm, toasted light. "It's pretty special."

He glances over at me then, holding the eye contact a beat too long for it to feel strictly casual. My whole body warms in spite of the stiff, chilly breeze ruffling my hair. "So what happened, huh?" I can't help asking, clearing my throat a bit and taking half a step away from him, reminding myself what a bad idea it is to get too close. "Sadie wasn't into this?"

Gabe makes a face, glances out at the skyline. "She's afraid of heights, remember?"

I roll my eyes. "That's not really an answer." I feel bad for ruining the moment, but not bad enough to keep on pretending like everything's fine among the four of us. I don't know if it's the bird's-eye view or what, but something about being up here makes me feel like it's time to cut the crap and tell the truth. "Come on, dude. What's going on with you guys, huh?"

"What happened to not talking about anything personal?" Gabe asks; his tone is teasing, but underneath is a flash of the craggy irritation I've gotten used to from him over the last few days. Then he sighs. "I don't know," he admits, shaking his head. "This has been . . . not a great trip for us, clearly. Like I said, most of it is my fault. I think she

233

thought I was a certain way, back at school? And maybe I was, a year ago. But now I'm not."

My heart pings with recognition, a circuit lighting up inside some complicated machine. "You seem the same to me," I tell him honestly. "Like you're going through a thing, maybe. But not, you know. Fundamentally altered."

Gabe smiles—not as broadly as he was a minute ago, but it's something. "Thanks," he says. "I mean, I think."

We gaze out at the view for another long minute, neither one of us saying anything. In the distance the sun is getting heavier, the sky turning orange and pink. There's a question mark hanging in the air between us, the conversation not quite finished; sure enough, after a moment he looks over at me one more time. "So what about you?" he asks, rocking back on his heels and raising his eyebrows. "What's up with you and Louis XIV?"

I roll my eyes. "Shut up," I scold, though truthfully—guiltily—I have to work not to laugh. "Don't call him that."

Gabe must sense he's almost got me: "Oh, come on," he says, eyes widened like a standup comedian delivering a punch line. "You didn't even know he was a secret billionaire, apparently. Like, listen to that sentence for a second. That is an *absurd* fucking sentence."

My whole body prickles, red and embarrassed. "Enough." I push myself away from the railing. He's laughing now, like he wants me to share this inside joke with him, two Star Lake kids having one over on my dopey outsider boyfriend.

And I'm not going to do that. "You don't know anything about my relationship with Ian, okay?"

Gabe shrugs. "Maybe not," he admits easily. "But I know you. I've known you almost my whole life, and I know you can't possibly be happy."

That galls me—the presumption of it, maybe, the sheer leap on his part. "Oh, *really*?" I counter, drawing myself up like the heiress to a ball-bearing fortune affronted by a mouthy peasant kicking mud onto her dress. "And why's that, exactly?"

"Because all of a sudden you're so—so—" He breaks off in frustration. "You're just—"

"*What*?" I demand. "Oh my God, just say it already."

"*Tidy*," Gabe spits out finally.

"Tidy?" Now I do laugh, loud and barking, though it's not like I don't know what he's getting at, exactly. More like I don't want to think about it. "Wow, Gabe. You really know how to insult a girl. Next thing you'll be telling me I practice good hygiene or have elegant penmanship. Really putting me in my place, there."

"I'm not *trying* to insult you," Gabe snaps, like I'm being stupid on purpose. "I'm trying to tell you what I see. And what I see is you turning into this small, inoffensive, terrified version of the person I used to know." He shakes his head. "You said it yourself a minute ago when you were talking about your roommate, that you're tying yourself up in knots trying not to give anybody a reason not to like you. And that's a ridiculous way to live."

Oh, I do not like him saying that to me. I do not like it at *all*. I feel like he's caught me at something obscene and perverted; I feel careless and ashamed for letting him get close enough to look. "Okay then," I reply, voice brittle. "Thanks for the professional diagnosis. Any time you want to stop mansplaining me to myself, that'd be great."

Gabe rolls his eyes. "I'm not mansplaining anything to you, Molly," he counters, openly annoyed. "I'm saying that I have noticed, over the course of this weird, miserable week, that you're putting on a twenty-four-hour stage show like you're headlining at the fucking Copacabana for everyone else's benefit, and I'm asking if it doesn't get tiring sometimes."

My mouth drops open. "That's not—" I start, then immediately break off because of course he sees me just like he always has; of course we both know it's true. It's *exactly* what I've been doing, actually, and it *is* tiring, but at this point I don't know how I'd possibly go about dropping the act even if I wanted to. Still, Gabe of all people calling me out on it makes me want to run all the way down to the bottom of this tower.

"None of this is actually even your business to begin with," I counter finally. "We don't date, I'm not your problem, so—"

"Yeah, well, whose fault is that, again?"

"Oh my God!" I gawk at him, stunned by the bald unfairness of it. "You want to relitigate our breakup right now,

Gabe? Fine. Our breakup was my fault. I fucked up. I own it. I have *been* owning it, I promise you. Basically everything I have done all *year* has been about me owning it, so . . ."

I trail off as Gabe's eyes narrow. "What does *that* mean?" he asks.

"Nothing," I say, too quickly. "Forget it."

"I don't want to forget it," Gabe presses. "Tell me."

"Why?" I ask—cornered and fearful, all talons and teeth. It occurs to me that we're making a scene, inviting all manner of curious glances in our direction, but for the first time since I left Star Lake last summer, I don't actually care. "Seriously, why are we even having this conversation? You said yourself we've never been friends, and for some reason I've been trying to convince myself that we were, or at least that we *could* be, but you're right." I shake my head at my own stubborn stupidity, counting off on my fingers. "If we were friends you wouldn't have fallen off the face of the planet after last summer. If we were friends you wouldn't have lied to me and said we were cool. If we were *friends* I would have mattered enough that you could have been bothered to call me back sometime between last October and the moment we ran into each other in freaking London, Eng—"

"I didn't call you back because you broke my fucking heart, Molly!"

That stops me, baffled and blinking; for a moment the whole world seems to go quiet. "I *did*?" I ask, and my voice sounds very small.

Gabe gapes at me. "You know you did," he says immediately. "Are you seriously going to look at me right now and say you didn't know that you—"

"No, I just—" I break off. I remember the moment last summer when he found out about Patrick and me, the hurt and betrayal and bewilderment on his face. "I mean, of course I know I did. I guess I just . . . thought you were over it."

"Yeah, well," Gabe says flatly, that belligerent shrug of his shoulders. "I'm not."

"But the way we left things last summer—" I shake my head, stubborn. "You made it seem like we were okay."

Gabe makes a face. "Come on, Molly. What was I supposed to say to you? You were going to Boston, you know? You were starting fresh."

I consider that for a moment, the last twelve months reshuffling in my mind like the vacation photos my mom used to get developed at the drugstore in Star Lake. I thought about Gabe this year—in the stairwell as I left him a voicemail and in the waiting room at the clinic, sure, but also a million other times: eating a really amazing slice of pizza at a hole-in-the-wall restaurant in the North End with Roisin. Sticking a carrot I'd begged from the dining-hall guys into the smiling face of a snowman on the Esplanade. At the very end of the semester when all the trees exploded into spring on Commonwealth Avenue, a canopy of pink flowers up above my head. I thought about Gabe every time I heard a dumb joke in the elevator, every time I went to the movies, every time our song came up on Spotify while I ran.

It never once occurred to me that, halfway across the country, he was thinking about me, too.

"But—" I don't understand. "You're here with *Sadie*."

"And you're here with Ian!" Gabe explodes, looking at me like I've totally lost it. "Jesus Christ, Molly. Obviously you've moved on. You can't possibly be angry with me for trying to do the same thing."

"I'm not *angry*," I protest, though as I say it I realize that's not true at all. Suddenly everything from last fall comes back in a rush: the loss and the loneliness, the dull certainty that he'd moved on without a backward glance, while—just like always—I was the one facing the fallout. "I needed you. And you weren't there for me."

Gabe's face darkens at that, confusion and worry. "Needed me how?" he asks urgently. "Molly, what *happened*?"

I shake my head again, knowing there's no way to say it. Knowing in my bones that it's time. I look at him for a moment, standing here tall and honest in the most beautiful place on the planet. "I was pregnant," I finally say.

For a second Gabe just blinks at me, uncomprehending. "Wait, what?" he asks, shaking his head. "When?"

"When I got to school," I tell him. "Last fall."

"Last fall—" The realization creeps up his face, his lips thinning half a second before his eyes go sharp and wary. "So it was—?"

"You and me," I say. "Yeah."

He tilts his head to the side. "But we were careful," he says, "right?"

"I thought so," I say, shrugging. "I guess we weren't as careful as we thought."

"And you—?" Gabe doesn't finish.

"I had an abortion," I tell him. My voice doesn't waver at all.

Gabe doesn't say anything for a long moment. Then his eyes go wide. "Holy shit," he blurts out, like he's only just connecting the dots for the first time. "You're saying that's why you called me? And I didn't—*fuck*, Molly." He shakes his head. "I am so fucking sorry."

I shrug. All around us crowds shuffle along the observation deck in a colorful blur: families with balloons tied to their strollers, groups of teenagers shoving each other playfully, two middle-aged women using a cell phone camera to fix their wine-colored lipstick. I wonder if this is how I'll remember this trip, as a long series of emotional crises conducted while strangers Instagrammed themselves all around me. "You didn't know," I remind him, all the hot fury burning just a moment ago drained suddenly out of me. "I could have kept trying."

"It's not your fault." He lifts his hand to the back of his neck, like he's checking to make sure his skull is still attached to it. He looks shell-shocked. *"Shit."* He wraps his fingers around the guardrail and stares out at the city for a moment, like we're back in the pine-scented quiet of Star Lake and not here, in this bustling, cacophonous place. It's full sunset now, the sky red and dripping; all around us, the world seems to glow. "I am really, really sorry you had to do all that on your own."

"I wasn't alone," I promise him. "My mom and Imogen were both fantastic." Even Roisin, who I barely knew back then, somehow seemed to figure out something was going on—she brought me Rice Krispies treats from the dining hall and a month-old *Cosmo* she'd filched from the big recycling bin on our floor. "I was way luckier than a lot of people would have been."

"I know," Gabe says. "But still, I wish I'd known. I wouldn't have tried to get you to change your mind or anything, I don't want you to think that. I just wish I'd been there to hang out with you. I would have brought you all the fucking Red Vines in Massachusetts." He lets a breath out. "I'm just sorry I wasn't *there*."

He wraps his arms around me then, squeezes; I hold on just as tightly, breathe him in. "I'm sorry too," I say into his chest, not even sure which part of it I'm apologizing for. All of it, maybe. But underneath the regret relief is blooming, slow and soothing: telling the whole truth is like aloe on sunburn, the balm of finally being totally seen.

I take a step back, or try to; Gabe catches my waist and holds on, like he doesn't want to let me go. I hesitate as the air between us changes, getting heavier; my breath catches in the cavern of my chest. When he looks at my mouth I can feel it in my elbows, the hot zing of desire. When my forehead brushes his cheek I can feel it behind my knees. It's like my heart is being squeezed for juice as we stand here, dripping wet and sticky down my ribs.

Still: "We can't," I remind him again, though it feels physically painful to say it. But I'm not going to do that to Ian, even if I know—and I do know now, with a certainty that thuds like my own heartbeat—that things between us are never going to be exactly right. And it's not because of Gabe, or because Ian isn't wonderful. It's because it's time to be who I really am.

Gabe holds me for a minute longer, strong and steady. Then he squeezes one more time and lets me go. "We're good?" I ask as the sky detonates in the distance. "For real this time?"

Gabe smiles at that, just faintly. Then he nods. "Yeah, Molly Barlow," he promises, and I believe him. "We're good."

It's almost ten by the time we finally make it back to Ian's parents' house, the wide, leafy street gone purple-dark and quiet. Both of us pause on the doorstep like there's some kind of invisible force field preventing us from going in, Gabe shoving his hands into his pockets and me rubbing my arms against the chill. I want to stretch this moment out as long as possible. I want to cup it in my hands to protect it like a flame.

"Look," Gabe says. We were silent all the way home on the Metro, up the steep hill back to the house, and his voice sounds deeper than I think of it as being, more grown-up. "Can I just—" He breaks off, taking a step toward me. Thinking again. "I don't want to do anything out of line. I just want—"

"*Yes*," I say, popping up on my tiptoes and wrapping my arms around his neck, hard and impulsive; Gabe holds on so tight and desperate I almost can't catch my breath. I want to unzip my body and put him inside it, for us to become one person. I feel like I can't possibly get close enough.

I don't know how long we stand there frozen in place like two magnets, Gabe's hand on my neck and my face pressed into the hollow at the center of his rib cage, breathing in his warm, slightly sweaty smell. All I want in the world is to keep him. But I know that he's not mine to have. We've never quite managed to get it right, me and Gabe, the two of us all near-misses and missed calls and dangling conversations. I still love him so ridiculously much.

"Okay," I say finally, taking a step back and breaking the moment, knowing I have to say good-bye. "Um. Travel safe, yeah?"

Gabe nods, clearing his throat. "Yup." He and Sadie have an early morning flight, need to be at the airport before seven; on one hand I'm sorry I won't get a chance to see her off properly, but on the other I can't imagine what I could possibly say that wouldn't taste like a lie or a betrayal. I'm a damage doer, no matter hard I try not to be. Maybe every-body is, in some way. "I'll see you around, Molly Barlow," he says quietly.

"Yeah," I promise, swallowing down the longing, hold-ing my hand up in one last wave. "I'll see you." The tips of our fingers brush again, so lightly I think I might have imag-ined it, in the moment before I turn and go inside.

Ian's asleep in the master bedroom when I get up there, French TV flickering blue in the darkness and a paperback splayed open on the mattress beside him; I root around in the sheets until I find the remote, clicking it off and plunging the room into deep, velvety silence. He rolls over on the mat-tress, blinking awake. "Hey," he murmurs. He looks younger than usual in the slice of white moonlight sneaking through the linen curtains, his face smooth and unguarded. "How was it?"

I swallow. It feels like I've lived a whole year in the last twelve hours. It feels like I've lived an entire life. "It was good," I tell him finally for lack of a better answer, climbing under the covers beside him. "It was a really good day."

Ian smiles sleepily. "I'm glad."

"Me too," I say, laying a gentle hand on his back. In the morning I'm going to set about fixing. Tonight, I'm going to let him rest. "Go back to sleep."

DAY 8

I wake with a start the next morning, the knowledge of something undone humming like a power grid deep inside in my bones. When I look over Ian is still asleep beside me, limbs sprawled in all different directions and his face creased from a kink in the pillow. I slide out of bed as quietly as I can.

The house is calm and quiet, morning sun spilled in yellow-white puddles on the honey-warm hardwood floor. Gabe and Sadie are already gone, their water glasses rinsed on the drainboard and their sheets in a heap on top of the washing machine in the alcove off the kitchen. I catch sight of a note beside the coffeemaker in Sadie's handwriting: *Didn't want to wake you up to say good-bye! Thanks SO MUCH for everything.*

I pick up my phone, click the icon for my travel app. We're supposed to fly back to Boston this afternoon; I'm supposed to spend the week before school starts with Ian in his Fenway apartment, watching old movies and reading in the park and eating late-night dollar slices from the pizza place downstairs. We were going to ride to the end of the Orange Line and go to the Arboretum. We were going to go to the beach.

Instead I switch my ticket to a flight to New York, so I can't chicken out at the last second. I text my mom to let her know I've changed my plans. I make two careful cups of coffee in the fancy machine, adding milk and half a sugar to Ian's the way I know he likes it. Then I gather my courage and climb the stairs to the second floor.

"Hi," I say, sitting down on the edge of the mattress and setting the cups on the nightstand. It occurs to me, with a flicker of dark hilarity, that I've never actually broken up with somebody before. Every other romantic relationship of my life has imploded in the middle of a screaming fight about my own infidelity, my own failures, my own wrongness; this feels oddly civilized even as I think I'd do anything in the world to avoid it. I wonder if I might actually prefer the other way. "I have to tell you something, and you're not going to like it."

Ian blinks awake. "Good morning to you too," he says sleepily. He sits up, scritching a hand through his bedhead. "What's wrong?"

"I think we have to break up," I blurt.

For a second Ian just looks at me, confused and bleary. Then he frowns. "What?" he says. "Why?"

I open my mouth, then close it again, weirdly embarrassed. God, I should have at least waited until he was up and dressed. Already I'm doing this all wrong. "I'm sorry," I say, biting my lip the moment it starts to tremble. It doesn't seem fair to cry.

"Is this because of the other night?" Ian asks. He's leaning forward, periodically jamming the heels of his hands into his eyes and rubbing vigorously. I didn't even let him pee first. "I was a dick the other night, Molly, I'm sorry. I shouldn't have given you a hard time like that."

"No, it's not about the other night," I tell him, voice as steady as I can manage. "Or maybe it is, but not the way you think. I mean, yes, the other night was kind of fucked up. But we could have figured it out, I think, or maybe it wouldn't even have been an issue to begin with if everything else between you and me felt . . ." I trail off, and then finally I admit it. "Right."

"Right?" Ian repeats, his face sharpening suddenly with hurt and surprise. "I mean, I guess I didn't realize it felt wrong to you this entire time."

I shake my head quickly. "No, it's not that, I just—" I break off. "Don't you think it says something that neither one of us felt like we could be completely honest with each other?" I ask him. "Like, that we got this far into it before we started telling the truth?"

"I *tried*, Molly." Ian's kind eyes flash then, all anger and frustration. "Don't you think I tried? I've spent the last eight months doing everything I can think of to try and get you to open up to me, and even after the other day I know there's still stuff about yourself you're never going to talk about. And I don't know how to be the kind of person you can tell."

"You're right," I tell him honestly. "And that's on me."

Ian shakes his head. "But I don't—*why?*"

I want to give him a neat, tidy answer. But all I've got left is the truth. "I just—when we met last year, I was trying so hard to re-create myself, you know? And you liking me—liking this new version of me, even if it wasn't always who I actually was—was, like, proof that it was working. I didn't want to wreck that." I bite my lip. "I honestly thought eventually it would start to feel normal and natural and like something I didn't constantly have to calculate for. But somehow it never totally did."

Ian frowns. "So being my girlfriend—that was *fake?*"

"*No,*" I tell him immediately, reaching my hand out and curling my fingers around his wrist, squeezing. "Not at all. I really care about you, Ian. I've loved being your girlfriend. I *wanted* to be your girlfriend. I just mean I think there was a part of me that felt like if you knew everything about me, warts and all, you'd run away like your hair was on fire."

Ian pulls away. "You keep saying that," he points out, sounding frustrated. "But when did I ever make you think I wouldn't like your warts?"

I hesitate at that, not sure how to answer. After all, he has a point. But if I've learned anything this week, it's that I've been holding on to the past a lot more tightly than I realized. Living in total opposition to something is just a different way of not getting over it.

"You're right," I tell him. "You never gave me a reason to think the person I used to be was so terrible. But I guess a lot of other people did." I glance down, remembering, then— finally, *finally*—letting it go. "I'm really sorry, Ian."

"I still don't get why this is something we have to break up over," he insists, stubborn. "Like, let's be up-front with each other from now on, that's all. Let's see how it goes. There's no reason to just throw our whole relationship away."

I waver for a moment, letting myself picture it: going back to Boston and papering over everything that's happened, convincing ourselves that what we have together is enough. It's tempting, that much is undeniable. But in my gut I know it wouldn't be fair to either one of us. "I think maybe it's too late for that," I tell him quietly.

Ian gazes at me for another long moment. Finally he sighs. "Yeah, Molly," he says, shaking his sandy head sadly. "I guess it is."

Ian calls me a car in a gesture of courtliness so simple and straightforward it almost breaks my heart. I stand by the door like a little kid waiting for a ride to camp, listening to him speak perfect French into the receiver.

"Thank you for this," I say as the car pulls into the drive-way, two neat taps on the horn to let me know it's arrived. Outside the sun is a ripe, dripping yellow, the sky a million brilliant shades beyond blue. "Not just for the cab, I mean. But for all of it."

"Yeah," Ian says, shrugging a little. "Of course." He takes half a step in my direction, then hesitates like he isn't sure if he ought to hug me or not. Finally he lifts his hand in an awkward wave. "Bye, Molly."

I smile faintly and press my palm against his, lacing our fingers together long enough to squeeze in gratitude. I pull him a little closer, plant a kiss on the back of his hand. "Bye, Ian."

DAY 9

One week later

I'm curled on a lounge chair in the lush green backyard of my mom's house in Star Lake when the back door creaks open. "Whatcha reading now?" she calls, padding down the steps from the deck with a massive coffee mug in one hand. She's wearing ripped jeans and one of her trademark long, thin cardigans, her blond hair in waves down past her shoulders.

I hold it up for her inspection as she crosses the late-summer grass—a fat paperback pinched from the overflowing bookshelves in our living room, a voluminous and wide-ranging cache that I never really paid much attention to until this week. It occurs to me to wonder if that will be the big take-away from my relationship with Ian, this newfound ability to lose myself in stories—to find myself less alone there, to find myself forgiven. I want to thank him for that, though it occurs to me that now probably isn't the time.

My mom takes the book from my hand and glances at the back before returning it with a satisfied nod. "I'm going to try and not take it as a personal failing that it took you twenty years to discover you like to read," she says, lips twisting. "What is that, your fourth book this week?"

"Fifth," I confess, settling back down into the lounge chair and tilting my face up toward the sunshine. I've spent the week since I got back from Paris almost as if this entire year had never happened at all, holed up at the house while my mom's cranky cat, Vita, wound wary circles around my ankles and industriously kneaded a pillow next to my head. Jet lag, I assured my mom when she periodically popped her head into my bedroom that first morning, but of course it was more than that; in the past she might have taken me at my word, closed the door and left me to my own mopey devices, but this time she sat down on the mattress beside me.

"Hey," she said, reaching out and straightening the sleeve of my T-shirt. "We don't do that anymore, remember? You don't have to tell me what's going on if you don't want to. But you also don't have to lie."

I hesitated for a moment, old suspicions creaking like a medieval suit of armor, but in my heart I knew she was right. I opened my mouth to tell her everything. "I broke up with Ian" was as far as I got before I burst into tears.

I cried for a long time with my head on my mom's shoulder, leaving dark spots on her delicate silk shirt—for what I could have had with Ian if I'd trusted either one of us enough to be myself around him. For whatever I might have had with Gabe. Finally I sat up on the mattress, wiping my wet, puffy face with the back of my hand. "You can't write a book about any of this, you realize," I warned her, sniffling wetly. "No matter how blocked you ever get."

My mom made a face at that, rueful. "I deserved that," she admitted wryly, then gathered me up one more time.

Now, a week later, she squeezes my knee and boosts herself up off the lounge chair, takes a sip of her coffee. "Corina is driving up from the city tonight to work on some marketing strategies for the new book," she tells me. "I thought we could go have dinner at the Lodge, if you're interested."

I nod, curious. "That sounds great." Then: "Mom," I blurt, before I can talk myself out of it. "Are you and Corina . . ." I trail off, not exactly sure how to continue.

My mom raises her sharp eyebrows. "Are Corina and I—" She stops short, and I think she's about to play dumb or deny it, or that maybe I really do have it wrong, but instead she tips her head to the side and looks at me for a long moment. "Would that bother you?" she asks. "If we were?"

I laugh a little, surprised. "*No*," I tell her, shaking my head. "Of course not."

Her eyes narrow. "Really?" she asks quietly, and it's the most vulnerable I've ever heard her sound. It occurs to me that all of us have secrets. It occurs to me that all of us are afraid.

"Mom!" I scramble up off the lounge chair, my book hitting the grass with a crinkly flop; I wrap my hands around her wrists, her coffee sloshing a bit. "Not at *all*. I want you to have someone, you know? I want you to be happy."

She flushes at that, pretty and pleased and young-looking. "All right," she says, gently shaking me off and making a bit of a face like she's the teenager and I'm the mom, like I'm embarrassing her. "Then yes, to answer your question. We've been seeing each other for a few months."

"That's amazing," I tell her, sitting back down on the lounge chair. "Seriously. I'm really glad."

"Well," she says, a little awkwardly. "I'm really glad, too." She clears her throat then, picking my book up and flicking at the cover with one painted fingernail. "That one ends happy," she tells me, then heads back across the grass toward the house.

That afternoon I lace up my sneakers and go for a long, sweaty run, perspiration dripping down my backbone and my sneakers hitting the hard-packed dirt with a satisfying thud as I loop the lake. I find myself smiling at moms with baby strollers and raising my hand to wave at tourists in kayaks, weirdly cheerful: I've spent so much of my time in this town hiding. It's nice to feel the sun on my face.

I take my old familiar route from last summer, along the trail that hugs the water and winds down past the Star Lake Lodge, the inn where I worked last year. I stopped by and saw my old boss, Penn, and her kids earlier this week, chasing sweet, mischievous Fabian through the lobby and lying on the floor of the office to color with Desi, who was completely silent for the entirety of last summer but chattered a blue streak as she dragged a crayon across the page with one chubby fist.

"Since when do you talk so much?" I teased her, and she looked at me like I was demented.

"Um, since *always?*" she asked with exquisite five-year-old exasperation, and dug another crayon out of the box.

Now I turn down the road that leads into town, passing French Roast and the tiny bookstore with its perpetual stack of *Driftwood* paperbacks in the window. The magazine rack outside is full of tourist-friendly gossip rags: *SABS HITS REHAB*, the headlines scream. Well, I think with a combination of sadness and admiration. Good for her. Probably both of us could stand another fresh start.

I keep going, down past Bunchie's Diner and the new, cursed juice place, but split off before I hit the block that houses Donnelly's Pizza. Gabe said Patrick was home for the summer, but even after all this time I can't imagine that running into me would be anything close to a kuddelmuddel for him. I hope he's happy, though, whatever it is he's up to. And I like to think he'd hope the same for me.

I'm starting to slow down when my phone dings in my pocket with a text from Roisin: Any requests from Costco? she wants to know. I'm here w my mom and she's buying us the whole store for the apartment.

I grin down at the screen: I'm headed back to Boston in a couple of days, and the closer it gets the more excited I find myself—for my very own campus apartment and long nights of bingeing sexy time-travel shows, yeah, but also to settle into myself again, to see who I might actually be now that I don't have to work so hard at being perfect. It's corny, maybe, but it kind of feels like Roisin isn't the only one I haven't seen in a while.

Nope, I promise, tucking my phone into my pocket and turning my face up toward the sunshine, heading for home. Got everything I need.

That afternoon I'm rinsing a coffee cup at the kitchen sink, the light spilling in warm and dappled through the window, when Vita lets out a sudden, affronted hiss; I jump as she darts from between my ankles, her patchy fur standing on end as she charges the back door. I turn around and gasp as a startled, high-pitched bark splits the silence: on the other side of the screen sits a tiny, wrinkly-faced beagle puppy.

And there, holding the leash, is Gabe.

"Hey, Molly Barlow," he says, raising his free hand in a greeting. He's wearing frayed khaki shorts and a soft-looking T-shirt, his face scrubbed clean and smooth. The bridge of his nose is faintly pink from the sun. "I was hoping you'd still be here."

I blink as Vita barrels toward the dining room in outrage,

her angry paws thumping a tattoo against the hardwood. "Um, yeah," I say slowly, my head falling to one side as I stare at him across the tidy kitchen. It feels like I'm seeing an apparition. It feels like I'm seeing a ghost. "I'm still here."

"I see that." Gabe smiles. "Hi."

"Hi." I motion to the puppy, who's standing up on four short, pudgy legs now, turning in snuffly circles on the porch. "Who's this?"

"This is Ellie." Gabe tugs her leash to get her attention, just gently; then, by way of explanation: "My mom got lonely."

"I know the feeling," I say, and Gabe nods.

"I got all the way back to Indiana," he confesses. He jams his hands deep into his pockets, Ellie's leash still looped around one wrist. "I got all moved in, I got my schedule and all that. But I couldn't do it."

I stare at him for a moment, heartbroken and hopeful. I wonder if this is our lot, mine and Gabe's, to surprise each other over and over until the very end of the world. "Do you want to come in?" I finally ask.

"Oh!" he says, like he'd forgotten he was standing out there. "Um. Yeah."

He opens the screen door, stepping into the kitchen and letting the leash go. Ellie runs over to Vita's water bowl and takes a few loud, thirsty slurps. Gabe and I watch her for a moment, neither one of us saying anything; suddenly some spell has been broken between us, awkwardness settling down like a fine, brackish mist. I clear my throat. Gabe scratches his collarbone. Neither one of us looks at each other. We're circling something, clearly, but it feels like neither one of us knows how to cross that final stretch.

"So what are you going to do instead?" I ask finally, my voice oddly jovial. Suddenly I don't know what to do with my hands. I clap them together for safekeeping, rocking back on my heels in a nervous little dance.

Gabe lets out a quiet laugh. "I have no fucking idea," he admits. He sits down with a heavy sigh at my mom's antique kitchen table, the polished wood knotted and scarred. "I was so busy trying to convince myself I wanted to be a doctor that I never really let myself think about anything else." He leans back, rubbing a hand over the top of his dark, shorn head. "I don't even *like* science."

I hide a smile. "I know that about you, in fact."

"You could have mentioned it," he says with a grimace.

"Seriously?" My eyebrows crawl.

Gabe holds his hands up in surrender. "Okay, okay," he concedes, lips twisting. "I guess you tried." He lifts his face and looks at me then, with an expression like he's about to dive into the deep end of the ocean. "I broke up with Sadie," he says.

I try to keep my face neutral, but the knowledge hooks itself into my rib cage and pulls the bones wide—my whole heart exposed and vulnerable, like he could reach out and cup it in the palm of his hand. "Yeah?"

Gabe nods, tilting his head back and looking at the ceiling. "That part wasn't right, either," he tells me. "She was great, but it wasn't—I mean, I didn't—" He stops, looks back at me. "I kept looking at the dumb picture I took of us," he says quietly, seemingly out of nowhere. "The one from Paris."

I wrinkle my nose at him, teasing even as my pulse races. "The one where I'm making the world's dumbest face?"

"It is a pretty ridiculous face," Gabe admits, grinning a little. "But we also just look really . . . happy in it? I *felt* happy that day, for the first time in a really long time. I felt like myself. And it wasn't 'cause things were fixed, necessarily, or because I had solved all my problems. The more I looked at the picture the more I realized that it was 'cause of you." He takes a deep breath and then he says it. "I love you."

I shake my head. My first reaction is bald denial, that *no you don't* ready on the tip of my tongue. *I don't deserve it*, I want to tell him. Instead I take a pause and remind myself that I do.

"I kind of don't think I ever stopped," Gabe continues, shrugging helplessly. "I thought if maybe I could cut off the oxygen to that part of myself it would be fine, you know? Like if I acted a certain way for long enough, then eventually it wouldn't be acting anymore."

That makes me smile. "I am sorry to inform you, turns out it doesn't work that way. At least, it didn't when I tried it." I sit down across the table, the side of my foot brushing his for the briefest of seconds. "Speaking of breakups," I begin.

Gabe raises his eyebrows. "You and Ian . . . ?" he asks.

"There is no more me and Ian," I admit.

That surprises him; I can see the relief—and the hope—on his face in the second before he schools his expression. "I'm sorry," he says quietly.

"I'm not," I counter. "Or, like, I *am*, but not because it wasn't the right decision. The truth is we probably shouldn't have been together from the beginning. Not when—" I gaze across the table for a moment. "You were right," I tell him, instead of continuing. "I was trying to be some perfect, brand-new version of myself who always had a plan and never screwed up or made a scene or embarrassed herself or offended anybody. But as much as I hate to admit it—and I really, *really* hate to admit it—it never felt totally normal. And being on that trip made me realize I just couldn't do it anymore."

"I don't need you to be perfect," Gabe promises. "I just want you to be you."

"But how do we know we won't just make a mess of things all over again?" I ask him. "How would it even *work*?" Ellie looks up at the sound of my voice, trotting over to sniff my ankles curiously. I bend down to stroke her soft, silky head. "Your whole family hates me," I remind him, grimacing at the thought as I straighten up again. "A hundred times more than they did at the beginning of last summer, probably. If we were just going to spend the rest of our lives ambling

around Europe far away from everyone here, maybe, but—"
I hold my hands up, baffled. "We just have so much *baggage*, Gabe."

"No shit," he agrees easily, and I like the fact that he doesn't try to argue. "That's kind of the whole point. Like . . . it turns out the only person I want to carry bags with is you."

That makes me laugh, a quiet exhale. "Because I'm such a train wreck?" I ask.

Gabe shakes his head. "Because you're *yourself*."

"A train wreck," I clarify.

"Stop saying that," he tells me. "Like, are you messy? Is our whole relationship so fucking messy? Yes, clearly. But so what? It's kind of liberating, isn't it?"

I think of jumping out of airplanes and splashing around in fountains and crying on top of the Eiffel Tower; I laugh again then, for real this time, resting my chin in my hands. "The idea that we're so messed up together that messed-up stuff happening is just par for the course?"

"That we can get *through* messed-up stuff," Gabe counters. "That at this point there's nothing we could tell each other that would automatically be a deal breaker." He shrugs. "I can be myself with you, even when I'm being a whiny, entitled asshole. And I think—I *think*—you can be yourself with me." He looks at me urgently. "Can't you?"

I think of spending eight months sure that if Ian knew the truth about me he'd run screaming for the Berkshires. I think of spending a whole year wanting to disappear. I open my mouth to tell Gabe that he's right, that we understand each other: "What if you came to Boston?" is what comes out.

Gabe's eyes widen. "Really?"

"Um. Yeah." I blurted it before I could even have the thought all the way, instinct and impulse, but as soon as it's out of my mouth I realize I want it desperately: I want to bring him to the place where I live now, to go to movies at the dilapidated old indie theater in Somerville and walk him by the tiny half doors in the brownstones on Beacon Hill and point to the place where the stolen paintings used to hang at the Isabella Stewart Gardner Museum. To make him a part of my life. "You could figure stuff out from there."

I fully expect him to say no. It's a random, ridiculous proposition: it doesn't solve the problem of what's going to happen to the pizza place, it doesn't solve the problem of what on earth he's going to do next. It doesn't solve anything but the problem of us not being together, and I'm opening my mouth to let him off the hook when he smiles. "I could do that," he says.

My mouth drops open. *"Really?"*

Gabe shrugs. "Why not?" he asks. "That's where you'll be, right?"

"I—*yeah*," I say slowly, letting myself imagine it—hockey games at the arena on Friday nights and coffee in the North End on Saturday mornings, fall settling down over the city like a blanket. "That's where I'll be."

Gabe gets up and comes over to my side of the table then,

the smell of grass and detergent and the lake at the very end of summer. Both of us have spent the last year trying to prove we were worthy of someone loving us—reinventing and remaking ourselves, tearing out the stitches and starting all over again to try and fit the patterns we thought other people wanted to see. But maybe that isn't what we need to do at all.

"Can I kiss you now?" he asks me, hands finding mine down at my sides and squeezing, a feeling like holding on for dear life. "Is that finally okay?"

"Yes," I tell him, standing up, the anticipation inflating like a hot air balloon inside my chest, like something big enough to cover long distances. "It's definitely, finally okay."

"Okay," he says.

"Okay!" I say, and then both of us are laughing, how it feels awkward but it also just feels *right*. He wraps one hand around the back of my neck and tilts my chin up, ducks his head. "I love you too," I tell him, or start to, but the words get cut off because he's already kissing me, his mouth warm and soft and familiar. I wrap my arms around his neck and we stand there for a moment, together in this place where we started.

I can't wait to see where we go next.

ACKNOWLEDGMENTS

This one was tricky but so worth the fight. A hundred humble thank-yous to my sharp-eyed, bighearted editor, Alessandra Balzer, and all the clear heads and generous souls at Balzer + Bray/HarperCollins—especially Kelsey Murphy, Bethany Reis, Jen Strada, Megan Gendell, Michelle Cunningham, Alison Donalty, Kristen Eckhardt, Vanessa Nuttry, Stephanie Boyar, Nellie Kurtzman, Bess Braswell, Ebony LaDelle, Sabrina Abballe, Andrea Pappenheimer, Kathy Faber, Kerry Moynagh, Jessica Malone, Jessie Elliot, Heather Doss, Jennifer Sheridan, Fran Olson, Deb Murphy, Susan Yeager, Jess Abel, and Caitlin Garing.

All my love and gratitude to Josh Bank, Joelle Hobeika, and Sara Shandler, who believe in me and make me laugh and listen with open hearts and minds to my half-finished sentences and middle-of-the-night worries and weird, complicated ideas. Les Morgenstein and everybody at Alloy, especially Stephanie Abrams, Laura Barbiea, Matt Bloomgarten, and Romy Golan, thank you for being so good at your jobs.

Lisa Burton, Jennie Palluzzi, Sierra Rooney, and Marissa Velie, forever friends and fiercest role models; Rachel Hutchinson, for always sticking; the Colleran and Cotugno families, especially my sister, for too many things to say. Tom Colleran, for being my buddy. I love you all the days that end in *Y.*